EMILY DICKINSON IS DEAD

The photograph has been taken in the form of a visiting card. It is
very small. On the back, someone has scribbled in a careless hand,
Emily Dickenson   1860.

WHO IS SHE?

EMILY DICKINSON IS DEAD

a novel of suspense

Jane Langton

Illustrations by the author

St. Martin's Press
New York

Reprinted by permission of the publishers and the Trustees of Amherst College from The Poems of Emily Dickinson, edited by Thomas H. Johnson, Cambridge, Mass.: The Belknap Press of Harvard University Press, Copyright © 1955, 1979, 1983, by the President and Fellows of Harvard College.

From Emily Dickinson Face to Face by Martha D. Bianchi. Copyright © 1932 by Martha Dickinson Bianchi. Copyright renewed © 1960 by Alfred Leete Hampson. Reprinted by permission of Houghton Mifflin company.

The daguerreotype on page 246 is in the collection of the Amherst College Library. The Frontispiece is in the possession of Mr. Herman Abromson of Rockville Centre, Long Island.

Design by Laura Hammond
Copyedited by Mildred Maynard

Library of Congress Cataloging in Publication Data

Langton, Jane.
    Emily Dickinson is dead.

    "A Joan Kahn book"—Verso of t.p.
    I. Title.
PS3562.A515E4   1984   813'.54   83-24451
ISBN 0-312-24434-7

First Edition
10 9 8 7 6 5 4 3 2 1

For David

. . . *is* there more? More than Love and Death?
Then tell me its name!

—*Emily Dickinson*

1

All but Death, can be Adjusted . . .

After the death of his wife, Owen Kraznik went on living and teaching in Amherst, but his days had become a bewildering fluster, a tangled wilderness, a formless and perplexing dishevelment. Snatching at the chaos as it hurtled past him, end over end, Owen struggled to arrange it in a rational pattern.

But the Emily Dickinson Centennial Symposium refused to be made sense of. It came crashing into Amherst like a loose boulder, ricocheting from College to University, crushing and grinding and destroying. Who was responsible? Owen didn't know. After the fire, after the disappearance of Alison Grove, after the awkwardness about the picture, after the attack in Emily Dickinson's bedchamber—with an axe!—and after all those other bizarre disasters, it was impossible to single out one human being and say, "Look, that person is entirely to blame."

But some of the guilt was his own. Wincing, Owen couldn't help pointing a finger at himself. Of course he wasn't crucially at fault, but there was no denying that it was Owen Kraznik who had given that boulder its first little nudge, way back in October. And then he had thrown up his hands in horror and galloped after it as it gathered speed and plummeted down into the peaceful valley of the Connecticut River, to bruise and shatter and lay waste, and change lives forever.

It was just an innocent little remark, that was all. If only he had kept his mouth shut!

2

Went home a century ago . . .

"*E*mily Dickinson has been dead for a hundred years." That was all he had said. And it had been true—well, almost true. On that October day last fall it had been ninety-nine years and five months since Emily Dickinson perished of Bright's disease in the big house on Main Street. And Owen had said it on the day the letter came, the letter from Peter Wiggins, the letter about the picture.

Owen had risen early that morning, as he always did, eager to get to his office at the University of Massachusetts before Winifred Gaw showed up. Now, taking the letter out of his mailbox, he held it in his teeth while he fastened the bicycle clips to his pants, and then he sat down on the top of the porch steps and looked at the return address:

> *Professor Peter Wiggins*
> *University of Central Arizona*
> *Pancake Flat, Arizona*

Pancake Flat, Arizona? Owen smiled. What an improbable-sounding place.

He pulled out a thick wad of paper from the envelope. It

3

was an article he had seen before, a study of a famous photograph of Emily Dickinson. Well, the photograph might or might not be a picture of Emily Dickinson. There was a controversy about it. This man Wiggins was trying to prove it was genuine. He had bought it from a collector. He owned it now, out there in Pancake Flat. He had examined the whole subject thoroughly. The photograph was authentic, he said. It was a real photographic portrait of Emily Dickinson, the celebrated poet of Amherst, Massachusetts, without a shadow of a doubt.

Well, good for Peter Wiggins, thought Owen, unfolding the xeroxed copy of the photograph. Turning it to the light, he looked at the face of the young woman in the picture.

Gravely the dark eyes looked back at him through the lens of the ancient camera and across the space of a hundred and twenty-five years. The woman was indeed good-looking. Owen wanted to believe it, that this was really the poet whose life and work had meant so much to him. What a fine and sensitive face! But did it match the younger face, the true face of Emily Dickinson as she appeared in the daguerreotype of 1848? Ah, that was the question. Some people thought they were the same, some didn't.

Owen put the picture back in the envelope and took out the letter. Peter Wiggins wanted to come East. He was inquiring eagerly: Would the English department at the University of Massachusetts be interested in a slide lecture on the subject of the photograph? Did Professor Kraznik know of a teaching position in New England? Résumé enclosed.

The letter had a panicky ring. The poor fellow seemed frantic to escape from Pancake Flat. Owen pictured him, this unknown Peter Wiggins, standing forlornly in some sunbaked desert landscape, stretching out his hand to the East. It was like Emily Dickinson's own yearning for the impossible—*"Heaven"—is what I cannot reach!* Well, poor Wiggins was out of luck, thought Owen sadly. Nothing could be done for him. All the colleges in the Connecticut River Valley were firing, rather than hiring.

Trundling his bicycle down the steps, Owen mounted and

4

rolled along the driveway, wobbling a little as he turned onto Spring Street, dodging puddles from yesterday's rain. Wet leaves were plastered to the pavement. Overhead the rising sun struck the lofty crowns of the sugar maples and set fire to them as with a match. Owen glanced up at the treetops and told himself he should take more pleasure in things like that. But it was no use. Since Catherine's death he found no savor in natural wonders. Today it was too painful to remember her delight in the autumn color of the Amherst countryside. Better not to notice anything, better not to be reminded, better not to think about that kind of thing at all.

Damp leaves spun around his wheels as Owen turned left on Dickinson Street, focusing his mind safely once again on the article by Peter Wiggins.

There was something about it that dismayed him. The flaw was a common failing—a note of ownership, of territorial arrogance. *My theory, my picture, my poet.* The inference was always the same, *Emily Dickinson belongs to me.*

On the surface it seemed innocent enough, this habit of grasping at the great and good after they were gone. And yet to Owen there was something violent about it. It was like grave-robbers stealing rings from the fingers of the dead, or groping in the lifeless jaws to extract the gold teeth. It was like an exhumation. *These bones are mine.* In the article by Peter Wiggins you could almost hear the ringing clatter of his wrecking bar against Emily Dickinson's tombstone.

Of course, Wiggins was not alone. In Amherst, Massachusetts, almost everyone laid claim to Emily Dickinson. She was like a colonial plantation, a piece of ephemeral real estate.

At Main Street, Owen swooped left and pumped to the top of the steep little hill. At the crest he stopped beside the Dickinson house and dragged the bike up the granite steps. THE DICKINSON HOMESTEAD, BY APPOINTMENT ONLY, said the sign at the front walk.

Owen didn't want an appointment. Owen knew every square inch of the public rooms. He glanced up now at the windows of the bedroom in which Emily Dickinson had written

nearly two thousand poems, the room that had been a haven from intrusion by fools, a place of retreat from the polite people of the town. She was still retreating, decided Owen. In death she had removed to the family plot under the white ash tree in West Cemetery. She had withdrawn to her narrow white coffin, six feet under the ground. But she could escape no farther. Any bunch of idiots could claw at the grass growing on her grave and hold up chunks of turf and claim them for their own.

Moving down the sidewalk, Owen gazed through the hemlock hedge at the sloping Dickinson garden. The grass was wet. In the oak tree a bird hopped from branch to branch. Owen stared through the hedge, wondering who really owned Emily Dickinson. If anybody in Amherst could be said to possess the woman in this ninety-ninth year after her death, who would it be?

Oh, Lord, there were so many claimants! In all the five

6

colleges of the Connecticut River Valley there were professors who regarded the poet as property—not to mention the fifty thousand students swarming on the streets of the local towns, Amherst and Northampton and South Hadley. Was there any other place in the world where one literary deity was worshiped so universally? Well, there was Stratford-on-Avon, and Concord, Massachusetts. Did everybody in Stratford own Shakespeare? Did everyone in Concord lay claim to Henry Thoreau? Here in Amherst even a piece of paper whipping down South Pleasant Street was apt to be a title deed, a page from *The Complete Poems*, unstuck from the paperback edition, fluttering out of somebody's motorcycle saddlebag. Impulsively, Owen covered his ears as he thought of the sounds of righteous Dickinson ownership, the rattle of a thousand typewriters, the battering of chalk on a hundred classroom blackboards.

Then he smiled. It wasn't just people, after all. Even that commonplace bird in the oak tree, there in the Dickinson garden, even that sassy robin who was whistling, head up, chirping a succession of phrases, spattering the whole side yard with cheerful melody, even that small bird could make a claim of its own upon Emily Dickinson. Maybe it was descended from the poet's own *Gabriel In humble circumstances* and owned the whole green lawn.

Mounting his bike again, Owen pushed off and sped along Main Street to the Common. The hour was still early. Except for a couple of joggers loping around its circumference, the Common was deserted. The sun was just surfacing over the Town Hall, shining on the snapping flag, casting a rosy glow on the brick cornices of Merchants Block. Leaning to the side, Owen whizzed around the corner onto North Pleasant Street. Later the crossing would be jammed with students and choked with motor traffic, but at this hour Owen had it to himself.

North Pleasant Street, too, was deserted. Racing left at the fork, Owen skimmed along too fast on McClellan Street and almost ran into Tom Perry.

Whoops! Dodging left, Owen shouted "Sorry!" at Tom,

7

who was standing in the street, opening the door of his car. Tom was one of Owen's superb successes, the youngest full professor at Amherst College, and another deed holder, of course, in the Emily Dickinson real-estate bonanza. Was that the girl he was engaged to, the fabled doctor from Northampton? Speeding away, Owen looked back to nod and smile at the girl, and then he nearly lost his balance in surprise.

It wasn't the doctor from Northampton. It was a sophomore English major from U Mass. Once you had seen Alison Grove, you didn't forget her. This morning Alison was coming out of Tom's front door, clutching a folded umbrella, teetering along in gold sandals, shivering in a skimpy outfit obviously left over from last night.

Owen whirled away, keeping eyes front. It was no business of his if Tom Perry brought a random girl home to share his bed. It was none of Owen's affair at all.

"Shit," said Tom Perry to Alison Grove. "The great Owen Kraznik. He would come along right now. Our iniquity is discovered."

"Well, who cares?" said Alison, getting into the car. "I mean, like you said you were going to tell your old girlfriend about us anyway. You said you'd break it off. You said she'll understand, because she's this really, really good sport."

Tom got in beside Alison. "Oh, sure. Next time I see her we'll have a heart-to-heart talk. But not now. I called her up yesterday and told her how busy I am." Tom grinned at Alison. "You know, all these midterms to correct, all these conferences with students." Bending his head, Tom kissed Alison's bare shoulder. "Like last night. Very important student conference. All kinds of"—Tom kissed Alison's throat and buried his head in her red-gold hair—"really important stuff to discuss. You know like this—and this—and especially this. Oh, Alison."

Alison Grove leaned back and allowed herself to be caressed. It was what she had been born for. She had always known it. But she had taken her time. Like in high school, she had been really just so incredibly fussy. But she had been right to wait for Tom Perry, who was really so incredibly good-

8

looking and just so fabulously important. Everybody said so. All the girls on Alison's floor at Coolidge Hall were incredibly jealous.

"Well, Owen won't tell on us anyway," sighed Tom, sitting up reluctantly. "The saintly Owen Kraznik, he'll keep it under his hat. Oh, say, that reminds me, didn't you say you were looking for a part-time job?"

"Oh, right. My clothing allowance, it's just so incredibly small."

"Well, listen, I understand they're going to fire Owen's assistant, Winifred Gaw. Dombey Dell told me. The whole department at U Mass voted to throw her out. So why don't you go over there this morning and talk to Owen? Maybe he'll hire you in her place. Tell him I sent you. Owen's a soft touch. You can wind him around your little finger."

"Well, I don't know. I mean, I don't know anything about Emily Dickerson. Isn't he this really big expert on Emily Dickerson?"

"Dickinson." For an instant Tom glanced sideways at Alison, aware of a flicker of doubt. He had felt it before, just once or twice. He banished it now by putting his arm around Alison's creamy shoulders. "An expert? That's putting it mildly. If anybody in this world owns the right to talk about Emily Dickinson, it's Owen Kraznik."

"Honestly?" said Alison, widening her eyes, really, really impressed.

"Oh, he'd probably never admit it, being a saint the way he is, but it's true. Owen Kraznik owns Emily Dickinson, lock, stock, and barrel."

9

3

. . . Estates of Cloud

Tom Perry was right. If some supreme judge had pounded his gavel and pronounced a ruling on the insubstantial domain that was Emily Dickinson, the title of ownership would surely have been awarded to Professor Owen Kraznik of the University of Massachusetts.

But Owen would never have accepted it. Fiercely, Owen repudiated all claims of vanity. It wasn't blindness on his part. It wasn't that he had never noticed his own moral and intellectual superiority to other people. He had discovered it in childhood. But at eight years old it had disturbed him as much as it did now, at forty. How sad for the human race if it could do no better than Owen Kraznik! In the simplicity of his nature and the clarity of his vision, Owen rejected self-congratulation. As his eminence grew, his eye grew milder still. The more he surpassed, the more helplessly he shrugged his shoulders, the more he refrained from needless victories.

Now, as Owen's bike plunged along Lincoln Avenue, the University of Massachusetts sprawled in front of him, forty-three acres of trampled grass. Owen swept past the long stretch of concrete sculpture that was the Fine Arts Center, dodged around Memorial Hall and Herter, skidded to a stop in front

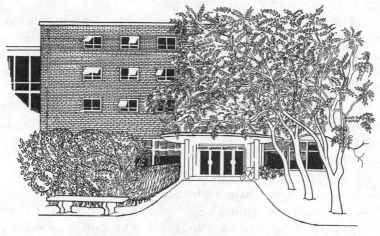

Bartlett Hall

of Bartlett Hall, chained his bike to a column, and opened the door. Running lightly up to the second floor, he felt his insides clench with apprehension. What if Winnie Gaw were there already, lying enormously in wait? Sooner or later Winnie would discover that her boss was coming in early. And then she would insist on getting there before him, to anticipate his every need.

Warily, Owen poked his head into the undergraduate English office, then breathed a sigh of relief. It was empty. Crossing to his own small study on the other side, he sat down at his desk and smiled with satisfaction.

But the telephone had eyes in its head. It began to ring.

Owen stared at it a minute, then picked it up. "Hello?" he said cautiously.

But it was all right. It was only his cousin, Dr. Harvey Kloop.

"Owen? How would you like to come fishing with me at the Quabbin Reservoir? I've got a free day at last. My patients are all behaving themselves and nobody seems to be calling on my services as medical examiner. I've got my boat all hooked up to the car and I'm ready to go."

Owen smiled, picturing the melancholy hollow-cheeked face of his old childhood companion. "Oh, Harvey, I'm sorry. I have to teach today."

"Oh, too bad." And then Owen heard a scuffling noise and a protesting shout, "Hey, wait a minute, Eunice Jane."

"Owen?" It was Eunice Jane. "Listen here, Owen, I'm sorry, but Harvey isn't going anywhere today. He's sorting his underwear."

"He's what?"

"And overcoats. He promised me. He said he'd sort his underwear and overcoats right away. Well, the time has come. Now, listen, Owen, while I've got you on the phone, I've got to tell you. You'll be amazed. I've been working on some more of those fascinating lines of Dickinson's, those *deeply obscure*

paooagco, rcmcmbci? Like *the sterile perquisite, Reportless Subjects, to the Quick, the peerless puncture?* Well, listen, I know what they mean. Those other fools were wrong. Wait till you hear."

Owen could have wept. The injustice of Providence smote him. How could fate have taken Catherine away from him and left Harvey saddled with Eunice Jane?

At last he made his escape and hung up the phone. Something fell with a crash. A heavy piece of furniture was squealing across the floor, hitting the other side of the wall with a jarring thud.

Leaping to his feet, Owen threw open the door. Two middle-aged men were flailing at each other in the outer office, tripping over the coatrack, plunging heavily this way and that in the small space between the windows and the door to the hall.

One of the combatants was Dombey Dell, chairman of the English department, administrator of one hundred and eighty-six separate sections of literature and composition and a teaching staff of seventy-five, to say nothing of an army of teaching assistants. As Owen watched in astonishment, Dombey landed a punch in the other man's solar plexus, then lost his balance and catapulted into Winifred Gaw's big potted plant.

"Oof," said the other man, swinging wildly at empty air. It was Owen's old friend from Concord, Homer Kelly, distinguished Thoreau scholar and professor of American literature, and ex-lieutenant detective for Middlesex County. Owen was chagrined to observe that Homer didn't seem to have any pugilistic know-how, in spite of his early background as a policeman. Homer was throwing his long arms around Dombey Dell in a bear hug and hanging on with all his strength.

"You lying alphabetarian," gasped Dombey, struggling to get his arms free. "You philological sneak!"

"Good heavens, gentlemen," cried Owen. "What's this all about?" Stepping bravely into the fray, he took Homer by the shoulders and dragged him away from Dombey Dell.

Dombey and Homer glared at each other, breathing hard. Then Homer turned to Owen angrily, and shrugged himself back into his jacket. "I think Professor Dell is troubled by a letter I wrote in the *Proceedings of the Modern Language Association*, disagreeing with some of his premises on nineteenth-century American usage. He seems to prefer fisticuffs to scholarly discourse."

Once again Dombey flung himself at Homer. Taken by surprise, Homer stumbled into Owen, who lost his balance and floundered backward through his office door. Together the three of them fell in a jumble against Owen's desk. "Look here," said Owen, his voice muffled under Homer, "why don't you people join me in a cup of coffee?"

Grumpily, Dombey and Homer stood up, and then Owen, struggling to his feet, began bustling around among his cupboards and shelves. "Sorry, but I don't seem to have anything to go with the coffee but these—ah—pretzels? I'm afraid they're two years old."

Dombey and Owen sat down sullenly, but Owen's clumsy hospitality soon broke the ice. Before long, Dombey was chaffing Owen about his terrible coffee and explaining what he had come for.

"We took a vote. The entire English faculty. I warned you, Owen. That girl has got to go. Winifred Gaw is no longer an employee of the English department. She is no longer a candidate for the doctor's degree. She leaves today, you hear that, Owen? You and your lame ducks."

Owen was dismayed. Picturing the scene with Winnie, he passed his hand over his eyes. How was he going to tell her? It would be an ordeal of the most harrowing kind.

But Dombey had no mercy. He turned to Homer. "You should see this Winnie Gaw. What a slob. You know what, Owen? If I looked like Winifred Gaw, I hope I'd have the grace to shoot myself." Then Dombey snickered, and gestured at the picture on the wall, Owen's precious copy of the daguerreotype of the young Emily Dickinson. "I must admit that's what troubles me about our famous local poet. Look at the woman! That's one plain little lady."

Homer Kelly was outraged. "My God, Dombey, that's the stupidest thing I ever heard. Listen, you dumb cluck, what difference does it make what a great poet looks like?"

Hostility was boiling up again. Swiftly, Owen pulled the envelope from Peter Wiggins out of his bookbag and waved it at Dombey and Homer. "But perhaps she was truly good-looking after all! I have a letter this morning from a man named Peter Wiggins in Arizona. He owns that controversial photograph of Emily Dickinson. He claims he can prove it's authentic. He wants to come and give a speech."

"Well, good for him," said Dombey, settling back in his chair. "Because, listen, Owen, I'm telling you a solemn fact. If Emily Dickinson was as homely as that picture on your wall, I hold it against her. I'm sorry to admit it, but it's something in my glands."

Homer said something rude about Dombey's glands, and Dombey snarled. Owen hastened to intervene. "My dear Dombey, how can it possibly matter? It was all so long ago."

And then Owen made his fatal mistake.

"After all," he said, "Emily Dickinson has been dead for a hundred years. Homer's perfectly correct. It's the poetry that counts. Nothing else."

"That's right," growled Homer self-righteously.

But Dombey was no longer listening. He was calculating under his breath. "It's true. It will be a hundred years next May." His eyes brightened. He grinned. "Say, listen, that gives me a superb idea. You know what I'm going to do? I'm going to organize an Emily Dickinson Centennial Symposium on the hundredth anniversary of her death, and invite people from all over the country." Dombey threw his arms wide and shouted, "All over the world!" Raising his fist, he brought it down on Owen's desk with a crash. Owen's books bounced. His coffee cup jiggled. "A hundred years dead! By God, I'll drag the woman out of her grave! And afterwards, when anybody thinks of Emily Dickinson, who will they think of first? Dombey Dell, that's who." Dombey smirked. "Me, in short. In person."

"Oh, for Christ's sake, Dombey," said Homer, exasperated. "If they think of anybody now and forevermore, it will be Professor Owen Kraznik, you big jerk."

1 5

"No, no, please, no." Owen shook his head and closed his eyes in silent suffering. It was the kind of talk that pained him most. He was repelled by Dombey's display of scholarly megalomania. He knew exactly what would happen. Dombey would organize his conference and prance around on the platform and make himself famous, and at the same time he would say condescending things about the poet. Not only would he be important in his own right, he would be more important than Emily Dickinson herself. It was sickening.

But Dombey was throwing back his head in a paroxysm of self-congratulation. "Oh, this is going to be a lovely, lovely symposium. We'll all get a chance to show off. You, too, Owen. You, too, Homer. And we'll get Tom Perry in on it. The University of Massachusetts and Amherst College, we'll run it jointly. And I'll get hold of that guy in Arizona. He can talk about his picture. Oh, wow, isn't this great. I've never had a whole entire conference to call my own. *The Emily Dickinson Centennial Symposium, brainchild of Professor Dombey Dudley Dell, founder, guiding star, principal factotum, and distinguished majordomo.*"

"Oh, Dombey, you big ass," said Homer.

But Dombey was jumping out of his chair. "Well, say, I'd better get right to work before somebody else thinks of the same thing. Get out my pick and shovel, start digging the woman up." Dombey jumped over Homer's huge shins, then paused in the doorway. "Metaphorically speaking, of course," he said, simpering. "I mean, just as a figure of speech."

He was gone, slamming the door behind him.

Owen stared at Homer, shaken to the core.

Homer stood up and tore angrily at his hair. "You know, Owen, the man scares me. He's dangerous. A conference like that is unhealthy. I mean it, speaking as an ex-cop. What you'll get is a collection of snarling tigers. Everything at a fever pitch of ambition and jealousy and character assassination. All those professors, they look so mild and easygoing on the surface, but underneath it's the law of the jungle. Violence, that's what you'll get! I mean, look what that fool did, Dombey Dell." Homer displayed the torn sleeve of his jacket. "He jumped me from the rear. A savage attack."

"Oh, yes, I know," murmured Owen, sinking his head into his hands. "And the man does have such an unfortunate way of expressing himself."

"You mean, all that stuff about digging Emily Dickinson out of her grave? Listen, Owen, I'll tell you what it's like. Remember those people who discovered the tomb of King Tut? You know, they broke the seals and burst in and took away all the mummies and the gold and everything? You know what happened to them? Death and destruction!"

4

. . . love got peevish, watching—

*H*omer helped himself to another petrified pretzel and told Owen his amazing news. He was living in Amherst now. "Renting a room on Route Nine. You know, Owen, bachelor quarters. It's got a kitchen. I'm cooking my own supper."

"Bachelor quarters?" Owen was dismayed. His fingers trembled with concern. "No trouble between you and your good wife, I hope?" he said anxiously, coming to the point at once.

Homer snorted in horror. "Good God, no. I rush home to Concord every weekend. I'm a guest lecturer at Mount Holyoke for the academic year. They wanted Mary too, but she's committed to that course we taught a couple of years ago in Memorial Hall at Harvard. Remember? All that hoopla with the music, and the explosion, and the poor chap who was buried alive?"

"Oh, yes, of course." Owen smiled. "The papers were full of it, even in this remote corner of the world. You attained a good deal of celebrity, as I recall."

"Notoriety is more like it," grumbled Homer. "Anyway, I'm supposed to tell you Mary sends her love." Homer cocked his great doggy head and looked wisely at Owen. "Wasn't it this month, two years ago, that Catherine—?"

"Yes, it was. Two years ago tomorrow. Thank you, Homer, for remembering."

Homer rumbled sympathetically, and thought how attractive the man was. There he sat, the great Owen Kraznik, looking like a child behind his big desk, his narrow chest concave beneath his shirt, his shirt cuffs nearly engulfing his small hands, his eyes wet—Owen was famous for bursting into tears at moments of emotion. Taken all in all, decided Homer admiringly, Owen was the very opposite of the popular image of the desirable American male, that cool, expressionless, jut-jawed hero. Jut-jawed! Owen didn't even have a chin. His face sort of disappeared into his collar. Nor did he, thank God, share Dombey Dell's cruel macho sense of humor. In fact, wondered Homer, did Owen have any sense of humor at all? Perhaps not, at least in the ordinary sense of the phrase. But it wasn't because something important was lacking in his makeup. It was simply his sober attention to the true terrors of the world.

"You're still living on Spring Street?" said Homer. "In that same big house?"

"Oh, yes. I know it's ridiculous. I just don't have the heart to leave it." Then Owen brightened, and he looked at Homer eagerly. "Why, Homer, of course, I should have thought of it at once. You must stay with me. There I am, all alone, standing up at the stove for meals, eggs for breakfast, eggs for supper. How about it? We could share the cooking, enjoy each other's company."

"Why, of course, I'd love to." Homer was delighted. "And listen, Owen, I'm developing a flair for gourmet cooking. Wait till you taste my salad dressing—corn oil, mayonnaise, mustard and ketchup." Homer smacked his lips and made a circle with thumb and forefinger. "I accept your offer. That's really great. I'll be on your doorstep Monday morning." Homer stood up to go, then leaned forward and tapped Owen's desk. "Listen, Owen, I should warn you about Dombey Dell. He'll want to rope you into that symposium of his as the central fixture and ornament. So watch out."

"Well, I won't do it," said Owen firmly. "And, anyway, everybody's sick of listening to me. There are plenty of people Dombey can call on. How about you, Homer?"

"Who, me? Do you think I want to watch Dombey swagger around, saying mean things about Emily Dickinson? Not on your life." Homer took Owen's small hand in his huge paw, shook it warmly, and walked out, shutting the door behind him.

In the outer office a pretty girl was waiting. The furniture was still askew. Homer smiled at the girl and righted the furniture. Then he looked at his watch. Good God, he would be late for his morning class in South Hadley. Charging at the door to the corridor, he collided with someone coming in.

Thump. Recoiling, Homer found himself enmeshed in the fringes of a giant shawl and the buckled strap of a mighty pocketbook. "Oh, sorry," he said, trying to disengage himself. He was belly to bosom with an immense woman. "Excuse me. All my fault. Oh, ha ha, whoops, is this your scarf? Just a sec. We seem to be entwined. Our rigging is entangled. I've been dismasted. There, now, are we squared away? Farewell, then. Ships that pass in the night!"

Winifred Gaw stared as Homer Kelly whisked away around the corner. But the man hardly registered on her consciousness. It was the pretty girl who had all of Winnie's attention. Winnie knew the girl's name. She was Alison Grove, a sophomore English major. She lived in Coolidge Hall. She was an enemy.

"What do *you* want?" said Winnie, hanging her coat on the coatrack. (Alison would see that Winnie belonged here.)

Alison Grove looked up at the huge girl in the tentlike jumper. "I'm just applying for a job," she said carefully.

"A job? What job? Have you got an appointment?"

"No, but Dombey said—I mean, Professor Dell—well, I mean, really it was Tom. You know, Professor Perry at Amherst College—"

"You can't see Professor Kraznik without an appointment. He's all booked up until January. There aren't any jobs anyway, okay?" Turning away from Alison Grove, Winnie wallowed across the floor, slapping down her sponge-soled wedgies, her thighs slubbing against each other under her dress. Opening the door to Professor Kraznik's cramped little office, she went in and shut the door behind her with a slam.

Professor Kraznik jerked and looked up. "Oh, good morning, Winnie. A little early, aren't you?"

"I just thought you might need me," said Winnie sweetly. "I just had this sort of a feeling." Winnie said nothing about Alison Grove, waiting in the outer office. Alison looked like a threat to the longing in Winnie's heart.

For Winifred Gaw knew love. Winnie was one hundred pounds overweight, but her love for Professor Kraznik was as powerful as if she had been slender and lovely, like the girl on the other side of the office door. Deep down inside, as a matter of fact, Winnie felt small and delicate, sort of like Emily Dickinson. The truth was, Winnie felt a special bond of closeness to Emily Dickinson. Actually, Winnie was more interested in Emily as a person than as a poet. Emily Dickinson had loved somebody, just like Winnie, and she had hoped and longed, just like Winnie, and she was homely to look at, sort of, the way Winnie was fat. The two of them had a bond in common, Winnie and Emily. Sometimes Winnie thought she was the only one who understood what Emily Dickinson had really been like, deep down inside.

So of course that gave her a special bond with Professor Kraznik, who was the top Dickinson scholar in the world. And he had seen it, her special closeness to Emily, because he had agreed to let Winnie be his personal assistant. She was one of his inner circle. She was almost in charge!

Now, squeezing past Professor Kraznik's chair, Winnie crouched down, wheezing with effort, and reached past his knees to inspect his wastebasket. It was empty. She bent over his chair, pillowing his shoulders with her huge bosom, and flipped up the back of the book he was reading, to see if it needed to be renewed. It didn't. Plucking the pencil out of his hand, she took it to the sharpener on the wall, ground it noisily to a point, and gave it back. Then Winnie took a tiny camera out of the pocket of her jumper—photography was Winnie's hobby—and backed up to get a good angle for a candid shot of her beloved professor.

There was a great flash of light. Professor Kraznik yelped. Leaning back in his chair, he put his hands over his eyes. Then he stood up and looked at Winifred Gaw with tortured wrinkles in his forehead. "Winnie," he said, "I'm afraid I have bad news."

Kindly but resolutely, he told her the decision of the faculty. She was no longer to be an employee of the English department. From now on she was not a candidate for the doctor's degree.

Owen had known the interview would be painful, but it was even worse than he had expected. He was astonished by the violence of Winnie's response. Hurling herself at him, she hung upon his neck, sobbing and beseeching. Owen had to stagger backward to keep his balance.

"I'll kill myself," said Winnie.

It was the worst day of Winnie's life. Well, as for worst days, it would have been difficult to discriminate among worst days. Sealed up in a bleeding package in Winnie's memory was the day she had lost the little finger on her left hand. "Paper cutter," she would say shortly, whenever anyone was bold enough to ask. But it had not been a paper cutter. And there had been a thousand other days in Winnie's childhood that could compete with this one for general misery. But Winnie had put them out of her mind. It was the kind of knowledge that tucked itself into hidden crevices in her layers of fat, deep down in the creases of her neck, or in the chubby folds of her knees.

"You're from around here, Winnie?" Professor Kraznik had asked her one day in kind inquiry.

"Oh, sure, I live in Ware. My father works at the Quabbin Reservoir. And we have, like, a farm."

And then Professor Kraznik had smiled at her and admitted her as a candidate for the master's degree—knowing full well he shouldn't do it.

It was out of pity, of course, pity for the immense pudgy body, pity for the doglike appeal in the brown eyes. And of course Owen had regretted it. He was fully aware of the fecklessness of his kindness, which made him do things that wasted his time, obliterated his leisure, and destroyed his peace of mind. Sometimes Owen thought he must emit some kind of odor that attracted pitiful human beings from miles away. Looking over a new class at the beginning of a term, his heart would sink as he recognized yet another sorry case. Their eyes would meet, a flash of terrible understanding would pass between them, and before long the tyrant would have fallen upon its greedy knees at his feet, demanding rescue.

It was his own fault, Owen knew. His kindness was merely laziness. Laziness and timidity. Sometimes it was easier to give in than say no.

But today he stood firm. "Now, Winnie, I know you won't kill yourself. Listen, I've been talking to the people in the Public Affairs Office at the College. One of the guides at the Dickinson house is retiring. They need another one, and I think I've persuaded them you would be perfect for the job. They pay the guides now, you know. It's not just a bunch of volunteers."

"But it's not with you," bawled Winnie. "I wouldn't be working with you." Her hold on his neck tightened. He was nearly strangled. She was rocking his frail body to and fro, so that he had to keep up a shuffling dance to stay on his feet. His ruthless conscience assaulted him. Why didn't he feel more pity for the girl? Her misery lacked dignity because she was fat, that was the reason. It wasn't any the less keen on that account, poor girl. "I'm sorry, Winnie," choked Owen, struggling to breathe, "but there's nothing else I can do. You'll like the new job, I know you will."

Slowly he disentangled himself from the powerful embrace, and at last Winnie turned, gulping, and pulled open the door. But then, at the sight of Alison Grove waiting outside, *waiting to take over Winnie's job with Professor Kraznik*, Winnie howled with rage and dismay.

Owen stood rigidly at his desk with closed eyes, listening as Winnie pounded down the corridor. Only when her lamentations at last faded into silence, trapped in the descending elevator, did he open his eyes and take a breath.

Then Owen did something he had never done before in all his life. At ten o'clock in the morning, he decided to get smashed.

Picking up his coat, he left his office, marched blindly and unsteadily past Alison Grove, stumbled down the stairs, mounted his bicycle, and rode home to Spring Street. There, without even taking off his coat, he took a bottle of whiskey from the mantelpiece and poured himself a stiff drink.

Therefore when Dombey Dell called to offer him the honorary directorship of the Emily Dickinson Centennial Symposium, and the privilege of delivering the keynote address, Owen said yes—partly because Dombey appealed so skillfully to his conscience, which was bleeding, but mostly from intoxicated befuddlement.

"If I didn't know any better," Dombey said happily, reporting to Tom Perry, "I'd say the man was squiffy, absolutely plastered."

.

5

The fire-bells are oftener now, almost, than the church-bells. Thoreau would wonder which did the most harm.

*T*he fire in Coolidge Hall was visible all over town from the cupolas of Amherst's nineteenth-century houses. The screaming fire trucks kept coming, roaring through intersections, clanging and clamoring, masters of the night. In the fire house on North Pleasant Street, the dispatcher's voice grew hoarse as he called for engine companies from Northampton and Hadley, Deerfield and Sunderland, ladder trucks from Chicopee and Springfield, rescue equipment from Easthampton, helicopters from the state police and the Coast Guard and Westover Air Force Base.

Owen Kraznik had gone to bed early, in his big dark house on Spring Street, his head awhirl. Besotted with drink, he hadn't even bothered to worry about the bad dream that so often plagued his rest, *that Vast Dark—That swept His Being—back.* His sleep had been dreamless.

But at eleven Owen woke up and lifted his head. A wild cry was trembling the window curtains, a rhythmical wail. It seemed to be coming from the direction of Main Street, but now there was another, whining farther away. While Owen listened, the caterwauling faded, then started up again. It sounded like a county-wide alarm.

He got out of bed, feeling muzzy. Throwing on his bathrobe, he hurried up to the attic and looked out the window. To the northwest there was a red glow above the trees. Good lord, it must be the University. Shivering, Owen hurried back to his bedroom and began flinging himself into his clothes. He got his pants on backward and had to take them off and start over, his fingers shaking.

Winifred Gaw's big van encountered the first engine companies from Belchertown on Route 9 as she drove home to Ware. They whipped past her, pounding down the road, heading for Amherst. Exhilarated, terrified, Winnie felt the blood rush into her face, flushing her big cheeks, pulsing in her forehead. Then she grinned with excitement as another ladder truck thundered past her in the dark, its red lights flashing, its siren howling. For an instant in the flicker of her headlights Winnie caught a glimpse of the polished gold letters on the side as they whizzed past her—WARE. The truck had been summoned all the way from Ware, Winnie's own hometown. Coolidge Hall must be burning down, it must really be burning down, the whole huge high-rise building. For an instant Winnie thought of people trapped in burning rooms, but then she put them out of her mind, and thought instead about what to do now. She was desperate to get home, to creep up to her room and hide herself in bed. But she couldn't go home yet. She had to do something with the extra can of lacquer, the propane torch, the shopping bag. She couldn't just put the stuff back in her father's garage. She had to get rid of it.
Well, there was a place. Winnie had thrown things to hell in that place before. She would have to get the key and go there, and throw the stuff down the hole. And that would take care of it forever. When things were thrown away in that special place, they stayed thrown away. . . .

The rescue at Coolidge Hall was under way, and going well. It looked like chaos, but it wasn't. The chief of the Amherst Fire Department and a quick-thinking major from the air base stood in the middle of the tumult, surrounded by firefighters, police officers, University functionaries, and barking dogs. In short order they had the helicopters taking off from the playing field on the other side of Commonwealth Avenue and landing on the flat roof of Coolidge Hall to pick up batches of frightened students.

Owen Kraznik waited at the edge of the field in a panic of concern, flapping his arms in the cold, watching the helicopters land and take off. He was inarticulate with anxiety. When he saw Tom Perry, he gripped him by the arms, unable to speak.

Tom Perry, too, was frantic. "Listen, Owen, have you seen Alison Grove? She lives in Coolidge Hall, right up there on the fourteenth floor. Look, see there, where all those flames are coming out?" Then Tom's face changed. "Oh, thank God, there she is." Jumping over a rope barrier, he raced across the field and embraced Alison as she descended from the bubble door of one of the Coast Guard helicopters.

Owen broke down and sobbed. But Alison was fine. She was rosy and clean. Her white sweater wasn't even smudged with smoke. She had combed her red-gold hair in the air. Tom took her home, and she called her mother to tell her she was all right, that she wasn't one of the kids who were being rushed to the infirmary or to the Cooley-Dickinson Hospital in North-ampton to be treated for smoke-filled lungs or minor burns or simple hysteria.

At the hospital, Dr. Ellen Oak was in charge of the emergency room when the first rush of ambulances pulled up outside. Ellen had been sleepily putting on her coat, thinking about bed. Instead she was up all night. By morning her staff had cared for nearly all of the Coolidge Hall residents who had come pouring in at midnight, carried on stretchers, walking, weeping, coughing. Dozens were put to bed on cots in the cleared-out cafeteria. Scores were calmed down and sent home. But no rescue techniques, no desperate lifesaving efforts, could revive the two sophomore men who had tried to descend the north staircase in Coolidge Hall, hoping to reach the ground in safety. Through one propped-open door the whole stairway had filled with smoke. For them it was a fatal mistake.

Ellen watched the two covered stretchers disappear

around the corner in the direction of Harvey Kloop's pathology lab. Worn out and disappointed, she swore under her breath, then indulged in a quick fit of tears.

The pathologist was not in the lab to receive the bodies. He was home in bed. No one had summoned Dr. Kloop. He slept through the whole thing. Not until five o'clock in the morning did his phone ring.

Harvey was used to calls early in the morning. Automatically he stretched out his arm to answer this one, keeping his eyes tightly closed on his dream, a vision of the shimmering surface of the Quabbin Reservoir. And on the shore—what a miracle!—a mountain lion was peering through the trees, the legendary catamount of old! They were rumored to be still lurking in the woods, but nobody was sure. It was Harvey's lifetime ambition to see one in the flesh. And there it was, with its big body and small catlike head, right there in the—

"Hello," murmured Harvey into the phone, not wanting to wake up.

It was the state police. "Hey, Harvey, big fire at U Mass, you should of seen it. Tower of flame, Coolidge Hall. A hundred students rescued from the roof by helicopter. Come on, you're wanted at the hospital. Couple of kids died of smoke inhalation."

"My God," said Harvey Kloop. For an instant his dream of the blue water of the reservoir remained upon the retina of his mental vision, and then it shriveled and vanished in the withering heat of the conflagration in Coolidge Hall.

6

The Horror not to be surveyed—
But skirted in the Dark . . .

*W*innie couldn't sleep. All night she floundered in her bedclothes. Not until dawn did she drift off at last. By the time she woke up, her mother and father had left for work and it was too late for the news on TV. Winnie was desperate to know what had happened. She wanted to go to Coolidge Hall and look for herself, but she didn't dare.

Instead she drove her van to the parking lot on the Amherst Common, and walked up to Amherst College to apply for the job at the Dickinson Homestead.

The woman who took her request in Converse Hall was distracted. "Oh, yes, I have a recommendation here somewhere from Professor Kraznik." She looked around vaguely. "Excuse me. This fire, it's got me all flustered."

Winnie's heart began beating furiously. "Fire? What fire?"

"At the University. Didn't you hear the sirens? They were going all night long. It was Coolidge Hall. Two students killed! It was dreadful, just dreadful."

Winnie stared at the woman and licked her lips. "Who were they?"

"Who—? Oh, you mean, who was killed? Oh, I don't know their names. A couple of boys. Sophomores, I think. Their poor parents! I've got a son at U Mass myself, only, thank heaven, he lives off campus."

"It was boys?" said Winnie, her heart lolloping in her chest. "Only boys?"

"That's right. Two sophomore men."

"But I thought there would be . . ."

"What did you say?"

"Nothing," said Winifred Gaw.

The fire in Coolidge Hall was big news. Television teams converged on Amherst. The president of the University was interviewed, and so were the helicopter pilots and the fire chief and the major from the air base and some of the students rescued from the roof and a bunch of miscellaneous people on the street and a handful of outraged parents who were calling for an investigation.

On the day after the fire, Owen Kraznik decided the best thing he could do was stay out of everyone's hair. He puttered around the house, trying to tidy it up for the arrival of Homer Kelly. The guest room was a problem. How could he make it look more comfortable? It smelled musty. It looked bleak. Owen didn't have the faintest idea what to do. There was a badminton net wrapped around a pair of poles in the corner and a dead typewriter on the dresser beside a jug of antifreeze. Opening the closet door, Owen was shocked to find an old gardening shirt of Catherine's hanging inside. It stopped him cold. He was still staring at it, wondering what to do, when the phone rang.

It was Mildred Crape, the provost of the University. Mildred wanted Owen to read a prayer at the memorial service for the two dead students.

"Oh, Mildred, I'm sorry," said Owen. "I can't do it. I'd break down in the middle. And that wouldn't help matters, would it?"

"Oh, honestly, Owen, it's too bad. Who else can I get? You're such an angel of light. That's what I keep telling Dombey Dell. That Owen Kraznik, I tell Dombey, he's an angel of light. Oh, that reminds me, Owen dear, Dombey and I have decided to enlarge your classes for next semester."

Owen gasped. "Enlarge my classes? But they're already too big as it is."

"I'm sorry, but we've got to quadruple the size of your lecture course. I mean, it's one of those famous courses everybody wants to take sometime in their college career. We'll get you another dozen teaching assistants and move you into Mahar Auditorium. Now don't groan, Owen. You're stuck with it, and that's a fact. Oh, by the way, I understand you've lost your secretary. Would you like a couple of new ones?"

"Oh, no, thank you, Mildred. I think I'll just carry on without a secretary for a while."

"Really? You mean it? Well, all right. It's your funeral."

"Or salvation," murmured Owen to himself as he hung up.

Homer Kelly moved in on Monday, with his Velveeta cheese, his tortilla chips, his Pizza Snax, his kosher dill pickles, his SpaghettiOs with Sliced Franks, his frozen fish sticks, his Grandmaw Butterworth's Homestyle Chicken Pie, his marshmallow cookies, and his instant banana cream pudding. He was full of news about the fire. "I stopped in at the police station to talk to Archie Gripp, an old friend of mine from Middlesex County. They've put him in charge of the investigation. Of course the insurance company will be looking into it too, you can bet on that. Hey, Owen, look at this. Mary sent along a pint of chicken livers. Fry them in butter, she said. I forgot to ask her how long. What do you think?"

"Half an hour?" said Owen doubtfully.

"Right-ho. Here they go. I'll just turn the heat up, and then we can have our drinks in the front room. It was arson, Archie thinks."

"Arson!"

"Strong smell of something flammable on the fourteenth floor, where the fire started. Couple of charred galvanized buckets."

"But why would anybody do such a thing?" Owen set a tray of drinks on the bench in front of the fireplace, moving

3 1

aside a shoe and a tin of shoe polish. "Do they have any idea who it could have been?"

"Well, they've got a list of people they want to find." Homer consulted his pocket notebook. "The kids in the building saw various strangers in the corridors on the day of the fire—an old guy with a beard, a woman with a cat on a leash, a guy selling a saxophone, a fat girl with a paper bag, and—here's the one I like—a gorilla."

"A gorilla?" Owen gasped. "Surely they must be joking."

"No, it's true. There was a gorilla wandering around on the fourth floor of Coolidge Hall last Friday night. It was just a gag, naturally. There's this guy who lives in the Orchard Hill student housing complex, owns a gorilla suit, his prize possession. He was just lallygagging around. But naturally he was dragged in by Archie Gripp and severely talked to."

"It occurs to me," said Owen thoughtfully, "that Hallowe'en is coming."

"That's right. That's what the gorilla said."

"The parents of those two poor boys are going to sue the University," said Owen gloomily, sipping his drink.

"Yes, I saw that on the news this morning," said Homer. "What's the University going to do about housing all those kids who were burned out?"

"Oh, everybody's doubling up. I offered to take some of them myself, but they said no. They're renting a couple of houses on North Pleasant Street to take the overflow." Owen coughed. "Homer, do I smell smoke? Good heavens, I wonder if the stove—"

"Good God," said Homer, leaping to his feet.

The chicken livers were tough black leathery nuggets. "I'm sure they'll be delicious," said Owen, scooping them onto the plates.

"You just have to—chew quite a lot," said Homer, chomping patiently. "Hmm, not bad—if I do say so—myself."

"Why, Homer, they're—really quite—tasty," said Owen, who had no taste buds at all, none at all.

*   *   *

And that was just the beginning. Encouraged by this culinary triumph, Homer began experimenting, branching out. By Christmas he had boiled, scorched, charred, and incinerated some fifty-five pounds of beef, lamb, chicken, fish, and pork. After the Christmas holidays he came back to Owen's house bearing a Christmas present, a French cook book, from his wife Mary. "From now on, Owen, it's *cordon bleu.*"

Owen was overjoyed to see him. "Oh, Homer, I missed you. Now things will feel normal again. And the University is back to normal too. I must say, it's a relief to see the place looking more like itself. The kids are moving into Coolidge Hall again, did you know that?"

"No kidding? Well, that was fast work."

"There was no structural collapse, as it turned out. Just surface disfigurement. A lot of smoke and water damage. I suppose young Alison Grove will be back there on the fourteenth floor where the fire started."

"Alison Grove?"

"One of the students in our department." Owen's forehead wrinkled in guilty recollection. "She wanted to work for me last fall. I had to say no. I hope she found another job."

But Alison Grove had not found another job. She hadn't needed one. Her wardrobe had been completely replenished free of charge. A special University fund had been set up to supply all the burned-out students in Coolidge Hall with cash for new clothing and new books.

And there was a new ring on Alison's finger. Tom and Alison were engaged now, officially engaged.

There was no engagement ring on the left hand of Dr. Ellen Oak, resident in charge of the emergency room at the Cooley-Dickinson Hospital. But that was only because Ellen had refused to wear a ring in the first place. It was true that she was seeing less and less of Tom Perry. Tom was always calling up to apologize. "I'm sorry I'm still so damned busy," he told her in February. "It's this symposium of Dombey Dell's. Dombey's asked me to help him out with this Emily Dickinson centennial conference. It's going to be a rat race, getting the thing organized in time."

Ellen was delighted. "An Emily Dickinson conference? Oh, say, that's just great. When is it? I'll come."

"Oh, no, you won't want to come. Boring speakers, a lot of claptrap. And I'll be so busy keeping the thing going, I won't have time to be with you."

Well, I'll come anyway, thought Ellen stubbornly, *I'll keep out of his way. I won't be a pest.*

Ellen wasn't the only one to be delighted at the news about the Emily Dickinson Centennial Symposium. Two thousand miles west of Amherst, in Pancake Flat, Arizona, Peter Wiggins was thrilled to find Dombey's invitation in his mailbox. Joyfully, he kicked a tricycle off the doorstep and brought the letter indoors to show Angie.

Angie was not impressed. Angie didn't want to be left alone with the children for days on end. "You're going to give another talk about that old photograph again? God! Who cares about a picture of somebody dead as a doornail?"

"You're jealous," said Peter angrily. "Just because she's so beautiful. You're jealous of my photograph."

"Jealous? Me? Jealous of an old photograph? Honestly, Peter, sometimes I think you've gone bananas. You've got this obsession. I mean, face it, that's what it is, an obsession with a dried-up old corpse in a cemetery."

"You ignorant little bitch," shouted Peter.

Nicole and Michelle began to shriek.

"Now see what you've done." Weeping, Angie gathered up the two babies and rushed out of the kitchen.

Left to himself, Peter went to the sink and gazed eastward out the window, hardly seeing the raw red hills, imagining instead some college in the East, with mellow brick buildings set tenderly around a tree-shaded lawn, where Peter would have an office to himself, a room like a green bower, engulfed with leafy growth, entwined with ivy, moist with dew.

3 4

7

The Sky is low—the Clouds are mean . . .

Spring was a mixed bag that year. There were balmy days in March, sucking the cold out of the ground, drawing everybody out-of-doors to admire the crocuses and quote Emily Dickinson—*We like March. His Shoes are Purple*—and cold, raw days in April, spitting rain and sleet. *Who knocks? That April. Lock the Door.*

The weather in Bartlett Hall was changeable too. Running into Dombey Dell in the corridor, Owen often found him testy. "Sensitive ladies, so far, that's all we've got. Bushels of responses from sensitive ladies. Marybelle Spikes, Jesus! Eunice Jane Kloop, my God!"

At other times, Dombey was jaunty and self-important. His big-deal arrangements were going well. The National Endowment for the Humanities had contributed ten thousand dollars, the University was going to pay the travel expenses of Peter Wiggins, and Amherst College had agreed to underwrite the cost of food and drink. *The New York Times* was sending a correspondent. There were applicants from all over the country, and from Sweden and Mexico. Far away across the Pacific Ocean, the Japanese Poetry Society, a men's club, was chartering a plane, an entire plane.

"Thank God, Owen, the Coolidge Hall fire isn't front-page news any more. Now we can get a little attention. We're going to restore the good name of the University in the public eye, right?"

"Well, I fervently hope so," said Owen. "Oh, Dombey, do you have a brochure? I don't think you ever sent me a brochure."

"A brochure?" Dombey shook his head. "Oh, too bad, Owen. As a matter of fact, I'm all out. Got to print up some more."

And therefore it wasn't until Dombey posted the new brochure on the bulletin board at the bus stop in front of Stockbridge Hall that Owen saw the list of symposium speakers. Only then did he discover that there were to be no women on the program. Instantly he called Dombey and complained.

"Oh, but you don't know about Alison Grove," said Dombey. "Alison's going to be on the program. She's going to wear Emily Dickinson's white dress and read a poem."

"She's going to wear the white dress? Listen, Dombey, you know that's a sacrilege. And, anyway, that's not enough. Alison Grove may be a woman, but she's certainly no scholar."

Dombey groaned. What the hell! Owen was so damned unpredictable. Most of the time the man was quiet and unassuming, and then for no reason at all he'd turn intractable and stubborn. "Listen, Owen, it's too late. And, anyway, there's no room in the Dickinson Homestead. That's where all the speakers are going to be staying. You and me, too. Special arrangement with the College. And the brochure has already gone out, all around the world. I can't change it now."

Owen was outraged. Dombey was surely headed for disaster. No women speakers at a conference on the nation's foremost woman poet? The man was asking for trouble.

And Owen was right. Trouble was already brewing in two separate quarters in the town of Amherst. But when Owen stumbled on evidences of it himself, later on, he failed to recognize them for what they were, the first fierce sputterings of two powerful engines of rebellion.

He came upon the first crackle of defiance at a meeting of

the Amherst Historical Society in the old Strong house on Amity Street.

As president of the society, Owen always came early to turn on the electric heater and arrange the chairs in a circle in the downstairs parlor. But now, hearing voices from above, he decided the meeting must already have gathered upstairs.

On the second floor he found another bunch of people entirely. It was the executive committee of the Amherst Women's Emily Dickinson Association. The guiding spirit of A.W.E.D. was his old friend Tilly Porch. There sat Tilly with Dottie Poole and Barbara Teeter and Marilyn Wineman and Carolyn Chin and all the rest, gathered around a big table with their needles poised over a large piece of cloth. It looked to Owen like a gossip session, an old-fashioned sewing circle. "Oh, good afternoon, Tilly, Dottie, everyone. Sorry, wrong meeting. I didn't mean to intrude."

He had taken them by surprise. Tilly took one look at him, then snatched up the piece of cloth and tossed it upside down on the table. Pins and needles flew. Sitting back in their chairs, the women gasped, and then began to laugh.

Strong House

"I'm sorry, Owen," said Tilly. "Big secret. You're not in on it, I'm afraid."

But then Dottie Poole clasped her hands and beseeched, "Oh, Tilly, don't you think we should tell Professor Kraznik? I mean, what if he thinks we shouldn't do it at all?"

The other women were horrified. "Heavens, Dottie, of course not. How can you say such a thing? Never!"

Owen put up his hands as if to say, Far be it from me to inquire. And then, smiling, he ran downstairs to find the other members of the Historical Society collecting in the parlor.

Afterward, when his meeting was over, when all the other members of the Historical Society had dispersed, Owen lingered for a moment and listened to the voices from upstairs.

Once again Dottie Poole was sounding a note of distress. "Oh, Tilly, do you really think we should? Now that we're all done—I mean, now that I really get a look at it, I just feel so uncertain. I mean, I didn't know how really huge and *real* it was going to look. I mean, I just wonder if we should really go through with it?"

"Nonsense, Dottie." Someone else was speaking up firmly. Again Owen recognized the voice of his widowed old friend, Tilly Porch, who had lived all her life in the house of her ancestors on Market Hill Road. "Of course we should go through with it. Shouldn't we, everybody? Are we mad at those men or not?"

There were cheers from the other women, and cries of defiance. Owen stood with his hand on the latch of the front door as Tilly's voice rose above the rest in gallant reassurance. "Courage, Dottie, you have nothing to lose but your good name, your family and friends, and your reputation as a law-abiding citizen. Forward, Dottie, forward!"

The rest of them were shouting it too, in exuberant chorus. "Forward, Dottie, forward!"

And then there was a pause. "Oh, well, then, forward, I guess," came the voice of Dottie Poole, faltering down the stairs.

8

How martial is this place!
Had I a mighty gun
I think I'd shoot the human race
And then to glory run!

Nor did Owen perceive the first signal flare of the second revolution against Dombey Dell's all-male Emily Dickinson symposium. Although it passed right in front of his eyes, he failed to recognize it as a flaming rocket in the sky.

It was merely a rectangular notice at the bottom of one of the soggy pages of *The Hampshire Gazette*, picked up from Owen's rain-soaked front porch and spread out to dry on the kitchen table.

Before supper Homer used the paper to catch the slop as he beat up his *omelette aux fines herbes*, a concoction of eggs, basil, taco seasoning, and hot dog relish. But Homer paid no attention to the little notice, and neither did Owen when he mopped at the front page after supper and looked the paper through. Even the forest of exclamation points didn't catch his eye.

!!! S I N G L E S   F O R   E M I L Y   D I C K I N S O N !!!
??????????? Are you a SURVIVOR ???????????
Somehow myself survived the Night
And entered with the Day . . .
Poem by E. DICKINSON

!!! WOMEN SURVIVORS!!! Are you SINGLE ??? HURT ???
EXPLOITED ???
??????? HAVE YOU *had it* with MEN ???????

!!! JOIN S.I.N.G.E.D.—"SINGLES FOR EMILY DICKINSON" !!!

!!! *Talk sessions every Tuesday night at 8 in the basement
of the First Congregational Church* !!!

!!!!!!!! NOW PLANNING ACTION !!!!! URGENT !!!!!!!!

But the ad was not lost on Winifred Gaw.

Since last fall, Winnie had been struggling to keep going.
Her panic over the investigation of the fire in Coolidge Hall
had quieted down. No longer did her heart pound when she
heard a knock at the front door or a shrill ring from the phone
in her mother's kitchen. "Fat girl with a paper bag," the TV
had said. They were looking for a suspicious fat woman. Well,
they hadn't come to the right fat woman. And the paper bag
with its contents was gone forever. On the night of the fire, the
heavy bag had plunged one hundred and twenty-five feet
down into the empty blackness of Shaft 12, and then it had
been carried away through the tunnel to Boston in the torrent
of water from the Quabbin Reservoir.

So the danger was over. And Winnie's van had stopped
smelling of flammable chemicals. Her clothes had been washed
ten times. The crisis was past. She could breathe more freely.

And Professor Kraznik had been right about the job at the
Homestead. The job was okay. Winnie liked going to Emily
Dickinson's house every Tuesday and Friday. She liked the nice
smell of the house. It reminded her of Professor Kraznik, because it was sacred to the memory of Emily Dickinson. And
Winnie was getting her self-confidence back. Standing spread-
legged in Emily's bedroom, saying her piece over and over to
clusters of visiting tourists, she was beginning once again to feel
in charge. The place was hers and hers alone, every Tuesday
and Friday. Emily Dickinson's white dress in the closet was
Winnie's own personal possession. She could show it or keep it

4 0

an arrogant secret. She could let people in the door, or slam it in their faces, if they didn't have an appointment. Serve them right.

It was only at night that Winnie's wretchedness came back. She couldn't sleep. All the things that had been tucked into the folds of her fat during the daytime came creeping out at night, from the rings of flab around her throat, from the deep dimples in her elbows. The two guys whose lives had been snuffed out in Coolidge Hall—they were a knobby bundle that refused to stay hidden away in a fatty cranny. And the thought of Alison Grove, sitting at Winnie's desk, waiting upon Professor Kraznik in Winnie's place, Alison Grove with her torrent of red-gold hair, her bewitching prettiness—that was another terrible thing that kept spilling out of hiding, night after night.

Therefore the ad in *The Hampshire Gazette* was heaven-sent.

Somehow myself survived the night
And entered with the Day . . .

It spoke to Winnie. It was just what she needed.

!!! Talk sessions every Tuesday night at 8 in the basement
of the First Congregational Church !!!
!!!!!!!! NOW PLANNING ACTION !!!!! URGENT !!!!!!!!

It was always hard for Winnie to enter a group of strangers. On the next Tuesday evening at quarter past eight, she stood for a moment outside the basement door of the Congregational church, gathering her courage, and stared at the sign that said TAG SALE ON LAWN MAY 15. It had rained all day, but now the clouds were clearing in the west. There was a tremulous glow of sunset in the air.

Winnie opened the door. Immediately she was confronted by a huge banner, declaring the church to be in favor of
JOY!
There were voices down the hall. They stopped as Winnie paused in the doorway. The women in the folding chairs

looked up. Winnie scowled. She knew what they were thinking: *fat girl.* Maybe in a little while they would notice her eyes. *My eyes are my best feature,* thought Winnie. Instinctively she put her left hand with its stump of a little finger in the pocket of her pants.

A tall, hollow-cheeked woman stood up. She had lank colorless hair and steel-rimmed glasses. "Come on in. Join us. I'm Helen Gaunt. Here, sit down." Then Helen Gaunt explained the business of the evening. "We have this really important item on the agenda. This is sort of an emergency meeting. But first we want to get to know our new members. We were just talking to Debbie Buffington. She's new too. Okay, Debbie, you were saying you decided to keep the baby? What's his name? Elvis?"

Debbie was a pale young woman who looked about twelve years old. There were blue shadows under her eyes. She sucked on her cigarette. "Like I thought it would be just so

great, having this, you know, cute little doll to play with. Like
he'd stay in the corner in his crib. Only, like, wow, it isn't like
that at all. I mean, *I'm* the teeny person in the corner, and Elvis
is this really gigantic—" Debbie waved her transparent hands.
"All he does is bawl." She sank back and took another drag on
her cigarette, her face empty of feeling. "Like tonight I
couldn't even get a sitter. I had to dump Elvis with the lady
across the hall, and she was really pissed."

One of the women was hugely pregnant. She gazed at
Debbie with frightened doelike eyes. Next to her a big-boned
woman spoke up with bitter emphasis. "Listen, you think *you*
got trouble. I am the mother of *ten*. Wait till Elvis starts running around and getting into everything." The mother of ten
shook her head in dire warning.

Helen Gaunt cut the whining short. "You don't need a
baby-sitter," she said to Debbie. "Why don't you just bring Elvis
along?"

"Oh, Jesus, I couldn't do that," said Debbie. "He bawls all
the time."

"So?" said Helen Gaunt. "What's this big guilt trip? We
were all babies once. All babies bawl. You can't let your whole
life-style be cramped just because your kid acts like a kid. And,
hey, listen, that baby will fit right in. Wait till you hear what
we're going to do. We're all going to be in it. Elvis, too. I've got
this plan. I mean, Emily Dickinson is our role model, right?
She was a single woman, right? She thumbed her nose at the
world, right? She's one of us, isn't that right? Well, okay, wait
till you hear about the latest insult to her memory." Helen
Gaunt looked around the circle. "There's this conference. This
big Emily Dickinson conference. All these big speakers are
going to talk about Emily Dickinson. And get this." Helen's
voice sank an octave. "They're all men."

"Men?" whispered the expectant mother.

"Men?" gasped the Mother of Ten.

"Men?" breathed Winifred Gaw.

"Every—single—one." Helen Gaunt sat back grimly.

Winnie Gaw was dumbfounded. Of course Winnie had

heard about the conference, because she had been asked to conduct special tours for visiting scholars. But nobody had said the speakers would exclusively be *men*. Winnie was flabbergasted.

"Wait till you hear my idea," said Helen Gaunt solemnly, leaning forward like a conspirator. Then she looked at Winnie. "Oh, I forgot. It's your turn to introduce yourself. Go ahead. Tell us all about it."

"Well," said Winnie, "like it said in the ad in the paper, people that have been hurt." To Winnie's amazement, her throat filled with sobs. "You know, when somebody—" She paused again, uncertain how to go on. "You know, when a man—I mean it's a lot like what they did to Emily Dickinson."

There were kindly murmurs, clucks of sympathy.

Winnie stopped. She had gone far enough. She let the implication hang in the air that her pain had been inflicted by a perfidious lover.

Helen Gaunt looked at the fat girl, and wondered how Winnie could ever have attracted a man, even for a moment. But she muttered gently, "Join the club."

"God, I don't know what I'm doing here," said Debbie Buffington, dropping her cigarette on the floor and grinding it under her heel. "I mean, like, Jesus! Who's Emily Dickinson anyway, for creep's sake?"

9

God keep me from what they call households . . .

*H*omer felt comfortable in Owen's house. For one thing, he didn't have to pick anything up from the floor, the way he did at home. And that was all right with Owen, who had little sense of house pride himself. And both of them enjoyed Homer's gourmet meals, which were new and different every day.

On Monday the twelfth of May, the day before Dombey Dell's symposium was to get under way, dinner was beefsteak. "Why don't we just put it in the oven and let it bake slowly during the happy hour?" said Homer. "And then I'll toss the salad and we'll be all set."

"Perfect," said Owen. "Oh, Homer, I've been meaning to ask you, has there been anything new in the investigation of the Coolidge Hall fire? Or is it hopeless? Have they given up?"

"Given up? Good grief, no. I talked to Archie yesterday. He says all the likely suspects have been cleared, but they're still working on the notion that it was some disgruntled psychotic student. Poor Archie. That means sifting through twenty-five thousand kids, one at a time. And of course they're still trying to track down the source of the kerosene, or gasoline, or whatever it was in those burned buckets. You know,

they're checking garages, hardware stores, talking to kids who pump gas."

Owen looked sadly at the empty hearth of the fireplace, where for some reason a volleyball lay behind the fender. "But, Homer, you can get kerosene in the supermarket. I remember buying it there. Catherine used to light the fire with kerosene."

"Oh, sure." Homer jumped up quickly, snatched the salad bowl, and got to work vigorously with spoon and fork. Soon fragments of cabbage and iceberg lettuce were flying all over the table.

But that night in bed the empty fireplace haunted Owen's dreams. It was a black pit, an endless narrow flue into which he was falling. When something shrilled at him, something insistent, something demanding, he opened his eyes and sat up. The window was gray with the half-light of early morning. The harsh noise was the telephone. Gratefully, Owen reached for it and said hello.

Once again it was his cousin, Dr. Harvey Kloop. Harvey's whisper came hissing out of the phone, inviting Owen to come with him to Quabbin.

Owen whispered too, aware of the sleeping menace of Eunice Jane. "You're going fishing again?"

"Again? This is the first time, and the fishing season started a month ago. I've packed a lot of sandwiches and beer. How about it?"

"Oh, Harvey, I'm sorry. Someday I hope to see that Quabbin of yours. But today I've got to be at the Homestead to greet the people who are coming to the Emily Dickinson symposium. I'm really sorry."

"Emily Dickinson? Not again? The hell with Emily Dickinson! Who cares about Emily Dickinson?" It was a joke between them. Owen didn't blame Harvey for being sick to death of Emily Dickinson, or at least of the tiresome incarnation of Emily Dickinson that loomed over the Kloop household in the dread imagination of Eunice Jane. "Well, too bad, Owen. So long, then. I'll get going right away. I've got to get out of here fast before somebody calls, Mabel Grout or somebody like that, with one of her spells."

"Why don't you just take the phone off the hook?"

"Oh, no. Can't do that. It's against my Hippo-something oath."

"Your what? Listen, Harvey," said Owen wistfully, "have a good time. I wish I could come with you."

At the other end of the line, Harvey Kloop put down the phone and crept back into the bedroom for his heavy sweater. Then he froze in his tracks. Eunice Jane was rearing up in bed. Staring straight ahead, she was croaking another weird passage from the insane poetry of Emily Dickinson: *"Below Division is Adhesion's forfeit."* But it was all right, decided Harvey. Eunice Jane was sound asleep. She was flopping back on the pillow with a snort.

Grinning, Harvey tiptoed downstairs. Already a picture was glowing in his head, a bright vision of the boat-launching dock at Gate 43. Already he could see the lively scene at the

4 7

pier, he could hear the scrape of the aluminum bottoms on the concrete ramp, the jocular greetings of the men in their orange flotation vests and duckbilled caps, and the sputter of the outboards as the boats curved away from the dock and headed for open water, to float for the rest of the day above the drowned cellar holes of the little lost villages at the bottom of the lake.

Picking up his fishing gear and his lunch box, Harvey struggled with the back door, thinking about those old ghost towns under the water and the empty cemeteries down there— even the coffins had been removed! And all those dislocated people whose houses and factories and churches had been destroyed back in the nineteen-thirties. It was terrible, really, what had happened, even though the resulting lake and its surrounding watershed were Harvey's idea of heaven on earth, the heaven that was to be his for the rest of the day, if he could just—get out—the back door. Carefully, Harvey closed the door behind him, tiptoed down the porch steps, climbed into his car, and rolled down the driveway.

But once again he was intercepted. There was a screech from the bedroom window: "Harvey, telephone!"

Wincing, he looked up to see Eunice Jane grinning cruelly down at him.

This time it was Mabel Grout, in person, flat on her back on the floor of her breakfast nook, with the telephone entangled, she said, around her neck.

10

. . . all is jostle, here—scramble and confusion . . .

*O*wen packed up the notes for his speech, his shaving kit, a clean shirt and his pajama bottoms, and said a regretful good-bye to Homer Kelly. Then he walked around the corner to the Homestead. From now on he would be at the mercy of Dombey Dell.

Walking up the driveway, Owen stood behind the Dickinson house for a moment, looking up at it, reluctant to go inside. It pleased him to think that the light must have fallen on the high bulk of the brick walls a century ago just as it did today. Lofty and solid, the house rose above him on its granite foundations. It was like the poet who had lived in it, decided Owen, in her hard-won sense of self.

> *The Props assist the House*
> *Until the House is built*
> *And then the Props withdraw*
> *And adequate, erect,*
> *The House support itself*
> *And cease to recollect*
> *The Augur and the Carpenter—*
> *Just such a retrospect*
> *Hath the perfected Life—*

A past of Plank and Nail
And slowness—then the Scaffolds drop
Affirming it a Soul.

For a moment as Owen stood on the back porch, house and poet became one. He put down his bag and rang the bell.

Dombey Dell opened the door. "Oh, there you are, Owen. Good." Behind Dombey a chambermaid from the College was carrying a pile of sheets. "Come on in. Your room's at the front, upstairs, across from the sacred bedchamber. Right this way." Briskly, Dombey ran up the stairs ahead of Owen, and threw open the door of Lavinia Dickinson's bedroom.

Owen wanted to protest, to ask for a different room, but he didn't want to be a nuisance. Here he couldn't forget Catherine, who had shared it with him once, back in the good days before she had become so ill. Painful memories crowded in upon Owen as the chambermaid ballooned a clean sheet over the bed and Dombey rushed away down the hall.

There is a finished feeling
Experienced at Graves—
A leisure of the Future—
A Wilderness of Size.

A Wilderness—that described it exactly. Since his wife's death, Owen had found himself stumbling through a wilderness, a bleak forest where no light fell.

The doorbell rang. There was an anguished shout from Dombey. "Get that, will you, Owen?"

Owen hurried down the stairs and opened the back door. There on the porch stood a slight young man with fair hair and high tense shoulders. He was carrying a square case and a heavy bag. "How do you do?" he said, speaking with painful care. "My name is Wiggins. I hope I am not—"

It was the professor from Pancake Flat. "Oh, Professor Wiggins," said Owen. "Come right in. We've been expecting you. My name is Kraznik. I'm eager to hear what you have to say about that intriguing photograph."

Peter Wiggins took a deep breath, and stepped inside. His shoulders relaxed. He put down his slide projector and his bag, and followed Professor Kraznik, looking reverently this way and that at the sanctified spaces of the house of his dreams. In the kitchen he sat down timidly, awed by the august presence of the great Owen Kraznik. But soon he was disarmed.

"Tea bag?" said Owen. "Good heavens, I wonder if you can help me figure out how this stove works. Milk? Sugar? Oh, sorry, no sugar, I'm afraid. Now where are the spoons?"

And then Owen expressed a flattering interest in Peter's precious picture. Soon Peter was removing it from his billfold and unfolding it delicately from its tissue paper.

"How fascinating," said Owen, gazing at it eagerly. "What a handsome young woman she is, indeed. Would you like to see your room? We'll have to find Professor Dell."

On the landing they ran into Dombey. Shaking hands with Peter Wiggins, Dombey was lordly and energetic. "Sorry, Wiggins, but we have to stow you on the third floor. We decided you were young enough to make it up two flights of stairs—not like some of us, cough, choke." Playfully, Dombey pounded his own chest. "Oh, say, Owen, did I tell you *The New York Times* is sending somebody?"

"Yes, you did. More than once, as a matter of fact."

"Well, listen. This is brand-new. I just got a phone call.

The Smith Brothers are coming. Do you know them, Wiggins, the two brothers from Harvard?"

"Well, of course, I've heard of them." Greatly daring, Peter ventured a joke. "I've often wondered—ha, ha—if they have short and long beards like the Smith brothers on the cough-drop box."

"Oh, yes, ha, ha," echoed Dombey. "Well, it's true, they do. They're famous for it. It's common knowledge." Then Dombey poked Owen slyly in the ribs. "Rumor has it they're head-hunting. Looking for somebody to replace that poet, Pulsifer Rexpole. Lousy teacher, apparently, Rexpole. So there'll be an opening at that distinguished institution of higher learning on the River Charles. What do you think of that?"

Peter's hand tightened on the strap of his canvas suitcase. *A job opening at Harvard. Perhaps when the Smith brothers hear my significant platform address, they might think*—Peter followed Owen to the third floor, thanked him effusively, closed the door, and turned around, grinning, to gaze at his room.

He was in the attic, Emily Dickinson's own attic. She had come up to the attic to read Shakespeare. The room was filled with cool green light. Hurrying to the narrow arched windows, Peter looked out upon a landscape thick with new spring foliage. Through the branches of the trees he could see the cupola of Emily's brother's house next door.

She must see everything too. Swiftly, fumbling at the latch, Peter took his slide projector out of its case and set it up on the top of the dresser. Soon the beautiful face of the woman in his photograph was looking back at him from the blank wall above his bed.

"You're home at last," said Peter softly. Smiling at her in congratulation, he imagined her great eyes staring out of the front page of *The New York Times* the day after tomorrow. And there would be a headline: WIGGINS PROVES VALIDITY OF DICKINSON PHOTOGRAPH.

And then, perhaps, by some crazy stroke of luck, he might win the job at Harvard. Or if not at Harvard, somewhere else, anywhere east of Albany. Anywhere in the green and wooded

5 2

East, far from the desert country of Pancake Flat, Arizona. "Dear God," muttered Peter, who didn't believe in God, "get us out of there." He closed his eyes and clenched his fists. "Soon, soon, soon."

11

Noon—is the Hinge of Day . . .

At lunchtime Owen managed to sneak off by himself, grasping at a last cowardly moment of anonymity. He felt a little guilty. He should have asked Peter Wiggins to go with him. But there was something about the naked want in Peter's face that suggested an incipient lame duck, and Owen was wary of encouraging him.

In the Gaslite restaurant he took the next-to-last empty stool, consulted the sticky menu, and ordered a Superburg Delite. As he finished it and pushed away his plate, someone sat down beside him, deposited her pocketbook nimbly on the floor, and opened a pamphlet. Recognizing the brochure, Owen spoke up amiably. "Excuse me," he said. "Are you attending the Dickinson conference?"

The woman took off her glasses and smiled at him. She had a thin face and keen eyes. "Yes, I came early to find a place to stay. Actually, my fiancé is helping to run the symposium, but I don't want to be in his way. He doesn't even know I'm coming."

"Dombey Dell?" Owen was astonished. "You're engaged to Dombey Dell?"

"Oh, no." The woman laughed. "Not Professor Dell. Tom Perry. My name is Ellen Oak."

So this was the doctor from Northampton. Owen was stunned. His irrepressible compassion rushed to the surface. Blushing scarlet in anguished sympathy, he mumbled something in congratulation, aware at the same instant of the arrival of Alison Grove. Alison was standing beside the door, looking for an empty stool. Heads turned. The boys behind the counter looked up. For a split second everything in the Gaslite restaurant came to a halt, then went on as before.

"The hamburgers are very good," said Owen courteously, pointing to a grease spot on the menu, "and the French fries are delicious."

"Oh, thank you," said Ellen. Promptly she ordered Lunch #17, Quarter-pounder with French fries and coleslaw.

Then Owen introduced himself. It was Ellen's turn to be surprised. "Oh, Professor Kraznik, I'm looking forward so much to your lecture tomorrow afternoon."

"Oh, no," said Owen. "I'm sure it will be dull. I don't think you should bother to attend."

"Come now," said Ellen. "I'm tired of being told that. Tom said it too. 'Don't bother,' he said. 'It will just be the same old stuff. Stay home.' But I decided to come anyway, on my own hook." Ellen's grin was dazzling, a flash of big white teeth. "After all, I'm the biggest Dickinson freak in Northampton."

Again Owen blushed for the dishonesty of Tom Perry. How could the boy be so two-faced? Getting up from the counter, Owen said a cordial good-bye to Ellen Oak and went to the cash register, nodding politely at Alison Grove as she moved forward to take his place. Paying for his lunch, Owen shook his head, wondering at the difference between Tom's two girlfriends. There was no comparison. One was so ordinary, the other so striking. What a foolish, careless boy!

Ellen's hamburger was enormous. Picking it up hungrily, she glanced at the girl who was settling herself on Professor Kraznik's stool, and felt a twinge of envious wonder. How lovely the girl was! A pinnacle of nature, a sort of masterpiece. In her presence everything else fell away—all achievement, all endeavor. Beside this physical perfection nothing else seemed important. And it was the kind of perfection you couldn't deserve. You could only be born with it. It was showered upon you from above—or else it wasn't. You couldn't get it by trying, by working, by any kind of strenuous effort.

Ellen chewed her hamburger thoughtfully. It occurred to her that Alison's beauty was like grace, the old-fashioned Calvinist concept of grace. Grace, too, came down from the sky, unearned, a present from God. Right here in Amherst, in the old days, people had prayed for grace, hoped for it, yearned to have it descend upon them. But sometimes in vain. Even Emily Dickinson had never experienced the miracle that was required for conversion. Somehow she could never get the hang of it.

"Anything else?" said the boy behind the counter, snatching away Ellen's plate, staring at the girl beside her.

"Coffee, black," said Ellen. And then she smiled to herself as she thought of conversion as it was practiced today, in all the little college towns of the Connecticut Valley, right here and now. These days it was sexual, not spiritual—a sudden overnight metamorphosis from virginity to rapturous understand-

The gaslite

ing. Every day in the week, women students came to Ellen's office to learn how to win this blessed transfiguration without embarrassing consequences.

The beautiful girl was ordering canned peaches and cottage cheese. Ellen found herself wondering how it would feel to look like that. She couldn't imagine it. But, after all, she told herself, it didn't matter. Even without that kind of birthright, she had been lucky. For one thing, she really liked her job at the hospital. She loved figuring out what was the matter with people. It was something she did well. And then this man had come into the emergency room with his inflamed appendix, last summer, and her life had suddenly changed—

As if I asked a common Alms,
And in my wondering hand
A Stranger pressed a Kingdom . . .

Alison Grove left half a peach uneaten, remembering what her mother said, always leave a little on your plate. Sipping her coffee, she was hardly aware of the woman sitting next to her except as part of the universe that wheeled around Alison Grove. Without glancing left or right, Alison knew that everyone in the Gaslite was aware of her, the other people at the counter, the girl at the cash register, the guys making sandwiches. In all her life so far, Alison had seldom beheld the profile of another human being, only full round faces staring at her. Even when Alison was a baby, her own mother had fastened her sad eyes upon her, she had dandled Alison in her lap, she had stroked Alison's pretty dresses, she had twined Alison's hair around her finger. Alison had been her mother's only darling. She would have been her father's darling, too, only Alison didn't have a father. Her mother never talked about him. He had vanished long ago.

But she was the world's darling as well. Whenever Alison walked into a room, she gathered all attention to herself and held it, without lifting a finger, without opening her mouth to speak.

It seemed natural to Alison that this should be so. She

hardly bothered to think that she had been especially chosen. But Alison knew one thing, and knew it well. She had not been made so beautiful for nothing. It was like something Emily Dickerson had said—Alison had heard this lecture in Stockbridge Hall—*there is always one thing to be grateful for, that one is one's self and not somebody else.*

Now Alison spared a glance out of the corner of her eye at the woman sitting next to her, grateful once again that she was Alison Grove, that she wasn't really, really ugly, with a long nose and sallow skin and those incredible skinny pigtails fastened on top of her head. How did the woman stand it when she looked at herself in the mirror?

"Oh, darling, there you are." Suddenly Alison was swept up from the stool, engulfed in a tweed jacket, embraced and kissed, while everyone else in the restaurant looked on, pleased at the sight of two marvelous-looking young people in one another's arms. And then the two of them made their way to the cash register, crushed together, the man's hand in the red-gold hair of the girl.

Tom Perry had not even noticed the drab woman in the brown dress, although he was still engaged to be married to Ellen Oak.

12

Behold! Whose Multitudes are these?

After lunch Owen felt restless. He was reluctant to go back to the Homestead. And he wasn't needed right away. Dombey had promised to play host for the afternoon. Actually, Owen knew, Dombey was lying in wait for the Smith brothers.

"Why not invite them to stay in the Homestead?" Dombey had said to Owen. "They could have my room, and I could move in with you."

"But I thought the house was reserved for the speakers," protested Owen. "The Smith brothers aren't going to speak."

"Well, what the hell," said Dombey Dell. "I just thought, considering their position—and, after all, it's *my* symposium." And then Dombey took Owen by the shoulders and shook him, rattling his teeth together. "Listen, Owen, they're *terribly* interested in Emily Dickinson."

Taking his time, Owen walked around the Common. To his nearsighted vision the sidewalks along South Pleasant Street seemed to be tumbling. Students were milling everywhere. A couple of girls were licking ice cream cones in the vast shade of the ancient katsura tree on Boltwood Avenue. It was almost time for exams, but the day felt festive. A pink balloon wobbled

The Common

on a parking meter. Owen could detect no tension in the air. Even the boy approaching him with an armload of books lost his look of studious solemnity as his bubble gum swelled and exploded all over his nose.

Duty was calling. Owen walked back to the Homestead. In the driveway he found Dombey abandoning ship. "The Smiths are at the Lord Jeffery Inn," said Dombey importantly. Slicking down his hair, he scuttled away up the street.

But Homer Kelly was shambling up the walk to keep Owen company. "Hi," he said. "Just thought I'd come along and help you hold the fort."

Afterward, remembering Homer's innocent remark, Owen was struck by its prophetic power. Within the hour, the Homestead was a besieged fortress, a stronghold under attack.

At first, settling to their coffee in the kitchen, Owen and Homer paid no attention to the commotion out-of-doors. It wasn't until the noise became insistent, like the rustling of a great gathering of birds, a shrill chattering like the mutterings of eagles or giant rocs, with a tenor undertone in some foreign tongue, that the two of them suddenly looked at each other and hurried to the parlor to look out the window.

"Dottie Poole, stop falling behind," cried Tilly Porch, marching backward at the front of the line, her glasses tipped wildly sideways. "Rachel! Carolyn! Hold the banner high!"

Obediently, Rachel Miller and Carolyn Chin lifted the banner of the Amherst Women's Emily Dickinson Association at arm's length over their heads. The women of A.W.E.D. were present in strength. Their banner was a freshly ironed sheet with huge letters appliquéd in calico:

EMILY IS OURS!

At the granite steps in front of the Homestead they suddenly stopped short and stared.

Another straggling line was advancing on the Dickinson house, another banner fluttered in the breeze, another pair of glasses sparkled in the sunlight. At the head of the other procession a tall thin woman marched sturdily forward. Behind her wallowed a vast shape in a denim jumper, then an expectant mother, leaning backward to balance her burden, and then a miscellaneous raggedy crowd. At the end of the line a girl lugged a whining child.

This militia too had a flag, a yellowed curtain crudely lettered with a marking pen. Tilly squinted at it. What did it say? It had folded over on itself again. But now it billowed wide.

BUILDING TAKEOVER!

"Good God," gasped Tilly Porch. Through her mind rushed a jumble of images from the late sixties and early seventies, the anti-Vietnam moratorium at Amherst College, the Quaker peace vigils on the Common, the sit-in at Westover Air Force Base. It was all so long ago. What sort of takeover was this? What building were these women planning to occupy? Not the Homestead? Surely they weren't about to trespass on the ancestral home of Emily Dickinson?

"Who are those people?" whispered Barbara Teeter.

"Isn't this insane?" said Rachel Miller, giggling.

"I want to go home," whimpered Dottie Poole.

"Hold it a sec," shouted a kid in the street. He had a camera. He was backing up to take a wide-angle shot of the two processions staring at each other beside the old wooden sign that said: THE DICKINSON HOMESTEAD, BY APPOINTMENT ONLY.

"Excuse, please," said someone to Tilly. "May I please? Excuse!"

From nowhere a third parade was emerging, a long line of Oriental-looking men in shiny black shoes and dark business jackets and open-collared sports shirts. Smiling, nodding, bowing, they pressed past Tilly Porch and Helen Gaunt, and moved up the walk in a thick flood. "Pardon! Please excuse!" Behind them on the street, a chartered bus released its brakes with a wheezing sigh and pulled away from the curb.

The two lines of women fell back. Tilly Porch gathered her wits. Stepping up to Helen Gaunt, she said crisply, "I think we ought to parley."

Owen couldn't believe his eyes. Leaning out the parlor window, he stared, gasping, at the men moving up the sidewalk, at the women spilling over the front yard. One of the women was Winifred Gaw. They were carrying signs and banners:

EMILY IS OURS!
BUILDING TAKEOVER!
EMILY WAS A WOMAN!
MOTHER OF TEN!

"Mother of ten?" cackled Homer Kelly. "How irrelevant can you get? What does motherhood have to do with Emily Dickinson? My God, Owen, it's Pearl Harbor. It's the Amazon army scaling the walls. Man the battle stations."

The boy with the camera was running up from the street. Winnie Gaw, too, was taking pictures. All the Oriental-looking men had cameras, and there was a continuous soft clicking of shutters as they recorded the front porch, the plaque on the wall, the blossoming dogwood trees.

Owen couldn't figure it out. He put a trembling hand to his forehead. Why were there no women among the invaders from the Far East, no men among the protesting white faces? What mad union of masculine East and feminine West was assaulting the Dickinson Homestead?

"Come on, old man," said Homer staunchly. "I'll stand beside you. Open the front door."

Owen got a grip on himself. Grasping the handle of the door, he swung it wide. Instantly, shining round faces pressed forward.

"Good afternoon, please?" A plump man in trifocals was smiling at him. "The bus, it deposit us at this address. Poetess live here, is it not so?"

"Merciful heavens," said Owen. "Professor Nogobuchi, welcome!"

It was the Japanese Poetry Society, at the end of its journey halfway around the world. From seven thousand miles away it had arrived at its destination, and now it was gazing at the sacred shrine with reverence and joy and humble eagerness to learn.

Owen stared wildly from Professor Nogobuchi to the women in the background. "Oh, sir, are they with you?"

Professor Nogobuchi turned to look at the swarming lawn He seemed astonished. His companions looked too. All of them shook their heads vigorously. "Oh, no," explained Professor Nogobuchi. "Ladies regrettably not of our party. Unhappy misfortune to be unrelated."

Then Homer saved the day. Stepping in with flowery eloquence, he saluted the gentlemen from Tokyo and explained that there would be an official welcoming tour of the house later on in the afternoon, at which time Professor Kraznik would be overjoyed to welcome them back.

"So happy!" exclaimed Professor Nogobuchi. "This visit in

politeness only. We go now to Lord Jeffely Inn. Four-thirty! Return sharp!"

Hands were shaken and glowing smiles exchanged, while the women dressed their lines, ready for combat. As the Japanese delegation retreated, bowing once again to the standard-bearers at parade-rest in front of the hemlock hedge, Tilly Porch exchanged a glance with Helen Gaunt, and raised her arm. Solemnly the women of S.I.N.G.E.D. and A.W.E.D. advanced upon Owen Kraznik and Homer Kelly at the front door of the Dickinson Homestead.

"It's not fair," said Helen Gaunt, staring angrily at Homer, her angular body pitched forward, her running shoes gripping the porch. "Singles for Emily Dickinson protests. We've got this list of demands." Helen gestured vaguely at the boy with the camera. "Everything you say will be taken down by the press."

"She's right, you know, Owen," said Tilly Porch, standing beside Helen, nodding her head wisely. "We don't like it either. I mean the rest of us here, the Amherst Women's Emily Dickinson Association. No women speakers on your program? It just won't do."

"After all," said Helen Gaunt loudly, half turning to look at the followers massed behind her on the lawn, "what was Emily Dickinson anyway? She was a woman, right?"

It was a signal. A chant struck up: *"Emily Dickinson was a woman! Emily Dickinson was a woman!"* They were all shouting at once, and waving their placards back and forth, and lifting their banners to dip and flap in the warm May wind.

"My God, Owen," murmured Homer Kelly. "What are you going to do now?"

But Owen had made up his mind. Gazing seraphically at the blue sky dotted with puffy clouds, he stretched out a welcoming hand. "Invite them in, of course."

13

Why cant I be a Delegate to the great Whig Convention?

*L*eading the way into the parlor, Owen felt wretchedly unequal to confrontation. But to Homer Kelly, Owen's handling of the explosive affair seemed just right. Perhaps *handling* wasn't the right word. Owen was merely listening, sitting patiently in a chair beside the display of Dickinson china, while the sunlight of early afternoon glittered on the gilt edges of the saucers and shone through the translucent porcelain of the teacups, and Helen Gaunt and Tilly Porch took turns bawling him out.

Homer sat back cautiously in his own chair, another fragile antique. (Homer had an unfortunate history of crushing valuable pieces of furniture.) Soon he stopped listening to Helen Gaunt and amused himself by imagining Emily Dickinson's father holding court in the same room, confronting some delegation of town fathers or state politicians or railroad men. What would Squire Dickinson have thought of the present circumstance if he could have foreseen it in a crystal ball? Homer's mind balked. He couldn't imagine Edward Dickinson even beginning to struggle to catch a glimmer of a speck of an idea of what this was all about. In the Amherst of Edward's time there had been no question about the proper behavior of men and

women. Men ran things, women kept the children and the house in order. And that was that.

But Owen Kraznik was not another Edward Dickinson. "You're right," he said softly, "of course."

There was an astonished pause. Tilly Porch smiled and glanced at Helen Gaunt, but Helen had been expecting some masculine trick. Narrowing her eyes in their hollow sockets, she waited for the betrayal.

But it wasn't a trick. With one gallant sweep, Owen over-turned Dombey Dell's schedule for the next day. "Professor Dell asked me to be the executive director of this conference, and therefore I will now make an executive decision. Which of you would like to speak tomorrow? I'll guarantee you a place on the agenda. Tilly? Aren't you the local expert on the Dickinson family tree? Won't you give us the benefit of your research?"

"Certainly," said Tilly promptly. "I've got a talk up my sleeve, all ready to go."

And then there was a volunteer. To Owen's dismay, Winifred Gaw raised her hand. Winnie was sitting on the floor at his feet, her jumper spreading around her like a wigwam. The fat hand she was holding over her head was not the hand with the missing finger. That one was tucked under her knee.

"Oh, Winnie, of course," said Owen, flinching. "Your essay on Emily Dickinson's method of capitalization? Well, why not?" Grimly, Owen reflected that the entire audience would now be punished for Dombey Dell's tiresome display of sexist chauvinism. He ran a finger around his collar. "Now, since the other speakers are staying in the house, I hope the new people on the program will stay here too. Tilly, how about you? The rest of us can double up."

"No, thanks," said Tilly. "Too many things to do at home."

"Winnie?"

"Yes," said Winnie, grinning, her great face flushed with triumph. Instantly her self-confidence swooped too far up the scale. Her sulky defiance vanished, and she became overbearing. "What about Emily's bedroom?" she said imperiously. "Who's going to sleep in there?"

"Oh, nobody will be using that room," said Owen. Reaching down in a gesture of good will, he took Winnie's hand.

The confrontation was over. Helen Gaunt unfolded her long bones from the floor, the Mother of Ten hurried home to make a vat of spaghetti, the pregnant woman staggered to her feet, feeling ready to give birth, and the members of the Amherst Women's Emily Dickinson Association burst into excited conversation as they drifted to the door. Dottie Poole was beaming with relief, overjoyed to have survived the afternoon without going to jail.

Only the baby seemed distressed. Elvis Buffington, a fat child of thirteen months, had been sleeping in his mother's arms, but now he woke up and howled with hunger. "Oh, Christ," said Debbie. Reaching into her bag, she took out a candy bar.

Tilly was scandalized. The baby was too fat. His mother looked starved. "Why don't you come to my house with the baby?" she said to Debbie. "I've got fresh-picked peas for supper." Picking up Elvis, Tilly held him at arm's length and tossed him playfully in the air. Elvis hiccuped once, and stopped crying. Tilly's grandmotherly face was the loveliest thing he had ever seen.

Outdoors on the sidewalk there was a flurry of mutual congratulation. Helen Gaunt slapped Winnie on the back and grinned at her. "Good for you, Winnie. You'll really sock it to them tomorrow, right?"

Winnie felt a frightening lurch in the pit of her stomach as she remembered the mishmash of her capitalization paper. But at the same time she was seized by fierce ambition. She would show them, all those stuck-up people who had thrown her out of the department! She'd show them she deserved to study with Owen Kraznik! Winnie hurried off importantly in the direction of her car. She would drive home for her notes and her nightie and something to wear tomorrow, and then she would rush back to conduct the official tour of the Homestead at four-thirty.

Hurrying around the corner of Triangle Street to her beat-up van, Winnie closed her eyes for an ecstatic instant and kissed the hand that had been held in the hand of Professor Owen Kraznik.

Homer Kelly, too, was enchanted with the afternoon. It wasn't the justice of the women's cause that had diverted him, it was the everlasting melodrama of human souls in conflict. It was the handfuls of gritty sand that were forever being sprinkled into the machinery of daily life, grinding the ill-fitting cogs against each other, warping the sprockets, jamming the mismatched teeth. It was always so fascinating, the way people went right on being so outrageously themselves, and therefore so eternally interesting. "Owen, old man, you were magnificent," said Homer.

Owen was deathly pale, his forehead beaded with perspiration. "Well, then, tell me—how am I going to tell Dombey Dell he's got to make room on his schedule tomorrow for a paper by Winifred Gaw?"

"Want me to tell him?" offered Homer amiably. "Look, if

he gives you any trouble, just call on me. I'll knock his block off. I'll wring his neck. Oh, say, Owen, that reminds me. I bought a chicken. How about coming home for supper tonight?"

"Oh, no, thank you, Homer. I've got to be friendly to all those people who are arriving today. I'm sorry."

"Oh, by the way, Owen, Mary's coming for the picnic on Thursday. Is it okay if she shares my room?"

"Why, certainly. I'll be delighted to see her."

"Well, so long then, Owen. Sorry about the chicken. I think I'll boil it in gin. That ought to sozzle its gizzard. Now, remember, Owen, if you have a hard time with Dombey Dell, just call me up. I'll come right over and bust him one."

14

Will the frock I wept in
Answer me to wear?

"What the hell?" said Dombey
Dell. "What the hell? What the hell? What the hell?"

Owen explained it again, from the beginning, and then he stood quietly beside the piano in the Dickinson parlor for fifteen minutes, enduring Dombey's rage and despair.

"Winifred Gaw? A platform address by Winifred Gaw? I'll be a laughingstock! How could you do it to me, Owen? How could you?"

But at last Dombey cooled down and accepted the additions with reluctant grace and only a mild sprinkling of extra what-the-hells. When Alison Grove appeared beside the teacups, Dombey goggled at her with lecherous enthusiasm and hurried to pick up her bag and guide her upstairs to the sacred bedchamber.

"Are you sure it's, like, okay for me to sleep here?" Alison put down her coat on the bed and looked around doubtfully.

Dombey's eyes flickered guiltily over the cradle in which the infant Emily had been rocked, the Franklin stove that had kept the grown woman warm, the bed in which she had died. "Oh, sure, sure," said Dombey hastily, "of course it's all right. After all, Owen Kraznik has been pretty high-handed himself.

Well, never mind about that." Dombey opened the closet door and took out Emily Dickinson's white dress. "Don't worry your pretty little head."

"Oh, wow," said Alison. "Is that what I'm going to wear?"

"It is indeed." Dombey held the dress high on its padded hanger. In the slight flow of air from the door the white gown trembled. The long pleats lifted at the hem and fell back. The soft cotton had a glistening surface, a small pattern of woven flowers.

"Was it really hers?" Alison took the dress from Dombey. "I mean, honest to God?" Holding it up against herself, she looked in the spotted mirror over the dresser. Wide-eyed, she turned to Dombey. "Where can I change?"

Dombey went to the door and pointed down the hall. Then he grimaced. Owen Kraznik was coming up the stairs.

Owen looked doubtfully at Alison as she hurried past him with the dress. Gravely he walked into the bedroom, wanting to

interfere, to protest. But then he thought better of it. He had already been at odds with Dombey. Perhaps he had better let this transgression pass. But when Owen saw Alison's overnight bag flung down on the small green sofa, it was too much. He couldn't quell the reproach that rose to his lips. "Now, see here, Dombey—"

Dombey was expecting it. He jumped in with a counter-attack. "Oh, for God's sake, Owen, you've already wrecked my carefully planned schedule for tomorrow. What the hell is it now?"

"This room," said Owen sternly. "Is that girl going to be sleeping here? Don't you think that's a little—?"

"Irreverent?" Dombey looked sour. "Good God, Owen, it's just another bedroom. Alison deserves a room in this house, just like all the other speakers. I see no harm in putting this one to good use."

Owen thought of a rejoinder, but he didn't know how to put it into words that would mean anything to Dombey Dell. Owen was remembering the story of a particular day when Emily Dickinson had refused to see a caller, because, she said, *My own Words so chill and burn me.* Those words had been hundreds of poems, written within these four walls. For an instant Owen felt in the gooseflesh on his arms and legs the fever of that unearthly chill. But it was no use. If Dombey felt no such bodily alarms, there was no way to transfer the sense of violation. Owen knew he would merely sound stuffy. He shook his head and kept still. Then Alison entered like a vision, and he caught his breath.

Dombey clapped his hands and crowed with delight. "My dear, you look charming. Your hair, you've done it just right. Emily Dickinson in person. Well, you're a damn sight prettier than she ever was, but, what the hell, who cares?"

Owen spoke up honestly. "Lovely," he said. "I must say, my dear, you look lovely." Then Owen turned in surprise. "Oh, Winifred, there you are. Come in."

But Winnie couldn't budge. She stood massively in the

doorway, staring in horror at Alison Grove. "You're not going to let her," she gasped, glowering at Owen and Dombey Dell. "She's not going to wear that dress? She can't. She just can't."

"Well, she is," said Dombey angrily. "What's all the fuss?"

Winnie tramped into the room, struggling for words. "But I need it. I've got to conduct a tour of this house in half an hour, okay? She's got to take it off right now."

Alison looked archly at Owen, dimpled at Dombey Dell, and swept past the fat woman without a glance.

"Oh, well, in that case," said Dombey, looking at his watch, "we'll all clear out. Come on, Owen, help yourself. Bring on the Japanese Poetry Society. The place is yours. For a while, anyway. Then it goes back to Alison."

Owen nodded graciously at Winnie, and left the room with Dombey. Only then did Winnie see the overnight bag on the sofa, the coat on the bed. The truth dawned on her. She,

Winifred Gaw, was not good enough to sleep in Emily Dickinson's bedroom! Instead, they were giving it to Alison Grove, her mortal enemy.

Rushing out into the hall, Winnie bawled after Dombey and Owen as they started down the stairs, while Alison disappeared in a flutter of white pleats around the corner, "She's not *sleeping* in there? She can't. I thought you said—"

"Oh, dry up, Winnie," said Dombey Dell.

15

. . . a Lynx like me . . .

By four-thirty Dombey was getting itchy again. "Say, Owen," he said, "would you take over now? I think I'll drop over and have a drink with the Smiths. So if you see the guy from *The New York Times*, just send him up to the Lord Jeff. I mean, he'll want to talk to me. I'll be in the bar."

So it was Owen, single-handed, who acted as welcoming committee for the official symposium tour. In flocks and batches people came to the door and rang the bell. Owen invited them in and shook their hands warmly and urged them to sign the guestbook. And then he handed them over to Winifred Caw, who dragged them upstairs to Emily Dickinson's bedroom for one lecture, then down to the parlor for another.

Winnie was in her element. Grandly she commanded each squadron of visitors, marching them up to the second floor, growing ever more domineering as the afternoon progressed, giving orders—"Stand here, not there!" For this fleeting moment Winnie was happy. Once again she was working with Professor Kraznik. Once again it was just the two of them, paired together like a team. Her heart beat with triumph. Her face flushed red. Her voice rose louder and louder.

People kept surging in the front door, college professors from Illinois and California and Arkansas, grammar-school teachers from Stockholm, two middle-aged women from Queens, a salesman for wood-burning stoves from New Hampshire, an endless stream of poetry-lovers from Tokyo, and droves of Dombey's sensitive ladies from everywhere, including Marybelle Spikes from Springfield.

Among the last to arrive at the front door of the Homestead was Dr. Ellen Oak.

Owen was delighted to see her. "Come in," he said, smiling with pity, remembering the shabby behavior of Tom Perry, her two-timing fiancé.

Ellen smiled wanly back at Professor Kraznik, hoping the physical signs of her wretched afternoon didn't show on her face. In the Gaslite restaurant she had discovered why Tom Perry had been so busy lately, so very much too busy to see her. It had not been meetings and student conferences and departmental affairs. It had been a girl with red-gold hair. The revelation had come as a brutal blow. Ellen had locked herself in her rented room and given herself up to misery. If only she had never met Tom Perry at all!

> *Had I not seen the Sun*
> *I could have borne the shade*
> *But Light a newer Wilderness*
> *My Wilderness has made—*

A wilderness, that was what her life would be from now on, a landscape of bleak loneliness—not so much a jungle or featureless plain as an enormous cold warehouse filled with meaningless machinery.

Professor Kraznik was looking at her, waving a pen. "Would you like to write your name and address? I'm supposed to ask everyone to sign the guestbook."

Ellen took the pen and stared at the space where she was supposed to write her name, *Ellen Oak*. With a pang she remembered the name that was to have been printed on her office door, *Dr. Ellen Oak Perry*. It wasn't going to happen. She would always be *Ellen Oak* now, never anything different. The split with Tom was final. She had made the break herself. She had written a letter, a dignified letter, and dropped it in Tom Perry's mailbox.

Her hand was still shaking from the feel of the envelope slipping from her fingers into the slot. And now she was exactly the same person she had been before Tom came along, *Ellen Oak*. But that wasn't such a bad thing to be, was it, after all?

Ellen Oak, Northampton, she wrote in the guestbook.

"The last tour is just beginning," said Professor Kraznik. His face bobbed in front of her, smiling gaily. "Well," he said, "I think I'll come along myself."

They were late. Winnie had already started her memorized recitation in Emily Dickinson's bedroom. With her feet planted heavily on the floor, wide apart, she was taking command of her miscellaneous captive charges and possessing herself of the writing table, the sleigh bed, the Franklin fireplace, the dresser, the windows, the view of the front walk and the driveway, the light of afternoon and the flowers of spring. In a flat drone she said her piece, hurrying along too fast, glowering at the Seth Thomas clock, the ruby glass decanter, the hatbox, the pictures of George Eliot, Elizabeth Barrett Browning, Thomas Carlyle. "Please don't touch that," she said sharply as someone's hand reached out to rock the cradle.

In the faces of her listeners Owen sensed a patient disappointment. Totally absent from Winnie's talk was any sense of the woman who had lived and worked in this room. Closing his eyes for a moment, Owen tried to imagine her for himself, Emily Dickinson, a small woman with dark red hair, moving quickly from door to window, from table to dresser to bed. *I rise because the sun shines and sleep has done with me. I brush my hair and dress and wonder what I am and who made me so.*

7 7

One of the women from Queens was asking a question. "Could she see the hat factory from the window?"

The hat factory? Winnie quailed. She didn't know. And at that instant Winnie caught sight of Professor Kraznik standing modestly in the rear. She was flustered. Craftily she decided not to hear the question. It skittered away from her ears and lodged between the folds of fat where she kept secrets from herself. Turning away, she pointed to the other pictures on the wall, the photographs of Samuel Bowles and Charles Wadsworth and Otis Phillips Lord. Scowling, unable to look at Professor Kraznik, Winnie talked of love. Then she pushed her way shakily past three or four members of the Japanese Poetry Society and threw open the door to the closet.

"This was her dress," she said, hauling it out, holding it high.

There were exclamations of pleasure. One of the sensitive ladies reached out her hand impulsively, then snatched it back. The dress hung among them, glistening.

Marybelle Spikes summed it up. "It was her father's fault, right? He wouldn't let her go. So she couldn't get married, so she was unhappy in love, and that's why she retired from the world and wore white dresses and wrote her beautiful poems, right?"

Owen cringed. He wanted to speak up and say, She retired from the world to get away from people like you, because *they talk of Hallowed things, aloud, and embarrass my Dog.* But he kept still and studied Marybelle's neck, a plump expanse of flesh rising from a nest of ruffles. A bizarre vision was appearing in his mind, a dream of Emily Dickinson as a great spotted cat, leaping at Marybelle's throat. Emily, he knew, had often thought of herself as a leopard, or some other kind of catlike beast. It made a pleasant picture, Emily Dickinson tussling with Marybelle Spikes like a lion worrying the carcass of a wart hog. In spite of himself, Owen smiled.

But Marybelle was still alive and well, callow and inquisitive. "Do you think she was pretty?" she asked Winifred Gaw. "I mean, really, really pretty?"

This time Winnie heard the question with painful clarity. She blinked sideways at Owen, then answered loudly, "No, she wasn't. You don't have to be pretty to have beautiful thoughts, okay? Emily Dickinson had a beautiful soul, deep down inside."

Owen closed his eyes again, wishing he could leave the room and go downstairs. But that would hurt Winnie's feelings. He glanced at Dr. Oak, but she seemed distracted. She was gazing at the floor. Then someone spoke up behind Owen. "Ah, but that's where you're wrong."

Owen turned in surprise. It was Peter Wiggins.

"A photograph exists," said Peter boldly, "so we know very well what she looked like." His pale eyes shone. "And Emily Dickinson was very beautiful indeed."

Winnie put the dress back in the closet and turned to him scornfully. "Oh, that. If you're talking about that dumb picture that turned up in New York City, nobody believes in that. That's not a photograph of Emily Dickinson, okay? The whole thing has been disproved."

"On the contrary," said Peter Wiggins, "it's a genuine

photograph of the woman who lived in this house. I'm going to prove it tomorrow."

It was a kind of battle. Owen could feel the tension in the air. The Japanese visitors were looking back and forth between Winifred Gaw and Peter Wiggins, obviously embarrassed. One of the Swedish schoolteachers giggled. The wood-burning-stove man whistled ironically through his teeth.

Owen felt sorry for Winnie. It wasn't Peter's beautiful photograph that was on trial, it was Winifred Gaw herself, in her obesity and ugliness. Somehow she had climbed gigantically into the balance, and her overloaded side of the scale was crashing to the floor. Owen wanted to warn her, to tell her to let it go, to move on to something else. But Winnie wouldn't.

"What does it matter, anyway, okay? What a poet looks like?" Her voice was too high, too sharp. "When you're, you know, a genius, okay? Who cares about looks? Who cares?"

But they all did, that was the trouble. They cared about looks, and they condemned Winnie for hers, for the grossness of her bulk, for her swollen arms, for her slablike hips, for her massive ankles, for her flat feet in their gum-soled shoes. And Winnie cared, too, thought Owen. You could sense the invisible track of her caring in the expressionless mask of her face. For an instant something irrelevant whisked into Owen's mind— "fat girl with a paper bag," the fat girl who had been seen in Coolidge Hall—but then it whisked out again, and he wondered what to do now.

The tour had come to an awkward halt. Peter Wiggins was nodding his head wisely, and leaving the room. The others were shuffling out after him to find their own way downstairs. Two members of the Japanese Poetry Society nodded graciously to Winnie, murmuring their thanks. Dr. Oak turned to go.

But Winnie stood frozen in the middle of the room. She was ponderously stranded. Owen decided it was up to him. He would have to take over for Winnie. Hurrying out into the hall, he ran downstairs to deliver the second lecture in the parlor.

Winnie watched him go. Her breast heaved, her disfigured

left hand opened and shut in her pocket, as Professor
Kraznik's light voice began drifting up from below. He was taking her place downstairs. Winnie didn't move until his voice
stopped at last, until the noise of departure swelled and faded
in the hall. Then she went to the window and watched the visitors saunter to the street in twos and threes.

And then her heart stopped, and began thumping painfully. Professor Kraznik was walking down the porch steps. He
was not alone. He was accompanied by Alison Grove. They
were wandering to the left, moving out of Winnie's sight
beyond the blossoming dogwood tree. Now she could see only
their legs. The legs were slowing down, standing still. Winnie
craned her neck. To her horror she saw Alison's white sandals
turn toward the feet of Professor Kraznik. The toes of their
shoes were touching. The heels of the sandals were rising. Alison was standing on tiptoe.

A sob rose in Winnie's throat, and she whimpered out

loud. Alison Grove had stolen Winnie's job, she had stolen Emily's bedroom, she had stolen Emily's white dress, and now she was stealing Professor Kraznik! Hot tears streamed down the pinched passages between Winnie's nose and her fat cheeks, and she lifted her fist to the ceiling.

Alison Grove was not going to get the dress! She was not going to get this room! And she was not going to get Professor Kraznik, not if Winnie could help it!

"It must be some kind of pollen," murmured Owen, "from one of these flowering trees." He stood very still with his eyes closed, while Alison Grove worked on him with his handkerchief, pulling his eyelid down, trying to swab away the obstruction. "There, that's better. Good for you."

"Is it gone?" Alison backed away, looking at him doubtfully. "I'm not much good at first aid, or, you know, anything like that."

"Yes, it's much better, thank you." Owen took back his handkerchief. "Tell me, Alison, are you and Tom planning to get married? Or is that an interfering question?" He smiled at her shyly. "Forgive me."

"Oh, right, we certainly are. Well, okay, there's this little problem. Tom's sort of mixed up with some girl over in Northampton. This woman doctor. But he says it's okay. He says she's a really good kid. You know, just an incredibly good sport. He says she won't mind."

Once again Owen felt intensely sorry for Ellen Oak and disappointed in his friend Tom Perry. "Well, after all," he said politely, "love will have its way."

16

The Soul selects her own Society—
Then—shuts the Door . . .

W hile Owen was changing his shirt before dinner, someone rattled his doorknob and shouted at him. Fumbling with his buttons, Owen opened the door and found Dombey standing outside, a pillar of wrath. Behind Dombey stood Alison Grove. Alison was pouting.

"Now, listen here, Owen," hissed Dombey in a kind of whispering roar, "what are you going to do about this one? I mean, Winifred Gaw is your problem." Dombey jerked his head at the door of Emily Dickinson's bedroom across the hall. "It was your big idea to bring her here. Now she's locked herself in and she won't come out. You and your lame ducks! I told you what would happen. Didn't I? Didn't I?"

Owen closed his eyes. For an instant he was transported to the sky-reflecting surface of the Quabbin Reservoir, drifting with his cousin Harvey over the drowned steeples of lost churches and the smokestacks of abandoned factories while silver fish darted below them in the limpid water. Then Owen opened his eyes and stiffened his shoulders and walked across the hall.

The locked door was blank and featureless. Behind it Owen could sense the morbid presence of Winifred Gaw, breathing heavily on the other side of the door. Alison's coat and overnight bag lay tumbled on the floor of the hall.

"Winnie?" said Owen.

There was no answer.

Dombey Dell watched with satisfaction as Owen drew his hand over his face. The great man had certainly got himself in a fix this time. "Tell her to get the hell out," said Dombey.

Cautiously, Owen put his ear against the door and listened. Immediately he could sense a slight vibration. Winnie was leaning her full weight on the other side. Shuddering, Owen stepped back.

The whole thing was beginning to strike Dombey funny. He pictured himself making a joke of it at dinner. He could see the Smith brothers throwing back their bearded heads to roar with laughter as he described the grotesque behavior of that fat pig Winifred Gaw. Fat pig? No, he would call her *Brobdingnagian,* and chalk up a few Brownie points as a learned wag. "Have you got another key?" said Dombey.

"No, I haven't," murmured Owen.

"Well, then, we'll have to get in through the window." Dombey grinned at Alison Grove, who was standing limply beside the door, her exquisite lower lip sagging a little.

"No," said Owen sternly. "Why don't we just let her alone?"

"But the dress," whimpered Alison.

"Damn it all, Owen, it's Alison's room now," said Dombey.

Owen shook his head. "Alison can stay in your room, and you can move in with me."

"Oh, well," said Dombey, "what the hell. Come on, Alison." Picking up her overnight bag, Dombey shepherded Alison down the hall. He was furious.

Owen went back to his own room and closed the door. The word *key* had triggered another scholarly memory. Once Emily Dickinson had lifted her hand in the air as if to turn an imaginary key in an imaginary lock, and then she had said, *It's just a turn—and freedom!*

Maybe Winnie, too, was enjoying the exhilaration of that kind of freedom. Owen, at any rate, wasn't about to disturb her.

But it wasn't freedom Winnie wanted. On the other side of the door she listened to the retreating footsteps and the sound of the door closing across the hall.

They were going away. The room was hers. She had won.

She had no feeling of victory. Leaning against the door, Winnie yearned after Professor Kraznik. She had hoped that he would plead with her until she opened the door, and then maybe he would put his arms around her and console her.

But he hadn't. Disappointed, Winnie sank down heavily on the bed. It creaked and groaned.

There was one small comfort. At last she had Emily Dickinson's room all to herself. She could commune with the soul of Emily. Emily would understand Winnie's feelings. Surely Emily would sympathize with Winnie's dread of the beautiful Alison Grove.

At suppertime Winnie stayed put. She didn't dare leave, for fear Alison would find a key and move back in. But Winnie had plenty to eat. She had brought a lot of stuff in a paper bag. Munching on taco chips, Winnie sprawled on the green velvet sofa and tried to make sense out of her paper on capitalization in the poetry of Emily Dickinson, that old seminar report with Professor Kraznik's praise at the end, *Good Work, Winnie! C+*.

For Owen Kraznik, the dinner hour was another sociable chore. In the ceremonial comfort of the Lord Jeffery Inn, he sat at a long table with Professor Nogobuchi and the Japanese Poetry Society, playing the gracious host with all his strength.

Across the dining room Owen could see Dombey Dell at a cozy table for three, and he was fascinated to observe that the black whiskers of the Smith brothers did indeed reach to the top and middle of their neckties, respectively. When Peter Wiggins came into the dining room and gazed uncertainly at the crowded tables, Owen wondered if Dombey would get up to

Lord Jeffery Inn

welcome him. But Dombey was obviously in the middle of some jocular story, and he didn't look up. Owen waved at Peter and pulled up a chair beside his own.

Tom Perry, too, was ignoring his duties as co-chairperson of the symposium. Tom was dining with Alison Grove in Plumbley's Restaurant a block away. Blond head to red-gold, they sipped their drinks and studied the menu.

"Alaskan crab legs?" said Tom, picking the most expensive item on the list.

"Oh, yuck," said Alison. "Have they got, like, a steak?"

Dr. Ellen Oak decided to go back to the Gaslite for supper. Sitting once again on a stool at the counter, she ordered a bowl of New England clam chowder with oyster crackers in a cellophane package on the side. Keeping her eyes firmly fixed on her spoon, she was careful not to look up, for fear of meeting anyone's eye.

And three miles north of the center of town, on Market Hill Road, as the blossoms of Tilly Porch's apple orchard glistened in the twilight and dusk settled in the deep cleft of Cushman Brook, Tilly shared the last of her early peas with Debbie and Elvis Buffington. Elvis loved Tilly's peas. Sitting on two sofa pillows at the kitchen table, he wolfed them down, shoveling them into his mouth with both hands. Debbie ate them grudgingly, and refused a second helping. Then Tilly drove Debbie and Elvis back to the apartment where they were living on welfare, dropped them off, and raced madly back to her own house.

Tilly still had three things left to do. She had to wash the dishes, she had to go over the notes for her talk tomorrow, and she had to go up-attic to take a look at some of those old boxes. The visit to the Dickinson house this afternoon had whetted Tilly's appetite to look at that old stuff. After all, some of Tilly's ancestors had known the Dickinsons—good heavens, some of them had actually been Dickinsons themselves, members of that enormous Connecticut Valley family. Maybe there would be something really interesting up there in the attic—notes from Emily, or letters from her relatives. Well! Who knew *what* Tilly might find up there? She was eager to get started.

But just as she put her hand on the latch of the attic door, the phone rang.

It was Professor Dombey Dell. "Oh, Mrs. Porch, good evening. Excuse me, I've just got a minute. I'm calling from the Lord Jeff, where I'm entertaining distinguished guests. Oh, Mrs. Porch, I just want to say how fine I think it is that you'll be one of our speakers tomorrow. I just want to welcome you to the platform officially. Oh, and, by the way, Mrs. Porch, speaking of tomorrow's program, I wonder if it might be possible— that is, I was hoping you might just have time to help us with a little problem that has arisen. Do you happen to know where we might find a white dress? Something suitable for a young woman? You know, sort of old-fashioned? A long skirt, that kind of thing? The truth is, Mrs. Porch, we were wondering if you might be able to run up something very quickly on your sewing machine?" Then Dombey explained Alison Grove's predicament, and the importance of her appearance as Emily Dickinson tomorrow morning.

Tilly thought at once of her old lace curtains. "Well, I'll do my best," she said. "What size is the girl?"

8 7

Dombey passed along the measurements Alison had given him, then hastened back to the dining room of the Lord Jeff to hustle around and shake hands, and settle down again with the brothers Smith. So far neither of the brothers had said anything about a job opening at Harvard. At last Dombey brought it up himself, making a joke out of it. "Say, tell me, how's good old Rexpole? Still blundering around the department? Writing his so-called masterpiece?" But the two Smiths merely looked at Dombey blankly, and there was an awkward silence.

"Oh, say, that reminds me," said Dombey, changing the subject in a panic, "I forgot to tell you about this girl named Winifred Gaw. I mean, you should really see this woman. She used to be Owen Kraznik's girl Friday. She's huge, I mean really enormous, positively Grobdingdongian. . . . ."

17

The Show is not the Show
But they that go—
Menagerie to me
My Neighbor be—
Fair Play—
Both went to see—

*I*t was Wednesday morning, Dombey Dell's great day. By the time Owen Kraznik walked into Mahar Auditorium, the place was packed. Owen looked for an empty seat in the rear of the hall, but soon Dombey caught sight of him and motioned him grandly to the front. Obediently, Owen walked down the aisle, inspecting the crowd.

At first glance, the devotees of Emily Dickinson's poetry looked like ordinary people. On the surface they didn't appear to be helpless in the grip of greedy aspiration and territorial ardor. But strong passions were surging just under the skin, Owen knew, even now during the taking off of jackets, the settling of posteriors in the rows of seats, the crossing of knees and the blowing of noses, the courteous introductions, the pleasant chaffing. Listen! In the high pitch of the voices, in the tendency to laughter, you could detect the presence of all those underlying obsessions. You could see them in the sidelong glances left and right, in the craning of necks over shoulders— *Do I see anyone I know? Does anyone else know me?*

Owen sat down and glanced at the newspaper on the seat beside him, where someone was saving a place. There was a grouchy headline, COOLIDGE HALL FIRE INVESTIGATION ZILCH SO FAR.

Tom Perry picked up the paper and sat down. "They tell me *The New York Times* man is here," he said, leaning over to Owen. "Over there on the aisle in the third row. See that guy in the seersucker suit?" Then Tom moved one seat away. "Save that one for Alison," he said. "Look, here she comes."

The hall was darkening. A spotlight drifted across the curtain. Owen looked up and gasped. Alison Grove was stepping into the ring of light.

The rest of the audience was electrified, too, at the sight of Emily Dickinson in person. They clapped. They made happy chirrupings of appreciation. What a lovely facsimile! On the platform Alison stood quietly in the dazzling glare, waiting for the applause to stop.

But for a moment longer they kept it up. The wood-burning-stove man uttered a shrieking whistle through his teeth. Professor Nogobuchi applauded in a transport of enthusiasm. Tilly Porch, too, was pleased. Alison's dress was a success. Tilly had sat up till four in the morning to finish it. Did the tucks show in the back where she had tightened it this morning to fit Alison's slender waist? Did the hem look bunchy where she had turned it up a second time? No, the dress was lovely. Tilly smiled and clapped.

Ellen Oak steeled herself to endure.

At last the room grew still, and Alison read her poem. It was a familiar one:

> *"This is my letter to the World*
> *That never wrote to Me—*
> *The simple News that Nature told—*
> *With tender Majesty*
>
> *"Her Message is committed*
> *To Hands I cannot see—*
> *For love of Her—Sweet—countrymen—*
> *Judge tenderly—of Me"*

As Alison glided back through the curtain, there was a general exhalation of suspended breath, then a roar of approval. *Judge tenderly?* They would show her how tender they could be! The clapping went on and on.

Homer Kelly's applause was feeble. He soon gave up and sat on his hands. As for Winnie Gaw, she couldn't bear it. Turning to Dombey, she whispered scornfully, "Emily didn't look like that."

"Well, what the hell," said Dombey Dell, still applauding violently. "Who cares?"

And then someone sitting behind Winnie leaned forward and offered her own opinion. It was the sentimental lady from Springfield, Marybelle Spikes. "I bet her soul sort of shone in her face, you know what I mean? Like some people have these really, really beautiful faces, because their spirit just really shines out of them, you know? You don't even *look* at their features. Well, okay, maybe they're not so great to look at really, but you just say '*Hey*, there goes a beautiful *woman*.'"

18

His Mansion in the Pool
The Frog forsakes—
He rises on a Log
And statements makes . . .

Peter's talk was second on the program, right after Dombey Dell's opening speech. Tom Perry introduced him. "Professor Wiggins comes to us from—ah—the University of Central Arizona. He brings us a fascinating investigation of a famous and controversial photograph. Professor Wiggins?"

Peter ran lightly up the stairs to the platform, his heart in his mouth. What if the audience ripped into him as it had just ripped into Dombey Dell? Poor Dombey had entirely misjudged his listeners. He had called Emily Dickinson a typical Victorian female poet of helplessness and fragility. He had been clever and sarcastic at her expense. His pose of *enfant terrible* had enraged them all. There had been boos and catcalls, and during the question period Dombey had been dismembered.

Peter's talk was altogether more successful. As his slides succeeded one another in the darkened auditorium, he could feel the silence of complete attention. Relentlessly he had stricken from his speech all sentiment, all subjective response to the face in his photograph. He spoke only of facts. Shrewdly he allowed the eloquent eyes to speak for themselves. Carefully he raised the issues that cast doubt on the identification of the woman in the picture with Emily Dickinson, and then he destroyed them, one by one. Why, for example, was she not wearing a white gown? Because in 1860 Emily was still dressing in fawn and blue and brown, in *gay muslins in summer and bright merinos in winter.*

And then Peter launched into a detailed comparison of the photograph with the daguerreotype, displaying his diagrams of facial measurements and angles. Thoughtfully he discussed the ratio of facial length and breadth, the relative heights of forehead, nose, upper lip, and chin, the deceptive difference in the arrangement of the hair. From the massed audience in front of him, Peter was beginning to hear signs of approval, murmurs of pleasure. As he compared his findings with those of a cosmetic surgeon and a forensic dentist, there were outbreaks of spontaneous applause.

It only remained to read the verbal descriptions of Emily Dickinson, written by those who had known her, while the photograph remained on the screen. As Peter quoted from friends and relations, the words seemed to drift over the handsome face and settle there. *A pair of great, dark eyes set in a small, pale, delicately chiseled face; beautiful eyes and an exceedingly pale skin; the wine-brown eyes that could flash with indignation or soften in approval; unlike anyone else—a grace, a charm; a wealth of auburn hair and a very spirituelle face; a beautiful woman dressed in white, with soft, fiery, brown eyes and a mass of auburn hair; to the funeral of that rare and strange creature Emily Dickinson . . . E.D.'s face a wondrous restoration of youth . . . not a gray hair or wrinkle, and perfect peace on the beautiful brow.*

As the lights came on again, there was a standing ovation. Owen stood and clapped with the rest. There were more whistles of approval from the wood-burning-stove man. On the platform Peter's cheeks flushed, and he blinked in the glare, then jerked with surprise as a flashbulb went off in his eyes. Tom Perry shook his hand and laid a fraternal arm around his shoulders, then turned to the audience. "I know you liked it, but does anyone have any questions?"

9 3

Hands shot up all over the auditorium. But Peter's listeners wanted to praise rather than interrogate. Only Eunice Jane Kloop and Winifred Gaw had questions.

Eunice Jane stood up in the front row and quoted an obscure line from an obscure poem—*Her countenance it did inflate*—then fixed Peter with her fierce little eye. "Don't you agree, Professor Wiggins, that this is surely a reference to a disease, so far unnoticed by scholarship, which must have afflicted Emily Dickinson? I am referring, of course, to a case of mumps?"

Peter was too startled to reply, but fortunately Eunice Jane seemed to expect no answer. She sank back into her seat, having, she felt, made a contribution to learning.

Winnie Gaw was more pugnacious. She spluttered at Peter Wiggins, "It's wrong. That picture isn't her. She didn't look like that."

"Why not?" said Peter mildly, remembering that this woman had been an easy prey the day before.

"You left out that other thing Higginson said, okay? He said she was plain. I mean, that's what he said."

"Ah, but don't forget," said Peter, pouncing, his pale eyes alight, "he said it in a letter. A letter to his *wife*."

"I don't see what difference—" began Winnie, but the audience was erupting in laughter all around her. *A letter to his wife.*

Winnie couldn't bear it. She shouted above the laughter, "But I can prove it. I can prove that picture isn't Emily Dickir · son."

Peter waited for the laughter to die down. "What sort of proof do you have?" he said politely.

Winnie was cornered. "Well, I've got this—you know, documentary evidence, okay? Documentary evidence," she finished stiffly, "will soon be forthcoming."

"Very good," said Peter Wiggins, bowing. "I will be happy to examine it when it—ah—comes forth."

There was more laughter, more spontaneous applause. Angrily, Winnie prodded Dombey Dell and pointed to the watch embedded in the fat crease of her wrist. "Make him stop. It's my turn now. It's half an hour late."

Dombey was in a sour mood. It occurred to him that the damn fools who had repudiated his brilliant lecture deserved a dose of Winifred Gaw. He stood up and roared at Tom Perry, "Time for the next speaker."

"Right you are," said Tom. From the platform he nodded at Winnie Gaw, and turned to shake Peter's hand. Flushed with success, Peter Wiggins gathered up his papers and went back to his seat.

It was Winnie's turn at last. Breathlessly she heaved herself up the steps. But then as she took her place behind the rostrum, she was horrified to see a mass of retreating backs. Half the audience was surging out of the hall.

Dismayed, Winnie glanced at the front row where Professor Kraznik was smiling up at her encouragingly, nodding as if to say, Carry on, Winnie. For an instant she was comforted, but then she saw the girl sitting next to him. It was Alison Grove. Winnie's heart sank. What was *Alison* doing there? Gulping, almost in tears, Winnie began to read her paper on capitalization in the poetry of Emily Dickinson. "Speak up!" shouted someone in the back. Winnie spoke up, but now her voice was too loud and rasping. The diagrams she displayed were too small to be seen, her subject was tedious, her theory impossible. And it was time for lunch. Below her in the auditorium there was a steady leak from the audience as one person after another gathered up clothing and possessions, fumbled past other people's knees, and dodged up the aisle, head down. A plague of coughing swept the hall. The coughers, too, rose to their feet and hurried away.

The baby was the last straw. It was Debbie Buffington's big baby, Elvis. Debbie and Elvis and the Mother of Ten had come just in time to hear Winnie, their personal representative from S.I.N.G.E.D., and they had made straight for the front row, where Helen Gaunt was saving them a bunch of seats.

But Elvis was soon bored. He began to yell.

Winnie stopped reading, and glared at Debbie.

Debbie was miffed. She shrugged her shoulders. Elvis hollered louder.

"Bounce him up and down," whispered Helen Gaunt.

"Smack him, why don't you?" urged the Mother of Ten.

Debbie bounced Elvis up and down and smacked him, but it didn't help. Soon he was hurling himself backward in her arms, roaring, his face empurpled with rage.

"I will not go on," cried Winnie.

"Then why don't you stop?" shouted a well-wisher in the back.

Tilly Porch saved the day. Jumping out of her seat, she rushed down the aisle and gathered Elvis up in her arms. At once Elvis recognized his fairy godmother and stopped bellowing. Debbie, relieved, went out to the lobby for a smoke. There she fell into conversation with a guy from Shutesbury who was repairing a broken light fixture. It turned out that the guy had seen Debbie at a Flaky Jake concert. He had noticed her particularly when he was having a beer at intermission. "No kidding?" said Debbie.

In the auditorium Winnie carried on. But the worst was yet to come. Glancing up from her eleventh page, she saw something terrible. Professor Kraznik was rising from his seat. With his arm around Alison Grove, he was hurrying up the aisle and leaving the hall. Tom Perry's chair scraped across the floor behind Winnie as he too got up and ducked behind the curtain.

Again Winnie nearly broke down. When she finished her paper at last, there were only a few compassionate listeners left in the auditorium. As she closed her folder with shaking fingers, as the thin applause stopped and the audience began to bolt, Winnie saw Professor Kraznik appear once again at the door and begin to beat his way down the aisle.

But Winnie was too hurt. Turning away, she fumbled blindly through the folds of the curtain and broke down altogether beside a dusty piano and a pair of kettledrums.

19

❧

. . . I cross the river—and climb the fence—now I am at
the gate. . .now I am in the hall—now I am looking your
heart in the eye!

*I*t was lunchtime. Owen
Kraznik was weak with hunger. Deftly he escaped the clutching
fingers of sensitive ladies and fellow scholars and biked home
to his own house on Spring Street. There he found Homer
Kelly warming up the contents of a can of spaghetti. With a
flourish, Homer dumped a jar of bread-and-butter pickles into
the pot and stirred them around. Then he unwrapped a pair
of Hostess cupcakes and parked one beside Owen's plate, the
other beside his own.

"Homer," said Owen admiringly, "this is truly haute cui-
sine."

Everyone else in Amherst, too, was putting aside the work
of the morning to pause for lunch. In the Wildwood Elemen-
tary School the children were lining up in the cafeteria, and in
the Gaslite restaurant the counterman reached into the fridge
for a big bowl of shredded cabbage. Hikers at the top of Mount
Holyoke stood on the porch of the Summit House and ate their
sandwiches, looking out over the broad landscape of flat green
fields and winding Connecticut River. And in the neighboring
valley of the Swift River, the chief engineer for the waterworks
at the Quabbin Reservoir left the Administration Building and

Judie's

drove to the Crystal Springs Dairy Bar in Belchertown. There, sitting at the counter, he ordered a tunafish sandwich and wondered when to close off the Ware River intake and open the valve at Shaft 12, to begin the annual surge of water through the tunnel to Boston. Soon now. He would call up Jesse Jack Gaw today or tomorrow.

And in the reservoir itself, eighty feet down, lake trout nosed for smelt around the stone cellar holes of the lost towns of Greenwich and Prescott, Dana and Enfield. Dr. Harvey Kloop thought about the trout and yearned after them as he pushed his tray along the cafeteria line in the hospital in Northampton. Once again he had been delayed. Once again Eunice Jane had thrown a monkey wrench into the works. Before he took off for his little fishing expedition, Harvey was supposed to scrub out the birdhouse and paint the furnace. How long would that take? If he did a really slapdash job on the furnace, surely he would at last be on his way to Quabbin by late afternoon?

Tom Perry spent the lunch hour with Alison Grove in the cozy intimacy of Judie's Restaurant on North Pleasant Street. "Good God, Alison darling," he said, looking across the tiny table with concern, "are you really all right?"

"Oh, sure. It's just that I had this really incredible headache. I mean I felt really, really dizzy. You know, like I might faint. So Professor Kraznik brought me out to get some air. I'm okay now."

"My poor darling."

But after two glasses of white wine Alison confessed she had merely been pretending. "It was just such a drag. I mean, everybody else was leaving. You know, I mean I thought it over and decided it wouldn't be, like, polite to leave from the front row, not with this white dress on and everything. So I had to pretend to be really, really sick. I mean, wasn't she incredible?" Alison showed her perfect teeth in a rare smile. She had taken down her hair, and it gushed in a red-gold flood over the white sleeves of her long gown.

Tom laughed. "It's so funny, the way you were acting out Dombey Dell's thesis about Emily Dickinson as the pathetic Victorian female. There you were, fainting up the aisle, leaning on Owen. Well, the truth is I was glad to get out of there myself. That Winnie Gaw is certainly impossible."

And then Tom tackled his spinach quiche, while Alison babbled about some of the girls on the fourteenth floor of Coolidge Hall. Tom nodded and smiled, but he was barely listening. He was thinking instead about Ellen Oak. This morning he had spotted Ellen in the audience, and it had been a shock. What the hell was *Ellen* doing at the Emily Dickinson symposium? He had specifically told her not to come. Why hadn't she warned him she would be here? And then Tom remembered the letter from Ellen in his mail. Oh, God, he should have taken the time to read it. He had rushed home in a terrific hurry to change his clothes, and he had snatched his mail out of the box, glanced at it, and dumped it on the kitchen table. Now it occurred to Tom that Ellen's letter had not been stamped. She must have delivered it in person. He squirmed. He was beginning to get a nasty uncomfortable feeling about his old girlfriend and about what she might have said in the letter that was lying there at home on the kitchen table.

It was a sticky wicket. What was he supposed to do about the woman, now that she was here? The trouble was, he didn't have time to talk to her, not now. By rights he ought to take her aside and tell her about Alison and say how sorry he was, and how grateful, and so on. But he couldn't do a tricky thing like that in a big hurry. Not on a day like this, when the most important speech of his life was coming up this afternoon. After all, the Smith brothers from Harvard would be listening, and everybody said they had this job at their disposal, this big Aldershot Chair of American Studies, or something like that. Tom smiled to himself. Poor Dombey Dell. Dombey thought he had a chance at having the chair bestowed on his own fawn-colored polyester backside. He didn't have a prayer.

In the noisy cheerfulness of Judie's, in the jolly flicker of the lamps on the little tables, with waitresses squeezing past him and a lot of genial uproar in the background, Tom struggled painfully with the problem of his two girlfriends, then hardened his heart. It was just too damn bad about Ellen Oak. Oh, she was a fine woman, of course! No question! And back there in the hospital when she had diagnosed his inflamed appendix, there had been a kind of glamour about her, an air of distinction. But now, compared with Alison Grove—!

Then Tom winced, and put a hand on his abdomen, at the spot where his appendix had once festered. It was as if a thread were attached to the spot, and it was stretching away from him, right through the wall of Judie's and the row of stores next door, then trembling and thrumming along the sidewalk past the bus stop and glistening in the sunlight as it pulled taut across the fork where East Pleasant Street separated from North Pleasant, then poking through the clapboards of his own house on McClellan Street and fastening itself to the white envelope on the kitchen table. The thread tugged at the clean scar on Tom's belly. Oh, God, he ought to go back there and read the fucking letter.

But not now. There just wasn't time. There was too much to do.

Did Ellen Oak know he had seen her, there in the audience at Mahar Auditorium? Tom had an unhappy suspicion that just for a fraction of a second, just for the merest instant before he flicked his glance away, his eyes had met her steady gaze.

For Peter Wiggins, the lunch hour was the most exciting of his life. Peter had been invited to dine in style at the Lord Jeffery Inn by the correspondent from *The New York Times*. To Peter's surprise, the correspondent turned out to be a rather dowdy woman from the borough of Queens. She was fascinated, she said, by his talk.

Peter was flattered. Nobly he refrained from drinking

more than one vodka and tonic, even though he knew he deserved a whole bottle of champagne. Smiling modestly at his luncheon companion, he was keenly aware that everyone in the dining room was staring at him. People kept coming up to shake his hand. "I'm just so grateful," gushed Marybelle Spikes. "It's like you've given us this really fabulous treasure." And when one of the Smith brothers paused at Peter's table to ask him to join them for a drink after the afternoon session, Peter's cup was filled to overflowing.

But he didn't allow success to go to his head. The moment was too important. The woman from the *Times* was asking him questions, writing down his replies. Peter was careful to mention his various contributions to the *New England Quarterly* and the *Proceedings of the Modern Language Association,* to make it plain that he wasn't just a one-issue scholar. The *Times* woman wrote it all down, and asked for a copy of the photograph that had been the subject of his talk. Then she hurried upstairs to her room to tap out her article on her portable typewriter.

Left alone, Peter was relieved. The pressure was off. Grinning to himself, he took a long shaky breath and walked out the side door of the Lord Jeff, smiling cordially at a few more admirers who rushed up to shake his hand. There was just time before the next session to go back to the Homestead and call Angie from the phone in the hall outside his room, and tell her the good news.

But Angie didn't seem to be listening. "The kids," she said, "they're driving me bananas."

"But, Angie, listen. Wait till you hear—"

"It's the weather. God! The minute you stick your head out the door, you're fried. I took the kids to the K-Mart, and the blacktop in the parking lot was so hot I nearly fainted. I had to race the car out of there before I lost consciousness. The kids were screaming."

As Angie talked, Peter gazed through the open door of his bedroom and saw the sunlit leafy paradise beyond the windows dissolve and become an image of the blazing sun itself, filling the windows, dazzling out over the walls until they faded away, until nothing was left but a ruthless blinding light. He hung up the phone a little sadly, remembering how important to Emily Dickinson had been the noonday sun.

> *You'll know it—as you know 'tis Noon—*
> *By Glory—*
> *As you do the Sun—*
> *By Glory . . .*

Well, good for Emily Dickinson. But she had not perceived the sun as he did, as a brutal object in the vast metallic sky. She had merely beheld it tremulous among the foliage of her father's trees, its image dappled in little circles on the shady lawn. Or she had watched it drop slowly westward in the small New England heavens, veiled in pretty colored clouds. She had never known it as the fiery withering destroyer that blazed in the white-hot oven over Pancake Flat, Arizona.

20

My God—He sees thee—
Shine thy best—
Fling up thy Balls of Gold . . .

The afternoon session of the Emily Dickinson Centennial Symposium was called to order by Dombey Dell in Johnson Chapel at Amherst College.

Owen Kraznik sat with Homer Kelly in the front pew and looked out over the audience crowded together in the handsome columned spaces. At this moment it was almost possible to regret his refusal to teach at the College instead of at the University. Tom Perry was always needling him about it. "Owen, I just don't understand it. Why would you want to stick with that ex-cow college when you could be part of the Amherst faculty? You should hear Dombey hint around about transferring over here from U Mass. He'd give his eyeteeth. Why not you?"

Well, why not? wondered Owen. For an instant he imagined himself talking comfortably to a small class of selected students in this sanctified place instead of shouting through a microphone to a faceless mass in Mahar Auditorium. The thought was tempting, but Owen knew he'd never do it.

His address was the last of the afternoon, after Tilly Porch had been informative and brief, Tom Perry witty and sound, and Professor Cobb from Minneapolis boring and repetitious.

Dombey Dell rose to introduce him, but then Dombey had to wait. There was a hushed chaotic pause. A crush of new people was wedging its way into Johnson Chapel and spreading into the side aisles. Owen's speech was what everybody had been waiting for. Homer Kelly straightened his slumped spine and sat up as Owen began to talk.

His address was simple and lucid, reverent and sane. The poems he examined were not in the anthologies. They came from his lips majestic, tragic, vast. Veils were withdrawn from central mysteries, trivialities vanished in the breath of the poet's ethereal wind, immensities spread outward from her short quatrains, the sea parted to show a further sea. For a moment Emily Dickinson stood before them in all her amplitude, her grandeur and strength, her melancholy power, her quivering vulnerability. Then, as Owen finished his brief address, she rose in sober stature and withdrew into a sublimity of privacy.

With one motion the audience stood up. There was massive prolonged applause. Owen answered a few questions, then
called a halt. The audience began shuffling from their pews
into the aisles, satisfied, solemnized, transfixed.

Tom Perry was desperate to get back home and read
Ellen's letter. The white envelope on the kitchen table had
been pulling at his gut all afternoon. He drew Alison across the
hall into an empty classroom. "Say, Alison, listen. I've got a lot
of stuff to do right now. And I'm having supper with those
guys from Harvard. I'll meet you at that recital this evening,
okay? You know, at Merrill Hall."

Alison was peeved. She was not used to being set aside. "So
what am I supposed to do in the meantime?" she said angrily.

"Oh, Alison." Tom put his arms around her and kissed
her, feeling his body engorge with thick warm blood. Once

again he understood the necessity of breaking off with Ellen Oak.

But Alison jerked out of his embrace. Turning her back, she flounced away down the hall. Alison was really mad.

Our first quarrel, thought Tom sentimentally, letting her go, watching her turn swiftly to descend the stairs. Peering over the iron railing, he caught a last glimpse of her bright hair against the dark stone of the granite steps. Then Tom remembered Ellen's letter. He walked down the stairs slowly, to avoid encountering Alison again, and raced down the hill in the direction of McClellan Street.

There on the kitchen table, waiting for him, was the letter. Tom tore open the envelope, read the letter hastily, and smiled with relief.

Ellen was breaking it off herself. She wasn't accusing him of anything. She didn't seem to have heard any rumors. She was just taking a serene farewell. Somehow she seemed to have grasped the fact that things had changed, and she was bowing out gracefully.

You had to hand it to the girl. She was a damn nice woman. Smart, too. Had Ellen heard his talk? Tom preened himself on the thought, and then his love-fogged mind cleared. For an instant he saw Ellen and Alison side by side, not in their physical embodiments but in their essences and selves, and he was shaken. He remembered something Emily Dickinson had said. *A Letter . . . is the mind alone without corporeal friend.*

But people were not just minds, Tom reminded himself. Ellen had a body as well as a mind. What a shame her ancestors had been so stingy in handing out corporeal goodies! It was really too bad.

As it happened, Tom's vainglory about Ellen was wrong. She had not come to Johnson Chapel to hear his lecture. She had been one of the crowd that pressed into the hall just in time to hear Professor Kraznik.

Now, walking down Boltwood Avenue in the direction of the Gaslite, Ellen's head was reverberating with the poems he had examined, and with the sound of his voice. For the first time in twenty-seven hours, Ellen was not thinking about Tom Perry and Alison Grove.

I could not have defined the change—
Conversion of the Mind
Like Sanctifying in the Soul—
Is witnessed—not explained . . .

At that moment Owen Kraznik himself was opening the front door of the Homestead. He was worn out. Dragging himself upstairs, he was glad to find the bedroom empty. Dombey was elsewhere. But Dombey's clothes were all over the bed—his sharp new blazer, his boots with the cowboy heels, his three-piece suit, his boxer shorts. Owen pushed everything to one side and crawled under the covers. Laying his teeming head on the pillow, he went to sleep.

Instantly he was in one of his spinning nightmares.

And then a Plank in Reason, broke,
And I dropped down, and down —
And hit a World, at every plunge,
And Finished knowing—then . . .

21

Success is counted sweetest
By those who ne'er succeed.
To comprehend a nectar
Requires sorest need.

*W*inifred Gaw was too miserable to attend the afternoon session of the Emily Dickinson Centennial Symposium. She had been planning to sit in the front row and clap loudly for Professor Kraznik. But this morning he had hurt her too deeply by walking out of her lecture in the company of Alison Grove.

With her bosom still heaving in long shuddering sighs, Winnie drove southeast on Route 9. In Ware, she pulled up in front of Astrella's Doughnut Snack Bar on North Street. Winnie needed comfort. More than anything else, she yearned for a certain kind of solace, and this was the place to get it. Good things lay on the paper doilies in the glass case in Astrella's. Winnie poured herself out of the front seat of the big van and crossed the street.

The shop was warm and fragrant. Avoiding the eye of the cute high-school girl behind the counter, Winnie peered hungrily at the piled-up doughnuts in the glass case. "I'd like some doughnuts, please," she said coldly. "A dozen glazed, a dozen chocolate, a dozen cinnamon." And then she saw the éclairs. "Oh, and a dozen of those too, okay?"

The high-school girl was slow. She picked up each dough-

nut daintily in a piece of tissue paper, so that it would be untouched by human hands, and put it carefully into a white box.
Winnie balled her disfigured left hand into a fist in her pocket.

At last the girl handed a stack of four white boxes across
the glass case. Each box was tied separately with white string.
The boxes and the string were the color of Emily Dickinson's
white dress, thought Winnie, the dress that still hung in the
closet, the dress she had saved from Alison Grove. They were
also the color of gluttony—the color of sugar, the color of
flour, the color of lard—but Winnie didn't think of that.
Quickly she carried them across the street to the van and put
them down on the front seat. Then she climbed in, fitted herself under the steering wheel, and tore at the string on the
uppermost box.

The doughnuts inside the waxed paper were covered with
a brittle sugary glaze. Winnie put one to her lips. The first bite
was rapture. Crystalline sugar flaked against her mouth,
crumbs fell on the shelf of her bosom, the airy interior dis-

solved upon her tongue. Holding the doughnut delicately between finger and thumb, Winnie started the car again. On the way home she polished off three more of the glazed doughnuts and two of the chocolate éclairs. The éclairs were delicious, eggy and soft in texture, and puddingy with filling.

Driving along Greenwich Road, Winnie forgot the woes of the morning. She chewed and swallowed and chewed, and thought, as she so often did on Greenwich Road, of the lost town of Greenwich to which it had once led. Greenwich was the village in which her parents had lived as children, in houses long since destroyed to allow the water of the Swift River to fill the valley, rising higher than the Town Hall, higher than the textile factory and the Walker sawmill, higher than the Village Hotel and Chamberlain's Store, higher than the steeple of the Congregational church, higher than the little one-room schoolhouse in which Winnie's father and mother had acquired all the education they were ever going to get.

Of course, Winnie herself had never seen any of these places, but she had heard about them all her life, in the angry reminiscences of her father. Her mother always said, "Forget it, let dead dogs lie," but her father couldn't let it alone. Even though he worked at Quabbin for the Metropolitan District Commission, even though his wages from the MDC had been supporting his family for years, Jesse Gaw's anger was alive and festering.

You would think it was yesterday instead of fifty years ago that the bulldozer had knocked down his old schoolhouse and broken the schoolhouse bell and run over his leg and crippled him.

Winnie hated her father. She felt no sympathy for his lame uneven walk, and she was sick to death of his rancid indignation.

Turning into her driveway, she was careful not to look at the house, because the sight of it depressed her. She ignored, too, the wrecked cars all over the front yard. But she couldn't avoid seeing her father working in the garage beside the house. JESSE JACK GAW, COLLISION, FRONT END WORK, said the sign over the garage. Bending cars back into shape—it was what her father did in his spare time. Sometimes the noise was unbearable, the violent repetitive crash of the sledgehammer against crumpled pieces of sheet metal, the clang of the chain and the frame-puller, the hissing throb of the compressor. Sometimes it drove Winnie right out of the house.

Jesse Gaw glanced up without expression as Winnie's big van pulled up beside him, and then he looked back at the object on his workbench. It's that damn bell, thought Winnie. The broken bell from the old schoolhouse in the valley was red hot under his torch. For years her father had been talking about replacing the broken fitting for the clapper. Now he was working on it at last. Would wonders never cease.

Winnie climbed down out of the van with her white boxes and stood watching him sullenly, but he took no notice of her. After a moment he abandoned the bell, limped to his workbench, and picked up the axe that lay there, gleaming on a heap of rags. Then Jesse Gaw began sharpening the edge of the axe blade on his grindstone. Sparks flew up from the wheel.

Only then did Winnie's father look at her with his small mean eye.

Clumsily, Winnie whirled around and lumbered up the porch stairs, aware of the furious beating of her heart. Carefully she opened the front door, hoping to creep up to her room unheard. But she couldn't prevent the creak of the treads under her weight. Her mother called out sharply from the kitchen, "Is that you, Winifred? I been waiting lunch."

"I don't care for any lunch," said Winnie daintily. Opening her bedroom door, she waited for her mother's reply. Downstairs there was a slam and a crash. Her mother was mad. But Mrs. Gaw said nothing more. Relieved, Winnie went into her room and closed the door, safe at last. Putting down the boxes on the dresser, she sat down beside them on the bed and began working her way through them methodically, alternating cinnamon doughnuts with chocolate, glazed with éclairs, until at last she could eat no more. She wiped her face, which was sticky with sugar and smeared with chocolate, and put a hand on her swollen midriff. The effort to digest was robbing her of strength. There was a feeling of tightness around her heart. She was suddenly thirsty. All that sweet stuff, it really made you thirsty. Winnie went to the bathroom, filled a cup with water, drank it, filled it again, drank it, and filled it yet again.

It was time to get to work. With an effort, Winnie dragged herself back to her room, took the second volume of Sewall's biography of Emily Dickinson out of her bookcase, and opened it to the controversial frontispiece, the so-called photograph of Emily Dickinson. It was the picture the man from Arizona had been talking about this morning. Carrying the book, Winnie tramped downstairs, all the way to her darkroom in the basement.

She had her work cut out for her, the manufacture of a solid piece of *documentary evidence*. It wouldn't be easy, but Winnie had figured out a way to do it.

And there in her darkroom Winnie forgot about the humiliation of the morning. She forgot about Alison Grove and Professor Kraznik. She forgot about the fire in Coolidge Hall and the two sophomore men who had perished in the choking smoke of the north staircase. For the next two hours, Winifred Gaw forgot about herself and all her troubles.

22

. . . death claims a living bride . . .

*O*wen Kraznik was still asleep in Lavinia Dickinson's bedroom in the Dickinson Homestead, groaning aloud, plummeting between vertical cliffs of basalt, when Winnie's van whizzed down North Street once again, on its way back to Amherst.

This time Winnie didn't give Astrella's Doughnut Snack Bar a second glance. Erased from Winnie's memory were the three dozen doughnuts and the twelve chocolate éclairs.

But even from herself Winnie couldn't hide the physical results of consuming a dozen custardy confections and thirty-six deep-fat-fried doughy morsels. There was a dull pain in her gut and a heavy pressure around her middle. She was short of breath. In her basement darkroom Winnie had managed to forget the chagrin and sharp dismay of the morning, but now the shame of her failure came back and flooded over her. Her mood collapsed into a poisonous settled depression.

She drove carelessly through Belchertown, her eyes glassy, her foot jolting from accelerator to brake, from brake to accelerator. In Amherst she tried to stop in front of the house where Helen Gaunt had an attic room, but she misjudged the distance to the curb and ran the van up on the sidewalk. Heaving herself out of the front seat, she plodded up the walk, dropped her envelope in the box labeled H. GAUNT, climbed back in the van, jerked it into reverse, careened down onto the pavement, and took off with a jackrabbit start.

There was a traffic light at the next corner. The light turned red. Winnie didn't feel like stopping, but at the last minute she jammed on her brakes. Her body lurched forward. In flatulent impatience she sat staring at the red light. There were no vehicles crossing the intersection the other way. There were no other cars on the street. There were no pedestrians. Then, just as the light turned green, someone appeared from the bushes screening the sidewalk of the cross street, and began to walk in front of Winnie's van.

It was Alison Grove, in her white dress. Alison Grove, the girl whose terrible prettiness had robbed Winnie of everything she held dear.

Winnie's grievances overwhelmed her. With one great sob, with no direction from her conscious brain, she lifted her right foot from the brake and jammed it on the accelerator.

Alison Grove went down, her destiny fulfilled.

23

To stir would be to slip—
To look would be to drop . . .
It was a Pit—with fathoms under it . . .

*T*he afternoon was waning as Owen woke up, more fatigued than when he had gone to sleep. In the bathroom mirror his face was haggard. Was there any cure for nightmares? Last year Owen had asked this question of his cousin Harvey Kloop, the medical man. But Harvey had merely looked at him without speaking, his face ashen. And Owen had understood that it was Harvey's problem too. The tendency to nightmare must run in the family. It was therefore hopeless.

Winifred Gaw, too, was having a nightmare, but Winnie's bad dream was real.

Getting out of her van, she stared down at the body of Alison Grove.

Alison's eyes were open. She was looking up at Winnie. She was not breathing. She was dead. She was really dead.

Winnie's heart began tumbling in her chest. She was frightened and exultant at the same time. *She's mine now,* thought Winnie. *She belongs to me.* All that loveliness of face, of red-gold hair, of dainty body, of tiny waist, of small soft breasts the size of peaches—they were Winnie's now. Alison didn't belong to herself anymore. No longer would she take things away from Winnie. No longer would she even have a will of her own. *From now on, Winifred Gaw was in charge of Alison Grove.*

Two streets away from the crossing where Winifred Gaw stood staring down at the body of Alison Grove, Dr. Harvey Kloop was making a right turn, glancing back at the boat-trailer behind his car. Out of the corner of his eye he saw something queer.

It looked like trouble. Dr. Kloop was in no mood for trouble. At last he was escaping from his tyrannical practice, from telephone calls at two in the morning, from the beeping electronic summons at his belt, from the nagging of his wife and her insane preoccupation with Emily Dickinson. He was going to Quabbin at last, with all his fishing gear and tackle, his pup tent, his sleeping bag, his six-pack of beer. His fishing license was pinned to his hat. Soon he would be alone on the water with silence all around him. The entire creation would not be buzzing and beeping. There would be no Emily Dickinson claptrap ringing in his ears. There would be no sound at all but the plunk of the sinker in the water and the tick of his reel, and maybe the occasional honking of a stray flock of Canada geese or the quack of a pair of ducks in rapid flight, or even—but this was merely fantasy on Harvey's part—the cry of the legendary catamount, howling from the depths of the forest.

But now this queer thing was happening down the street. Resolutely, Dr. Kloop turned his head away and refused to think about it. Shifting into third, he sped away. It was no business of his if some woman was standing in the road, picking up something white from the pavement in front of her car—a big woman, really big, positively huge, like that patient of his, Winifred Gaw.

Staunchly, Harvey Kloop drove straight down Route 9 in the direction of the Quabbin Reservoir, trying not to think about his Hippo-something oath.

Winnie was slow, but she moved with thick persistence, and her mind ran rapidly ahead, making a plan. As her car raced back along Route 9, the plan grew and blossomed until it included a scheme for Winnie's own future, one she had often dreamed of but had never quite dared to carry out. Swiftly Winnie itemized in her mind the things she would need to gather up at home.

Back in Ware, she was lucky. Her father had gone to work. So had her mother. Winnie was able to help herself freely to the stuff in her father's garage. She knew what she wanted, and snatched it up quickly. Therefore it was only five o'clock when Winnie's van slowed down at Quabbin Gate 43, with a miscellaneous collection of things piled beside her on the front seat.

Turning in at the gate, Winnie drove past the road to the boat-launching dock, with its big sign listing the rates for boat-rental and fishing and parking. Then she stopped her car in front of the long green boards that blocked the way to Shaft 12.

Winnie was familiar with those green boards. Once, a long time ago, when her father's car had been out of commission, its dismembered chassis hoisted over the grease pit, Winnie had driven him to work here, day after day. He had been doing a job at Shaft 12. Now, dragging the boards aside, Winnie felt like part of the administration of the Quabbin waterworks, a ranger or an engineer or something. She really knew her way around.

The paved approach to Shaft 12 was three miles long. Again Winnie's van was alone on the road. There were no walkers in the woods, no bird-watchers with binoculars searching the sky for eagles. There was nothing along the road but birches and pines and oak trees, and hemlocks with new green growth on the tips of their branches, and tall ferns, and maples with fresh green leaves. Here and there in the woods, she passed a stone wall that had once belonged to a house long since torn down because it stood in the Quabbin watershed. Some farmer's whole lifework had been destroyed, Winnie knew that. His white wooden church had been moved away, and the MDC had dug the bones of his ancestors out of the ground and buried them someplace else. Winnie knew the sad stories well. Altogether too well. She was sick and tired of sad stories about the vanished towns of the Swift River valley.

Shaft 12 was a solid little stone building right on the shore of the reservoir. Winnie pulled up and stopped in the clearing. Beyond lay the water, glittering and blue. Winnie had her father's key. She had taken it from a hook on the wall of the garage. Now she opened the the door and looked around, remembering.

Yes, there was the overhead crane. There was the great bucket, lying on its side. And there above the shaft were the wooden trap doors, flat in the cement floor.

Last fall, it had been dark. Winnie had found her way to one of the trap doors with a flashlight. And then the bucket of paint and the propane torch and the suitcase had plummeted into the bottomless hole. The water had been far down. The splashes had been faint and far away.

Now, seeing the place in the daytime, Winnie was reminded of the past, of that time when she had come here with her father. In those days the empty shaft had echoed with the immense noise of the work going on below, as the crew tore out the old wooden stop-planks that controlled the flow of water into the tunnel. Until then her father had come to Shaft 12 twice a year to throw the switch on the wall, so that the great hooks on the traveling crane would lift the planks or drop them down. But from now on there was to be a huge valve, opened and closed by a control switch far away.

It had been a big job. When the work was done, Winnie had knelt beside one of the openings in the floor and looked into the shaft, expecting to see the new valve far below. But the shaft had been full of water, and she had seen nothing. Would it be full today, or would the water be way, way down in the shaft as it had been last fall? Winnie didn't know what to expect. She was ready for anything.

It was going to be easy. She would pick up one of the trapdoors and drop the body down the shaft into the tunnel, and then the flow of water would carry it far from the town of Amherst, far from the town of Ware, far from a person named Winifred Gaw. And maybe the body of Alison Grove might never turn up at all. Winnie had a vague idea that there was a power station somewhere along the way to Boston, with big spinning turbines, turned by the water from Quabbin. She didn't know what a turbine looked like exactly, but she suspected it would mess up a body pretty bad.

Going back to the van, Winnie opened the back doors, dragged Alison out, and hoisted her with a gasping effort over her shoulder. Then she lugged her up the steps and into the building, and dropped her on the floor next to one of the trapdoors. She was careful not to look at Alison. Winnie was beginning to feel that the dead body of Alison Grove had nothing to do with her. It was just a piece of garbage to be thrown away. Then, puffing to regain her breath, Winnie went back to the van for the bell.

The bell had been an inspiration. There it had lain on her father's greasy workbench, still warm from the torch. It was just what Winnie needed. If there was water in the shaft again, she would use the bell to weigh Alison down, to make her sink all the way to the bottom of the shaft, to be carried away by the rush of water in the tunnel.

The bell was heavy, but not too heavy. Winnie dropped it on the floor next to Alison, and it rolled over with a hollow clatter. Then Winnie bent over the trapdoor and tugged at the rope handles. The trapdoor was stuck. She had to heave and heave before it suddenly came loose, throwing her off balance so that she staggered backward. At once the rope handles slipped from her fingers and the trapdoor fell, the noise of its impact with the floor making a tremendous hollow reverberation against the hard surfaces of the room. Gasping, Winnie knelt down and looked into the shaft.

It was a good thing she had brought the bell! Once again, the shaft was full of water.

Full of water? For the first time, it occurred to Winnie to wonder why the shaft should ever be full of water. Panting, she sat back on her heels to think. And then she groaned as she understood.

The shaft was full of water because this was the wrong time of year. The water in the tunnel wasn't going anywhere. The tunnel at Shaft 12 was closed off. Instead of flowing from the reservoir to Boston, the water was coming the other way, from the Ware River floodplain to the east. It was flowing all the way from Shaft 8 in the Ware River Valley *toward* Quabbin, entering the reservoir half a mile farther up the shore at Shaft 11-A, beyond the baffle dams. Sooner or later Winnie's father would throw a switch to close off the Ware River intake and open the valve here at Shaft 12. That was part of his job. He bragged about it all the time. And then the water would run through the tunnel the right way, from the reservoir to Boston.

But not now! Right now the water wasn't going anywhere! It was just standing there. It was dead water, dark and dank and still.

Until this moment a kind of desperate glee had kept Winnie going, an urgent obsession to carry out the idea she had worked out in her head. But now she was overwhelmed by a sense of nightmare. Her eyes filled with tears, and a painful lump rose in her throat. Weeping, she struggled to her feet, and then she made two trips back to the van—once with Alison, once with the bell. Slamming the rear doors, she climbed back into the driver's seat, her breast heaving with exhaustion, and headed for Shaft 11-A.

There was only one thing left for her to do. She would dump the body of Alison Grove directly into the reservoir, right there where the Ware River flowed out of the pipe into Quabbin, and trust to the turbulence of the water to carry it far out and away from the shore.

Behind her as she drove away from Shaft 12, the door of the gray stone building hung open, swinging on its hinges. In the empty room within, the long rays of the afternoon sun streaked through the high windows and shone upon the trap-door that lay half over the concrete floor and half over the watery abyss.

24

❧

*Oozed so in crimson bubbles
Day's departing tide . . .*

At six o'clock the air of Amherst was still bright with afternoon. The Common lay in shadow, but the whole length of Amity Street was flooded with sunset, and an old woman walking her dog across the intersection mumbled a line or two from Emily Dickinson—

*"Blazing in Gold and quenching in Purple
Leaping like Leopards to the Sky . . ."*

Once again it was suppertime. Brains were glutted, vascular systems were in need of alcohol, stomachs were hungry for food. In bars and restaurants all over Amherst, the cravings of the body were being satisfied.

In the Lord Jeffery Inn, the Japanese Poetry Society had taken over most of the bar. They were toasting the Swedish schoolteachers, clashing their wineglasses together in small tinkles of international congratulation.

In the Pub, a popular eatery off East Pleasant Street, Tom Perry and Peter Wiggins joined the Smith brothers in a couple of rounds of Scotch, and then the Smiths called for the supper menu and they all switched to Moosehead beer.

The *New York Times* correspondent had already finished her early supper at Plumbley's Restaurant, in the company of her friend, who happened to be a reference librarian, back in Queens. Now the correspondent was back in the Lord Jeff, sitting on the edge of her bed, phoning in her story, passing along a suggestion by the librarian that somebody in Rewrite consult a guy at Columbia about the photograph that had been the subject of the talk by Peter Wiggins.

In South Amherst, in her own kitchen, Eunice Jane Kloop was feeling sulky. Damn Harvey anyway! She had already prepared his supper, a bowl of cold boiled chicken necks, but Harvey had escaped. He had driven away with that damned boat of his to fish at the Quabbin Reservoir. It was too bad. For some reason Eunice Jane enjoyed serving chicken necks to Harvey. There was a peculiar pleasure in watching him spit out the bony bits onto his plate. Now she huddled alone at the table, gnawing at one of the chicken necks, peering at an article in a learned journal, "The Revitalization of Existential Contiguity in Deconstructive Metonymy," taking a swig every now and then from her bottle of sauerkraut juice.

Tilly Porch was used to eating alone. But tonight Tilly was having company. Once again Debbie Buffington was her guest at the kitchen table, while Elvis sat on the sofa pillows gobbling everything in sight. Tilly had been hoping to get up in the attic after supper, but instead she offered to babysit with Elvis, because Debbie had a date with this guy from Shutesbury. "I'm supposed to meet him at this tavern," said Debbie. "There's this group is going to play, The Soft White Underbelly, and they're raffling off this king-size water bed. Okay if I borrow your car?"

Homer Kelly was worried about Owen. The man looked positively ill. "Tell you what, Owen," Homer said. "I'll take you out to dinner in honor of your speech. What a noggin-dazzler that was, wow! How about someplace classy? Say, have you ever had a seafood platter at the Gaslite? Or their homemade chili? Or what they call their Junior Exec? Bulky roll, French fries, lettuce and tomato on the side?"

"Why, Homer, that's very kind of you," said Owen. "It all sounds delicious."

At the Gaslite, Owen was pleased to find Ellen Oak sitting at the counter, and he introduced her to Homer Kelly. After supper the three of them wandered across the Common and climbed a steep path to Johnson Chapel and the Octagon, to admire the view of the Holyoke hills. Then Ellen remembered the evening entertainment, and they ran all the way to Merrill Hall and sat down in the front row with hot faces. Owen hadn't done anything so sporting in years.

Tom Perry was sitting in the back. He looked up as they came in, hoping to see Alison Grove. When he saw Ellen Oak instead, he was jolted, and then a little miffed to see her red-faced and grinning in the company of Owen Kraznik and a tall stranger. Maybe Ellen was getting along without him a little too well. He looked up again as a flock of undergraduates streamed past him. Still no Alison. The program was begin-

ning. The dancers were running out, frisking to the music of harp and flute, while someone read a Dickinson poem, *Beauty—be not caused—It Is.* Triumphant leaps by the dancers, arpeggios from the harp, chirrups from the flute!

Tom couldn't keep his mind on it. He kept glancing over his shoulder. If Alison didn't come soon, he would leave. He didn't want to find himself face to face with Ellen Oak at intermission. *Tweedle-tweedle,* trilled the flutes while the dancers hopped and twirled.

Four blocks north of Merrill Hall, as the harpist plucked a delicate glissando, Winne Gaw's big van pulled up behind the Homestead and stopped with a jerk. Winnie's tank was almost empty, but she didn't care. After tonight nothing would matter for a while. Not until she was out of the hospital. Not until Professor Kraznik told her he was sorry. Not until he gave her back her job.

Winnie was worn out. Her heart was skipping and bobbing in her chest. At Shaft 11-A she had stood for only a moment to watch the body of Alison Grove disappear like a sliver in the boiling tumult and spray of the water in the cove. Then she had closed her eyes and dropped her head and slumped her shoulders, trying to recover her strength, and then she had driven back to the Homestead in the fading light. There was still so much to do. Her day was not yet over, her long day of tension and disappointment and greed and hard work and sudden violence and intense physical effort, her tortured day of grinding back and forth along Route 9 in the van, and up to Gate 43 and back along the Greenwich road.

Now Winnie struggled out of the van, slung her purse over her shoulder, picked up her basket, and reached into the back seat for the axe.

Winnie Gaw was not stupid. It was true that her mind had not been encouraged in childhood. It was true that her early education had been feeble. But Winnie had picked up a lot of miscellaneous information in other ways. Escaping from bad times at home, she had often holed up in the library or spent the afternoon at the movies in the Casino Theater in the middle of town. Sometimes Winnie stole dollar bills from her mother's purse and ran away as far as the bus would take her. The result of all this snatched education was not a collection of verbal skills but a kind of shrewdness, a cleverness sharpened by one violent compulsion after another. Chief among Winnie's obsessions were her passion for Professor Kraznik and—until today—her fear of Alison Grove. Now another tremendous urge had seized her, and it was focusing all her faculties on one thing, and on one thing only: her need to sleep—to sleep and sleep, to sleep so deep that she might die, only she wouldn't. She would wake up at last to find Owen Kraznik by her side.

Carrying the basket and the axe, Winnie shuffled across the driveway to the north door of the house. On the porch she put down the basket, leaned the axe against the doorframe, and turned her key in the lock. Cautiously she stepped into the twilit gloom of the central hall.

In Winnie's excited condition, the fragrance of the indoor air affected her strongly. Distilled in the scent given off by the polished furniture, by the paintings on the wall, by the ivory keys of the piano in the parlor, by the books on the shelves, was the ineffable presence of everything Winnie wanted, everything that was the opposite of her own life, everything that was of unutterable worth. Sniffling, she labored up the stairs in the dim light and walked along the hall. For a moment she stopped

to stare at the door of Professor Kraznik's room, where he would soon be lying softly under the bedclothes, only a few feet away. So close, and yet so far, so impossibly far away from Winnie Gaw!

The key to the door of Emily Dickinson's bedroom was different from the house key. Winnie extracted it from her purse, opened the door, and locked it behind her. At once she felt a return of proprietary confidence.

There was still so much to do. First, Winnie took off her clothes and put on her nightie. Then she examined her dress and sweater, her slip, her bra and panties, her shoes and socks. Miraculously there were no bloodstains on any of them, anywhere.

Alison's body had not bled at all, decided Winnie. She must have been, like, squeezed to death by the wheels of the big van. And then Winnie put the thought of Alison Grove

away from her. The memory of what she had done was beginning to fade, to be tucked away in the creases, like all unplea-
sant things. Winnie turned to her present task. What should
she do now?

The book. The book was next. Winnie put the book beside
the bed and opened it to the page where she had underlined a
passage with a pencil. The book was like a suicide note, a personal message to Professor Kraznik.

The pills. For weeks Winnie had been carrying around Dr.
Kloop's new prescription for sleeping pills. This afternoon in
the drugstore in Ware she had filled the prescription. And
then at home she had flushed most of the tablets down the
toilet. Carefully, Winnie dumped out the rest of the tablets and
arranged the two empty bottles—the new one and the old
one—side by side on the table beside the bed, next to the book.
Then she put the bottle caps and the two fluffy pieces of cotton
wadding beside the bottles. Now it would look as if she had
swallowed two whole entire bottles of pills. Spreading out the
remaining tablets on the edge of the little table, Winnie
counted them again. There were twenty. That was enough to
put her under, way under, but it wasn't enough to finish her
off.

Next, the glass of water. A lot of water. Enough water to help her swallow all those pills, and satisfy her burning thirst. Winnie was parched. She took the decanter of rose-colored glass from the dresser and filled it in the bathroom. There was a plastic cup beside the sink. Winnie filled it, too, and drank, again and again. Then she brought the decanter back to the bedside table and tipped it delicately over one of the rose-colored wineglasses. The water poured silently into the glass, filling it nearly to the brim. There was not a drop on the table.

What else? Was she ready? No, of course she wasn't ready. There was still the axe. How could she forget the axe? With trembling fingers Winnie picked up the axe from the floor and put it on the bed. The axe went with the passage in the book. Professor Kraznik would understand, and then he would be sorry.

How did she look? Winnie went to the mirror and took the clips out of her hair, so that it fell loosely beside her face. In the blotched old mirror she looked almost beautiful. Her eyes were her best feature, just like Emily Dickinson's.

She was ready. Winnie turned away from the mirror and lay down on the bed. Arranging her nightie around her ankles, so nestled the axe cozily at her side, and stretched out her hand for the wineglass and the first of the pills.

But then something occurred to her. She sat up and stared at the door.

If they saw that the door was closed, they might leave her undisturbed. They might not get to her in time. She might sleep and sleep, and then wake up alone, all by herself. No, no, they must see her sleeping on the bed, and realize something was wrong, and try to wake her and not be able to do it. And then they would know she was trying to kill herself, and they would take her to the hospital and Professor Kraznik would be there to comfort her when she woke up at last.

Therefore the door must be left open. Open wide. Winnie slid off the bed. Moving noiselessly on bare feet, she unlocked the door, pulled it open as far as it would go, and then lay down carefully again and put out her hand for the first of her Secanol tablets.

Again she stopped with her hand in the air.

Someone was coming into the room.

25

'Tis so much joy! 'Tis so much joy!
If I should fail, what poverty!

*F*or Peter Wiggins, the day had been one long triumph. When the Smith brothers said good-night to him at last in a back-slapping mood of tipsy joviality, he walked off into the dusk of evening feeling like a colleague already, a fellow faculty member, an associate professor in the English department at the most famous educational establishment in the East. Peter had visited Harvard once, last year, to look things up in the Houghton Library. It was green there, in the place they called the Yard. There were elm trees in a leafy canopy overhead. This evening, after two Scotches and a couple of beers, Peter had distinctly seen ivy gushing out of the Smith brothers' chins, twining down their shirtfronts, reaching to the top button in one case and the middle button in the other.

Of course, neither of the brothers had actually promised him the job that would soon be opening up, but they had made it clear that he was high on the list of candidates.

The back door of the Homestead was unlocked. That was lucky, because Peter had not been given a key. In the front hall he was shrouded in darkness. None of the lights had been turned on. The house felt empty. Everybody else was probably at that music and dance thing in a place called Merrill Hall.

Peter smiled as he felt his way along, recognizing the shadowy rectangle of the hall table and the dark squares of the portraits on the wall. He couldn't stop smiling. He smiled halfway up the stairs. But then as he paused at the second floor, something occurred to him with a shock. What about Winifred Gaw? Peter had forgotten all about Winifred Gaw. He had forgotten about her "documentary evidence." Documentary evidence! What kind of documentary evidence was the idiot female talking about? Good God, thought Peter Wiggins, standing in the dark hall with his hand on the banister of the stairway to the third floor, what if by some crazy miracle the woman had actually discovered something real? This morning in the auditorium he had made her look like a fool, but what if she actually possessed some nutty scrap of paper that identified his photograph as somebody else entirely, not Emily Dickinson at all? *Jesus*, it would ruin everything.

Peter took his hand off the banister and walked noiselessly along the hall toward the room Winnie Gaw had stolen from that beautiful girl, Alison Grove.

The door to Emily Dickinson's bedroom was open. The room was dark.

Winnie must have decamped. She must have gone with the others to the evening performance of music and dancing and poetry.

Peter stood in the hall listening. Was he still alone in the house? He heard nothing at all. No one was opening the door downstairs. In all the hollow spaces of the rooms, he was the only living soul. Peter felt a sudden access of freedom, an impulsive sense of adventure. It was like the first time his mother had left him at home by himself, in the family house in Providence, Rhode Island. Peter had opened the forbidden drawers of his father's desk and taken out the drawing instruments and played with the delicate little compasses. He had gone upstairs and fumbled in his mother's bureau drawers, inspecting her brassieres, trying on her gold wristwatch.

Now Peter peered through the open door of Emily Dickinson's bedroom. At first he could see only the two west windows, the last of the daylight moving in the leaves outside. But then his eyes accustomed themselves to the darkness, and he noticed the basket and the pocketbook on the floor.

That lumpy pocketbook was certainly Winifred Gaw's.

Peter was consumed with curiosity. He had to know. He couldn't allow some half-baked notion on the part of this ignorant woman to jeopardize his year of preparation, his hopeful future, all that had brought him so urgently across the continent to this place, to this moment of fulfillment.

Boldly he walked into the room.

And then he paused, awestruck, remembering that it didn't really belong to Winnie Gaw. It was Emily Dickinson's own bedchamber, sacred as a church. Here within these four walls the woman with the magnificent eyes had written nearly two thousand poems. In his half-drunken condition Peter was so moved, he almost sobbed aloud. Instead, he whispered to himself, *"Put off thy shoes from off thy feet, for the place whereon thou standest is holy ground."*

Therefore, when a massive shape loomed up beside him in the darkness, he gave a grunt of surprise and jumped backward.

"Who's there?" gasped the woman on the bed.

Peter could feel his face flushing with embarrassment and anger. The damned woman was here after all! He pulled himself together. "Oh, sorry. I didn't know you were in here. I mean, the door was wide open."

Winnie stared at Peter Wiggins. Never since she had grown up had she found herself alone in a bedroom with a man. She didn't know what to say. Peter Wiggins was looking at her so oddly. In the thin illumination of the streetlights beyond the hemlock hedge, his fine blond hair was a halo around his head. He was just standing there, staring at Winnie. This morning he had been part of the enemy, part of the world that always treated Winnie like dirt. But now he was a man in her bedroom. And he was looking at her so strangely! It was weird, thought Winnie excitedly, it was really weird.

She misunderstood the cause. To her amazement she, too, began behaving in a new way. Lying back on the pillow, she lifted her arms behind her head and raised one knee. Somehow she knew exactly what to do. "Well, hi, there," cooed Winnie softly.

"Listen here, Winnie," said Peter severely, "what did you mean this morning? You know, when you said you had evidence my picture isn't genuine? You said you had some kind of documentary evidence." Peter could see Winnie dimly now. She was smiling at him and lowering her eyelashes.

"I don't remember," teased Winnie, looking up at him again, remembering that her eyes were her best feature.

Peter was repelled. It dawned on him that the woman thought he had really come into her bedroom to—*God!*—make love to her, or something. Angrily he lashed back at her. "For Christ's sake, what the hell do you think you're doing in Emily Dickinson's bed? A slob like you?"

And then it boiled up in Winnie all over again. Everything that had been hidden in the crevices of her flabby body, everything that had been tucked into the fat creases around her neck, in the deep dimpled folds of her elbows and knees, in the crannies between breast and belly, now came raging forth, exploding like bubbles of gas. Seizing the axe that lay beside her, Winnie launched herself from the bed and lunged at Peter, swinging.

He was totally unprepared. With a yelp he jumped aside, and Winnie's blow smote the floor with a splintering crash. When she came at him again, he flung out his arms and grasped the handle and tried to wrench it away from her. Good God, an axe—the thing in her hands was an axe!

They were face to face, panting. Even as he struggled and jerked with all his strength, Peter thought, *This can't be happening.* The woman was pulling away from him. He couldn't hang on. She was stronger than he was. She had more mass to throw at him. And she wasn't dizzy from swallowing six ounces of Scotch and a couple of pints of beer.

Terrified, Peter stumbled backward, knocking over a small

table. Reaching for it, he snatched it up and threw it at Winnie as she rushed at him again. It hit her in the face and stopped her cold. Winnie groaned, and kicked the table aside. Again she came at him, flourishing the axe. Again he grabbed it by the handle. Again he couldn't hang on. Wrenching it from side to side, Winnie jerked it away from him, then threw him against the dresser. Sacred objects crashed to the floor. Glass tinkled and shattered. Peter's heart jolted in his chest. *This fool was trying to split his skull!*

Desperately he used his wits. When Winnie came at him again, Peter dropped craftily to the floor. She was taken by surprise. Tripping over him heavily, she fell with a sprawling thud that shook the house. Frantically, Peter scrambled up, hoping to make a rush for the door. But, quick as a cat, Winnie was on her feet, blocking his way, and immediately they were locked together. Again Winnie shoved him backward, and this time Peter's head cracked against the wall. Reeling, he braced himself as Winnie swept the axe violently upward.

And then, suddenly, it was over. She let go. The axe slipped from her fingers, fell against her, and clattered to the floor. Her body sagged. Peter saw the dim broad shield of her face tip away from him as she collapsed backward. A dark stain was spreading over her nightgown.

Peter too slumped feebly, and slid down the wall until he was sitting on the floor. In front of him lay the mounded shape of Winifred Gaw, her head bent sideways against one of the fallen chairs.

For a little while Peter merely breathed in and out, hardly able to believe he was still alive. What the hell had happened? The woman had been about to kill him! And then she had dropped the axe and toppled. Was she dead? Or was she only pretending? Was it some kind of trick? Was she about to spring savagely to her feet?

Cautiously, Peter got up on his knees and leaned forward. Winnie's eyes were staring upward. Her huge bosom was not rising and falling. To Peter she looked as dead as any corpse in the movies. Picking up her wrist, he felt for her pulse.

It was fluttering. She was still alive! But then the beat in her wrist hesitated under his fingers and stopped. She was dead now, for sure.

Peter's mind began to race. Even in his panic he thought of Dombey Dell and Tom Perry and all the rest of them coming back to the house very soon, probably any minute now. With prophetic clarity he could imagine how they would view this grotesque event, and instantly he was frantic to separate himself from it. After all, it was no business of his what happened to Winifred Gaw! How would he explain what he had been doing in her bedroom? How would he tell them that he had found himself in a battle to the death with a stupendous woman in a flannel nightgown? And, Christ, how would he make them believe that he, Peter Wiggins, had not slashed at the woman with that lunatic impossible weapon? What would happen to his precious photograph, what would become of his new destiny, if he found himself all mixed up in the public eye in a murderous scramble with a freakish fat lady in Emily Dickinson's bedroom?

Peter stood up shakily and looked at himself. There were a few dark splashes on his shirt. That was no problem. He could wash them out. Stepping carefully around Winnie, he went to the window and looked out. Someone was whistling beyond the hemlock hedge. Was Dombey coming home? The whistling stopped. He could hear laughter farther away. Was that Owen Kraznik coming along the sidewalk? No, the murmur of voices was trailing away toward the center of town. For a moment Peter held his breath and listened, but he could hear nothing else. No car was turning into the driveway, sweeping its headlights across the mirror and the pictures on the wall. There was no sound of an opening door. There were no footsteps in the hall downstairs.

He had time, then, a little time to recover, to retrace his footsteps and obliterate any sign of his presence. What had he touched? The fallen table? The handle of the axe? He could take care of that. He could wipe them clean. He could even take a minute or two to look for the thing he had originally come to find, Winnie's "documentary evidence." He could look through her pocketbook, her basket, the closet, the drawers of the dresser.

It didn't take long. In a moment Peter was once again standing in the hall, satisfied, pulling the door shut, his shoes under his arm. With his shirttail, he wiped the doorknob clean. Then he made his way back to his room on the third floor.

He was home free. He would examine the soles of his shoes for fragments of glass, he would wash his polyester shirt and hang it up over the tub in the third-floor bathroom, he would pay particular attention to his fingernails. And then he would be through with the matter.

Let them discover the body of Winifred Gaw whenever they got around to it! Let them invent whatever theories they cared to about the cause of her death. It was none of his business. He could go to bed with an easy mind.

Below Peter's attic room, at the end of the second-floor hall, in Emily Dickinson's bedchamber, Winnie lay still, her soft brown eyes fixed on the ceiling in an empty stare. Her long hard day had come to an end.

> *The longest day that God appoints*
> *Will finish with the sun.*
> *Anguish can travel to its stake,*
> *And then it must return.*

26

I meant to find Her when I came—
Death—had the same design . . .

Owen came back to the Homestead from the music and dance performance and went straight to bed, exhausted. But as he lay down he looked at his pillow with suspicion, dreading another nightmare.

As soon as he shut his eyes, there was a knock on his door. It was Tom Perry, opening it a crack, peering in at Owen. "Oh, sorry, Owen. I just wondered if you know where Alison went. She was supposed to meet me in Merrill Hall, but she never came. The fact is, we had a little tiff."

Owen lifted his head. "Alison Grove? She's not in the back bedroom?"

"No."

Owen was too drowsy to think. "What about her dormitory? Could she have gone back there?"

"Well, maybe. I suppose that's where she is. Wow, I didn't think she was *that* mad at me. Thanks, Owen."

Tom Perry closed Owen's door and ran lightly down the stairs to the telephone in the kitchen. He knew Alison's number by heart. It wasn't really Alison's own number. It was the number of the phone on her corridor on the fourteenth floor of Coolidge Hall in the Southwest Quad. Sometimes it rang for a long time before anybody bothered to answer it. But this time a breathless voice responded quickly. "Hello?"

"I'd like to speak to Alison Grove."

"Alison Grove? Wait a sec. Let me think. I'm from down-stairs, but I know who you mean. She's got this really red hair, right? Sure, I just saw her go into the john. Just a sec, I'll get her."

"No, wait. Don't." Suddenly, Tom was angry with Alison. Now that he knew she was all right, his relief turned to pique. He would let her stew in her own juice till morning. "That's okay. Never mind. I just wanted to be sure she got home all right. Thanks."

"Well, sure, okay."

On the fourteenth floor of Coolidge Hall, Sukey Darrow hung up the phone and went into the john with her bottle of shampoo and her towel and her blow-dryer. The john on her own floor had been out of whack since the fire, so everybody was using the bathroom on the floor above.

Pushing open the door, Sukey saw the girl with red hair. She was brushing her teeth.

"Oh, say, Alison," said Sukey, "some guy just called you up—only he said, never mind, like he didn't have to speak to you, he just wanted to be sure you were okay."

The redheaded girl spat out toothpaste and glanced up at Sukey. "Who, me? My name's not Alison. It's Rachel. Rachel Clapp. Alison Grove has like this really, really curly hair. Well, sure, mine's red too—only, see? It's straight. It's really, really straight."

"Oh, wow, I remember now. Right." Sukey turned on the water in the shower and tested it with her hand.

"Alison's not here anyway," said Rachel, shouting above the noise of Sukey's shower. "Her room's right across the hall from me, and she hasn't been there for a couple of days."

"Oh, no, oh shit," said Sukey, pulling off her bathrobe and jumping under the hot spray. "I just gave this guy a bum steer. I wonder who he was? Hey, Rachel, can you hear me? Aren't you in my chem lab? Hey, listen, do you know anything about all those creepy valences?"

27

The Heavens stripped—
Eternity's vast pocket, picked—

*T*he last morning of the Emily
Dickinson Centennial Symposium dawned pearly and warm.
Burning through a gold mist, the sun reached over the dark
water of the Quabbin Reservoir to light up the Pelham hills
and Sugarloaf and Mount Toby and Mount Tom, and skip
westward along the ragged peaks of the Holyoke Range. At the
University of Massachusetts it picked out the top of the library
and the upper floors of the high-rise dormitories in the Southwest Quad. Shining into Alison Grove's empty room on the
fourteenth floor of Coolidge Hall, it glistened on the cosmetics
lined up on her dresser, the lip moisturizer in cinnabar, the
contour blush in burnished copper, the liquid foundation in
Portofino Peach. On the top of Alison's bookcase it sparkled on
the silver frame of a studio portrait of Alison's mother. Below
the window the bed lay in shadow, the bedspread smooth and
undisturbed.

On the other side of town, the sunlight filtered through
the oak tree in the Dickinson garden and dappled the east window of Lavinia Dickinson's bedroom. Splashes of light wobbled
on the sleeping face of Owen Kraznik and woke him up. Lifting his head cautiously, he found himself alone in bed.

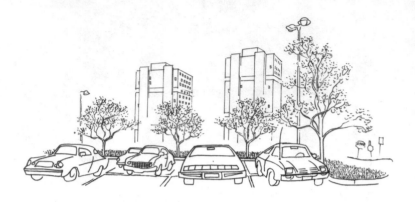

Dombey was up and gone. Dombey's clothes lay in a jumble on the floor.

Owen got up too. In the kitchen he was surprised to find Peter Wiggins standing in the middle of the room, looking around vaguely. Peter seemed relieved to see him. "Good morning, Professor Kraznik," he said, his voice high and sharp. "I'm just going out for breakfast. Will you join me?"

Owen looked at Peter curiously. The young man's eyes were glittering, but his face was very white. How did he keep so pale in a sunny state like Arizona? Maybe everybody in Arizona wore a ten-gallon hat, or maybe Peter suffered from a skin disease and had to stay indoors. "Well, of course I will, but you've got to call me Owen."

Together they walked up Main Street. Peter's head was in a whirl. His fingers trembled as he opened the door of the Lord Jeff for Owen, but his spirits were high. The scuffle last night with Winifred Gaw had been crazy, impossible, wild! But he had come through it unscathed. As for the shakiness in his limbs, that would surely disappear with a few bites of breakfast. Peter supposed he should not be spending his money at a fancy place like this—he should be eating in some greasy spoon instead. But at this point in his life, money was surely no object. He must continue to show himself drinking from fortune's cup.

But this morning, as Peter walked into the lobby of the Lord Jeffery Inn with Owen Kraznik, his brimming success suddenly drained from the bottom of the glass.

They were hailed by Dombey Dell. "What ho, good morning. Hey, looky here. See what I've got."

Dombey had a copy of *The New York Times*. The city edition had been trucked during the night from New York to the Holyoke News Company, and from there to the Hastings Stationery Store on South Pleasant Street, then rushed across the Common to the Lord Jeffery, to greet early-rising guests in this most perfect of rural New England inns.

Dombey tapped the newspaper and shook his head sadly at Peter. "Too bad," he said. "They're trampling all over you. Shame on them."

"They're *what?*" Peter's white face turned whiter still. His shaking fingers rattled the paper as he took it from Dombey.

"Good heavens, what do they say?" Owen stood on tiptoe to look over Peter's shoulder.

There at the top of the left-hand column was Peter's photograph of Emily Dickinson, right there on the front page of *The New York Times*. But the headline was a disaster—"EMILY DICKINSON" PHOTOGRAPH DECLARED FRAUDULENT.

Peter gasped. He couldn't believe his eyes. That woman from the *Times*, she had seemed so interested, so convinced. How could she do this to him?

Owen craned his neck to read the small print, feeling in the pit of his stomach Peter's disappointment and chagrin. But Dombey was looking on with vindictive relish.

"It's some Columbia professor," he said. "He's discovered who wrote the identification on the back of that picture of yours. You thought it was probably some relative, right? Well, he says it was the guy who originally sold the picture, back in the nineteen-sixties."

"Oh, God," whispered Peter. His eyes raced over the column of newsprint.

". . . If only Professor Wiggins had done his homework," said Dr. Ransome, "he would know that the handwriting on the back of the picture is that of a New York collector notorious for his overoptimistic attributions."

Peter's lifeless fingers dropped the paper. Owen picked it up and gave it back. "It's just one man's opinion," he said.

"No, it's not," said Peter, his eyes racing down the page. "Oh, God." An expert in the photographic identification of criminals had been given the last word.

"If Wiggins claims to prove his theory with diagrams, it's wishful thinking. Any quack can make diagrams. I could find you a hundred photographs of anonymous people you could diagram to prove they were Abraham Lincoln. If that woman is Emily Dickinson, I'm the Emir of Kuwait."

Peter lowered the paper and gazed at Dombey Dell, not seeing him, staring right through him. Peter's eyes had sunk back into their sockets. His body was covered with perspiration. The words *Any quack* were clucking in his head.

"Oh, well," said Dombey Dell, "what the hell? At least our symposium made the front page of *The New York Times*, thanks to you. That's a step up from *The Hampshire Gazette*." Dombey clapped Peter heartily on the back, almost knocking him down. Then Dombey turned with relief to the long stream of Oriental scholars flooding down the stairs. "Excuse me, chaps," he said. "I think I'd better continue my duties as the jolly host." Swiftly, Dombey deserted Peter's sinking ship.

But for Owen, a sinking ship was just another name for a lame duck. "Come on," he said cheerfully to Peter, "have something to eat. You'll see it's not important. Write a letter to the *Times*, why don't you? Refute everything they say. Nothing to it. This kind of thing happens to us all, every day."

But Peter was utterly shattered. He had lost his appetite for breakfast. He had no courage to enter a dining room in which the morning edition of *The New York Times* would soon be passing from hand to hand, accompanied by exclamations of surprise and terrible reorderings of opinion about Professor Peter Wiggins of the University of Central Arizona and his controversial photograph of Emily Dickinson.

Weakly, Peter fumbled for Owen's hand and shook it limply. Turning away, he stumbled out of the Lord Jeffery Inn. The bruises of his life-and-death battle with Winifred Gaw were beginning to throb in his arms and legs. Desperately his poor head tried to come to grips with the sudden collapse of his circumstances. He had hoped to sweep everything before him in total victory. Instead there was this sickening defeat.

On the way back to the Homestead it seemed surprising to Peter that nature was carrying on as usual. A bird uttered a ticking note in the bushes. A small blue butterfly folded and unfolded its wings on a flower in somebody's front yard. An insect was buzzing in the grass. Across the street a pine tree lifted and dropped its branches in the warm wind, then lifted and dropped them again, as though the world had not become an entirely different place, as though the claims of Peter Wiggins were still valid, as though they had not suddenly become sensational, a piece of charlatanry, a hoax—as if it were still possible that some respectable institution of higher learning would rush forward and award him a teaching appointment with cheery accompanying perquisites, a private office overlooking the college green, a carrel in the library, a membership in the faculty club.

But then Peter took heart. He reminded himself that all was not lost. There was an escape, a possible way out. He had prepared himself for trouble, for disbelief. He was ready with an alternative, a drastic fallback position in case of disappointment.

Turning from Spring Street onto Churchill, tripping over every twig in his path, shying at fluttering leaves like a spooked horse, Peter wondered if he could work up the nerve, the unmitigated gall, to carry out a thing like that.

Hoping for comfort, he called Angie, using the phone in the hall on the third floor.

But Angie had no comfort to give. "Oh, Peter, you woke me up. Listen to that. You hear that? The kids, there they go, the two of them. You might have had the courtesy—"

"Oh, I'm sorry, Angie, I forgot about the difference in time. How are things going?"

"Lousy. I mean it's just so incredible. There's green stuff dripping out of the air conditioner. Yesterday there was a scorpion in the bathtub. Nicole's diaper rash is back, and Michelle has these hives all over her neck. It's the heat."

Peter listened to his wife's complaints and made soothing noises and hung up at last, more miserable than ever, to find himself staring at the steep stairway to the cupola. The steps were bathed in dusty streaks of sunlight.

Careless in his wretchedness, Peter put his foot on the bottom step, climbed to the top, and stepped out on the cupola floor.

Around him lay the town of Amherst, with its airy domes of leafy green, the roofs of its comfortable houses, the pink blossoming of its apple trees. To the south he could see the hazy undulations of the Holyoke hills. It was easy to imagine Emily Dickinson climbing up here to gaze out at them, trying to look past them to Springfield, where Samuel Bowles was busy editing the Springfield *Republican,* cut off from Emily Dickinson by Long Mountain and Mount Hitchcock and Mount Holyoke, and by a much larger mountain range in the shape of Mrs. Mary Schermerhorn Bowles.

The solemn Alps—
The siren Alps
Forever intervene!

It struck Peter that Emily Dickinson's impossible longings were very much like his own. He too was reaching across a barrier. For him, too, there was a gap between desire and object. Like her, he was tottering across a shaking bridge, hammering at a door that was forever locked and sealed.

Slowly, Peter moved from one window to another, staring with greedy attention at the low hills of Pelham, at the cupola of Austin Dickinson's house next door, at the brick buildings of Amherst College, at the white wooden clock tower of Johnson Chapel. It was all so mellow—so mellow and old and green. Not red and raw and choked with dust!

A moment ago, climbing the stairs to the cupola, Peter had not yet settled the matter. Now, as he descended, he made up his mind.

He would fall back on his ace in the hole.

But first he leaned over the stair railing and looked down at the hallway on the second floor. Had Winnie's dead body been discovered? The house was quiet. There were no shouts of surprise, no tramp of running feet. How long would it take them to decide to open her door? Well, it didn't matter to Peter. His duty was simple. Until someone told him Winnie was dead, he would behave as if nothing had happened. Then he would register surprise and shock. Easy enough. There was nothing to worry about on that score.

Closing the door of his bedroom behind him, Peter took his wallet out of his pocket and reached into the secret compartment. In every wallet he had ever possessed, there had been a flap where you could secrete something, but this was the first time Peter had ever had anything to hide.

Like his original photograph, this one was protected by a wrapping of tissue paper. The second picture of Emily Dickinson was exactly like the first. And that was its glory, because Peter had manufactured it from nothing.

It had cost him a year of effort, a year of failure, a year of trying one thing after another.

One by one, the technical problems had been solved. An old photographic *carte de visite* had provided the right sort of paper and card stock. Peter had soaked them apart, then bleached off the old image in Farmer's Reducer, and resensitized the paper in baths of ammonium chloride and silver nitrate. Then, after taking a careful picture of the original photograph, he had worked over the new negative with a retouching tool until the image was a miracle of clarity. The perfection of the sepia coloration had simply been a matter of money—twenty-five dollars for a gram of gold chloride! And the glue was organic, a few scrapings from a horse's hoof, boiled down on the stove. (Angie had wrinkled her nose. "Peter, what are you doing? That stuff really stinks.")

But it was the writing on the back of the picture that would really prove his case.

Peter turned over his little forgery and smiled at the inscription. The oak-gall ink was organic, like the glue. The pen had been a sharpened goose quill. That part had been easy. It was the message itself that had called for all of Peter's scholarship and wit. It could not be too bald—*Emily Dickinson, poet, Amherst, Massachusetts*—that would never do. It must be the sort of swift identification scribbled on the backs of photographs by relatives as they sorted through old boxes of pictures, or the hasty comments jotted down just before a picture was slipped with a letter into an envelope—*Frieda's baby, six months old.*

Peter's choice had been clever. Looking at his forged inscription, he could almost believe it was real, it looked so right, so similar to Lavinia Dickinson's handwriting, so much like something Emily's sister might actually have said—

Emily don't like this much.

In one brisk sentence it identified the picture and explained why it had vanished from the family. *Emily don't like this much*—it was the perfect thing to say. After studying hundreds of Dickinson family letters, Peter was especially proud of his use of the word *don't*, rather than *doesn't*. It was the way they had talked. It was what they said informally, in writing to each other.

Holding the picture delicately, Peter went to the window and gazed at the distant view of housetops across the street. Somewhere in Amherst he must find it a home. His little counterfeit was small, after all. It wouldn't take much space, only a narrow slot two inches wide and four inches tall. Surely among these tree-lined streets there was a temporary hiding place for the woman with the magnificent eyes? A place where someone would discover her soon, and pounce upon her, and bring her to the light?

Peter Wiggins was no sentimentalist. He had been schooled in the dry astringency and healthy caustic skepticism of a great graduate department. But something had happened to him that was worse than sentiment, worse than slipshod scholarship. The single overwhelming reason why Peter was willing to sacrifice his principles and endanger his scholarly good name was simply that he had fallen in love with a dead woman.

28

There's something quieter than sleep
Within this inner room!

Owen, too, had lost his appetite for breakfast. Abandoning the Lord Jeff, he walked down Spring Street to his own house, where he found Homer Kelly making pancakes.

"Look at this," said Homer, handing him *The Hampshire Gazette*, tapping the front page with the pancake turner.

Owen took the paper cautiously, fearful of another brutal attack on Peter Wiggins. But it was only another report on the status of the Coolidge Hall fire investigation. Something had turned up in the bushes between the parking lot and Coolidge Hall. A guy looking for a lost hubcap had discovered an empty can of lacquer. The color of the paint was opal gold.

"Lacquer?" said Owen. "Not kerosene, after all?"

"Well, maybe. That is, if the can has any connection with the fire at all. It would narrow down the problem of the source, and that would be good. I mean, you don't buy lacquer at every supermarket, right?"

"But who uses lacquer?" said Owen, bewildered. "All I can think of is Japanese screens and lacquered boxes."

Homer laughed and waved the pancake turner. "I see. It was somebody in a kimono with long fingernails, skulking around in Coolidge Hall, setting the place on fire. Aha! A member of the Japanese Poetry Society, no doubt. Whee, whoops!" Homer flipped a pancake inexpertly, and it did a somersault in the air, then dropped with a splat on the floor. Picking it up, he dabbed at it with a towel. "I'll eat this one. You want to know who uses lacquer? I'll tell you, my friend. Guys who work on dented chassis. They repaint the cars with lacquer afterward. Spray the stuff on with a compressor. Archie Gripp will have his hands full, poking around all the body shops in Hampshire County. Here we go again, whoopee!"

This time the pancake hit the ceiling, stuck for a moment, then fell on a bicycle pump that happened to be lying on the counter.

"Oh, that's *quite* all right," said Owen. "I know it will be *delicious*."

After breakfast, Owen said good-bye to Homer and hurried back to the Homestead. There he found Dombey Dell storming up and down the front hall, waiting for him.

"Listen here, Owen, I promised the Smith brothers a private tour of the house before the memorial church service this morning. Get that Gaw woman up! She doesn't answer when I knock. It's just like the day before yesterday. She's sulking. Come on, if you can't get her out of there, I'll drag her out by the hair."

In Owen's stomach Homer's pancake lay like a stone. He followed Dombey upstairs. "Are you sure she's here at all?" he said, staring at the bedroom door. "Perhaps she's gone home to Ware."

"Oh, she's in there all right. Her van is still parked outside."

Owen knocked gently on the door. "Winnie?"

There was no answer, no sound at all but the drowsy buzz of a fly against the sunlit panes of the hall window.

He knocked again, and called louder. "Are you there, Winnie?"

Again there was no reply. Dombey swore under his breath.

Owen put his ear against one of the white-painted panels,

remembering the last time he had leaned against the door and felt it quivering with the suspended breath of the fat girl on the other side. Today the stillness was different. It was the un-speaking habit of voiceless, lifeless things, the staring pictures on the wall, the china bowl and pitcher on the dresser, the cast-iron fireplace. It was the wooden silence of tables and chairs. Surely there was nothing alive on the other side of the door.

"Go on in," demanded Dombey.

Owen tried the knob. It turned easily in his hand.

Bracing himself, he opened the door.

29

❧

Pain has but one Acquaintance
And that is Death . . .

"*O*h, God bloody damn," said
Dombey Dell. "What's the bloody damn woman done now?
Gone and got herself killed! Didn't I tell you she was going to
ruin me? Didn't I warn you she'd destroy the whole bloody
goddamn symposium? Look at that axe! My God, think how
that axe will look on TV! Think of the headlines! Axe Murder
at Emily Dickinson Conference! Bloody God, bloody damn,
bloody hell!"

Owen was on his knees beside Winnie, tears running down
his face. Picking up Winnie's hand, the one with the missing
little finger, he felt the pit yawning once more beneath his feet.
Grimacing painfully, he stared around at the chaos in Emily
Dickinson's bedchamber, at the fallen table, the upended
chairs, the tipped-over sofa, the broken glass scattered on the
floor. From a gold frame on the wall Edward Dickinson
frowned down at Owen. George Eliot and Elizabeth Barrett
Browning gazed at him blandly, indifferent to Winnie's fate.

Then Dombey discovered the pills. "Hey, look at this," he
said. "Pills all over the floor. A couple of empty pill bottles.
Look at that, two new cotton stoppers. Hey, maybe she took a
lot of pills, see? There's only a few on the floor. I bet she swal-

lowed the rest. So maybe she was committing suicide. Did she leave a note? Suicides, they always leave a note. Nope, I don't see any note. Just this book on the floor. Looks familiar. Library book, *Letters of Emily Dickinson, Volume Two.* What's this doing here?"

"I doubt very much it was suicide," said Owen sadly, getting to his feet. "You forget the axe."

"Oh, right, the axe. Well, what the hell do we do now? Listen, Owen, do we have to call the fucking police? I mean now? Do we have to call them right away? After all, our schedule for today is so harmless. All we're doing today is being pious, that's all. Can't we just go right ahead? We've just got a church service and a pilgrimage to the grave and a picnic, nothing but stuff like that. All in perfect taste. The symposium's practically over. Why can't we wait until everybody goes home before we call the cops?"

Owen shook his head grimly. "Of course we have to call the police. We have no choice." Then Owen's face brightened. "I know, I'll talk to my cousin Harvey. He's the medical examiner. He'll know what to do. And I'll get Homer over here. Homer used to be a policeman. Good heavens, why didn't I think of Homer right away?"

Dombey was flabbergasted. "You mean Homer Kelly, the big Thoreau man? *Homer Kelly* used to be a policeman?"

"That's right." Owen picked his way over the smashed fragments of the rose-colored wineglass and started downstairs.

"Oh, Lord," groaned Dombey, leaning over the railing. "It was spite, I tell you. The woman did it out of spite, just to make a monkey out of me. Listen, Owen, I don't care what *you* do, but I'm not going to say one word about this to anybody. Maybe by some miracle it won't hit the news until everybody's gone home. I'll give the Smith brothers some excuse, take them out for coffee or something before the church service. And then we'll cancel the open house this afternoon, during the picnic. We'll just let people use the garden and the kitchen, okay?" Dombey yelled louder as Owen moved out of sight at the bottom of the stairs. "Oh, God, Owen, do you know what day this is? It's May fifteenth! It's a hundred years to the day since Emily Dickinson died in that very room. Oh, God bloody Christ. Another gruesome headline, Axe Murder Commemorates Centennial of Poet's Death." Clapping his hand to his forehead, Dombey stamped down the hall to put on his churchgoing clothes and comb his hair.

Owen's cousin Harvey was not at home to answer the phone. At that moment Harvey was rolling up his sleeping bag in the state forest at Petersham, getting ready to spend the day on Quabbin's bright blue water. Therefore Owen heard only Harvey's recorded voice on the line, announcing with a hint of smugness that he would not be back in his office until Monday morning at nine o'clock, and in the meantime the emergency number at Cooley-Dickinson was . . .

But Homer Kelly picked up the phone on the first ring. When he heard the news about Winifred Gaw, he was darkly triumphant. "Didn't I tell you? Didn't I say these conferences are murder? An axe? Did you say an axe? And the medical examiner is unavailable? How about some other doctor?"

There was a pause. Then Owen's voice brightened. "Yes, I know another doctor. And she'll do very well."

30

Presentiment—is that long Shadow—on the Lawn—
Indicative that Suns go down—

The Notice to the startled Grass
That Darkness—is about to pass—

*T*om Perry was feeling pressured. He was late. He had forgotten to bring his alarm clock, so this morning he had overslept, and there was no time to have breakfast before the Emily Dickinson memorial service in the First Parish Church. He couldn't possibly be late for that, because he was supposed to stand up in the front of the church and read a passage from First Corinthians.

But he had to phone Alison first. Tom was feeling guilty about Alison. He should have talked to her last night. He should have made up with her on the phone. He shouldn't have been such a self-righteous asshole. Opening the door, Tom looked out into the hall, rubbing his frowsy hair.

Where was everybody? Well, Dombey was still here, banging around and cursing in Owen's bedroom. But the rest of the house was silent.

Dressing quickly, Tom plunged downstairs to the kitchen, picked up the phone, and dialed Coolidge Hall.

A voice answered briskly, "Fourteenth floor."

"Hello, who's that? Listen, I want to speak to Alison Grove. Right now. I'm in a hurry."

"Well, bully for you," said the girl at Coolidge Hall. "Sorry, but Alison hasn't been around for a couple of days."

Tom was nonplussed. His voice rose in anger. "But that girl last night, she said Alison was there."

"Who said? Listen, Rachel told me at breakfast this morning—Rachel Clapp, she lives right across the hall from Alison—she told me she hasn't seen Alison for two or three days."

"Well, where is she?" shouted Tom. "That girl last night—" Tom slammed down the phone and stared at the wall where someone had tacked up a reminder, *Get sugar.*

Where the hell *was* Alison? Could she have gone home to her mother, there on Pomeroy Lane? Tom didn't relish the thought of calling Alison's mother. Mrs. Grove would get all upset.

Tom had met Mrs. Grove, back in March, on Easter Sunday. Alison had taken him home to the big builder's Colonial, with its brick facing and white shutters and foundation planting and lamppost. Alison's mother had turned out to be a handsome woman, worthy of her daughter, but Tom hadn't exactly taken to her. Mrs. Grove had hardly noticed him. She had kept her huge blue eyes fixed on Alison. She had fussed with Alison's hair. She had painted Alison's fingernails. And she had seemed less interested in Tom, the bridegroom, than in the wedding to come. The wedding was going to be complicated and magnificent, with all the trimmings. More like a coronation, Tom had thought, watching Mrs. Grove run her hands under lengths of transparent tulle.

The last thing he wanted to do right now was get Mrs. Grove all worked up. Besides, he didn't have time. He was supposed to be across the street in the church, right now, ready to climb into the pulpit.

Jumping up, Tom strode down the hall, jerking at his tie. But when he flung open the door, he found Owen Kraznik on the porch, with—Jesus God—Ellen Oak, and that tall craggy-looking guy who had been with the two of them last night.

"Why, Tom, good morning," said Owen, startled. "Oh, Tom, have you heard what's happened?"

But Tom was staring at Ellen, a painful flush surging up from his collar. "Oh, Ellen," he said heartily, "there you are."

Ellen's face reddened too. "Hello, Tom," she said.

"I—uh—read your letter," said Tom.

Owen looked from one to the other. "I understand you two are old friends," he said lamely. "Oh, excuse me, Tom, have you met Homer Kelly?"

There were introductions. Homer shook hands with Tom Perry and wondered what was the matter with everybody.

"Well, Ellen and I certainly *are* old friends," explained Tom, suddenly overcome with joviality. It sickened him, but he couldn't help himself. "You see, Owen, Ellen is a *doctor*, and I was her *patient*. We met in the hospital when I was having my appendix out. I lost my *heart* as well as my *appendix*, ha ha!" Tom was appalled by his own idiocy, but he gibbered on. "Well, Ellen," he chuckled, glancing at his wrist, where there was no watch, "we've got to get together and *talk*, don't we? But right now, if you'll excuse me, I'm supposed to be across the street. So long." Nodding and beaming, showing his teeth, Tom dodged past them and escaped, running long-legged in the direction of the church.

"She says it wasn't the axe," said Homer cheerfully, coming into the kitchen.

"The axe hardly touched her," said Ellen. "I know it looked like a lot of blood, but it wasn't really."

"Well, then," said Owen, fumbling with the coffee cups, "maybe it was suicide after all? Do you think Winnie really swallowed two whole bottles of pills?"

"Well, I'm not sure," said Ellen. She sat down and looked around the room at the electric stove, the dishwasher, the bright wallpaper. For a moment she was disappointed that this was no longer the same nineteenth-century kitchen in which Emily Dickinson had baked bread. Then she chastised herself and turned to Owen. "The pills were Secanol, a very commonplace sedative. Not very potent. It would have taken at least ten of them to knock her out. You're not allowed to pre-

scribe more than thirty at a time. But Winnie had two bottles. That would have been sixty pills. I counted eighteen on the floor. There may be more in the bedclothes. If she swallowed all the rest, she would have taken about forty altogether."

"Would forty have been enough to kill her?" said Owen.

"Well, it certainly wouldn't have done her any good. Not a woman in her condition. We'll have to ask Dr. Kloop, whose name is on the prescription. He's a colleague of mine at the hospital. I never knew he had such a distinguished cousin." Ellen smiled at Owen, and made a gesture of resignation. "Now we'll just have to wait till he's back in his office. Then he can do an autopsy and make a blood test. He was perfectly correct in allowing her only thirty tablets in each of those prescriptions, a month apart. That's supposed to prevent this kind of overdose. But of course he couldn't stop her from saving two months' supply and taking them all at once. If that's what she did. Homer noticed something interesting."

"The decanter," said Homer wisely, holding up one finger. "The decanter was still nearly full of water. And so was the wineglass beside it. How could the girl have choked down a lot of large dry pills without drinking any water?"

Owen was puzzled. "But if she didn't take the pills, and if it wasn't the axe, how did she die? And who on earth was in the room with her, throwing furniture around? There must have been a knock-down, drag-out battle. The poor girl must have been fighting for her life. The noise—think of the smashing of glassware and the crashing of furniture on the floor! And yet none of us heard a thing. When could it have happened?"

"Obviously, when you weren't here," said Ellen. "Have you called the police?"

"Yes," said Owen, "just now. I spoke to a man named Archie something. They'll be with us shortly."

"Good old Archie Gripp," said Homer importantly. "Old friend of mine. I'll talk to him, if you like, and show him around."

"Poor Dombey," said Owen, shaking his head. "He didn't want us to call the police at all. He wanted us to go on as if nothing had happened, so that he could finish up his symposium in perfect decorum. Good heavens, that reminds me." Owen looked at the kitchen clock and jumped up. "They'll be leaving the church in a minute, and heading for the cemetery. I'm supposed to read a poem beside Emily Dickinson's grave."

31

"Called back."

*T*he ceremony was open to everyone. People came in throngs, and dropped their flowers over the railing of the Dickinson family enclosure. Schoolchildren reached through the iron fence to sprinkle violets around Emily's tall stone. The minister from the First Congregational Church said a prayer. And Ellen Oak recited a famous poem:

> *"Because I could not stop for Death—*
> *He kindly stopped for me—*
> *The Carriage held but just Ourselves—*
> *And Immortality . . ."*

It was Owen's idea. Owen was supposed to read the poem himself, but at the last minute he shoved the book at Ellen. She didn't need it. She knew the poem by heart.

Tom Perry was standing morosely at one side. Tom had come to West Cemetery in the hope of finding Alison Grove, but now he couldn't help listening to Ellen Oak. He couldn't help noticing that Ellen's way of saying a poem was different from Alison's. Altogether different. Different in a dozen ways,

a hundred, a thousand. Tom couldn't get over it. But then he told himself it didn't matter. Only one thing mattered—finding Alison herself. Stopping in at the Homestead after the church service, Tom had finally called Alison's mother. But Mrs. Grove had not seen Alison. And as he feared, she had turned hysterical. He had promised to go to the police.

Ellen finished the poem and moved away from the Dickinson enclosure, remembering what she had read about the burial that had happened here a century ago. It had been a day as fine as this. *The country exquisite, day perfect, and an atmosphere of its own, fine and strange, about the whole house and grounds. . . . The grass of the lawn full of buttercups.* Well, the buttercups were still springing up in the grass of the cemetery, but the mourners were not like the people who had followed Emily's coffin across the fields on that lovely May day in 1886. Today no one was wearing dark funereal colors. Only the shiny shoes of the Japanese delegation were black. Students from U Mass and Amherst College stood around in jeans and T-shirts. Some of the kids were barefoot. Everyone was talking cheerfully. After all, it had been a hundred years since that funeral procession had trailed among the buttercups to bury its dead.

The Amherst Historical Society was handing out paper cups of wine. Owen gave one to Ellen, and congratulated her on her recitation. Then, with an excruciating effort at conviviality, he introduced her to Eunice Jane Kloop.

"I suspect your good husband has gone fishing," he said kindly to Eunice Jane.

"Who knows?" said Eunice Jane darkly. Eunice Jane was not interested in her husband's foolish outing on the Quabbin Reservoir. She had no eyes for Ellen Oak. With a grip of steel she fastened her talons into Owen Kraznik and pinned him to the back of a granite slab. What did Owen think about her new analysis of Poem Number 1615, "Without Diminuet Proceed?" Had he read it in the church bulletin? He hadn't? Well, then, she would explain it from line one.

Ellen looked on for a moment in horrified amusement, then interrupted boldly. "Oh, excuse me, Mrs. Kloop, but I think Professor Kraznik is wanted over there." Waving her hand at the gravestones behind Eunice Jane's back, Ellen called out, "He's coming."

Swiftly she walked him away from Eunice Jane.

"Oh, how fortunate," breathed Owen. "Oh, what an escape! I must confess I find that sort of analysis very trying. Who wants to speak to me?"

Ellen looked at him sheepishly. "Well, no one, I'm afraid."

Owen's jaw dropped. "But how courageous! What a brilliant rescue! You are a woman of valor!"

Peter Wiggins, too, was wandering among the urns and obelisks. It was Peter's first venture into the world after seeing the article about his picture on the front page of *The New York Times.* Furtively he watched the Smith brothers. They were sipping wine, standing in a huddle with Dombey Dell. If he were to speak to them, would they still be as cordial as they had been last night? Courageously Peter moved across the grass, determined to brazen it out.

But as he drew near, Dombey turned his back and shepherded the two Harvard professors down the hill. Peter followed, hurrying his footsteps, but now the three of them were ducking behind the graves of eighteenth-century Dickinsons and sidling along the edge of the cemetery, becoming entangled with a cluster of children who were climbing the straggling trees. By the time Peter changed direction, Dombey and the Smith brothers were driving away in Dombey's car, the children were high in the branches, and a woman was running across the lawn.

It was the Mother of Ten. "You get right down from there, Ronnie and Richie! You hear me, Sharon? Kevin and Brian, I'll tear you apart! Donna and Diane—"

Peter's footsteps faltered as the car disappeared on Kellogg Avenue. He flushed with humiliation, then jerked violently as someone spoke up at his elbow. "You know what I think? That article in the *Times* was really dumb. That's what I think."

Peter turned in surprise to find a gray-haired woman at his side. She was carrying a small child. "Oh, excuse me. My name's Tilly Porch. I heard your talk yesterday. Those experts in New York, they didn't hear it. They didn't see your diagrams. What do they know?"

Peter was comforted. He smiled faintly at the baby. "Your grandchild?"

"Oh, no. This is Debbie Buffington's baby. She's staying with me for a couple of days. I'm just baby-sitting at the moment. His name's Elvis." The baby was squirming in Tilly's arms, and she put him down. "Come on, Elvis dear. Time for the picnic."

Peter fell into step with Tilly, and together they walked along Kellogg Avenue with Elvis toddling in front of them. Tilly didn't seem to notice the raw state of Peter's nerves. Instead she talked comfortably about the Amherst Women's Emily Dickinson Association and all the fancy cooking they had been doing for the picnic. The more she talked, the more interested Peter became. His false photograph was burning a hole in his pocket. He was going to have to put it somewhere, very soon. Time was running out.

1 6 5

"I wonder," he said casually, "how many of the people who are here today had ancestors in Amherst in Emily Dickinson's time?"

"Oh, not many." Tilly thought about it. "I guess, as a matter of fact, I'm the only one. Good heavens, Professor Wiggins, I'm still living in my great-great-great-great-great-grandfather's house on Market Hill Road."

"No kidding?" Peter's interest in Tilly became suddenly more intense. "Did your ancestors know the Dickinsons?"

"Oh, well, I suppose everybody in town knew everybody else in those days. Here, Elvis, hold my hand while we cross the street."

"Do you have letters and—you know, old pictures, things like that from those days?"

"Oh, yes, I guess so. I haven't worked my way through all of it yet." But Tilly wasn't interested in her own family history. She was fascinated by Peter's picture, and wanted to tell him so. "You know, there's something wonderful about that photograph of yours, isn't there? It's funny, I have this feeling I've seen it before."

"In Sewall's biography," agreed Peter. "That's where you've seen it." Peter in his turn didn't want to talk about himself and his photograph. He wanted to find out more about the old papers in Tilly's possession. "You mean to say you have more nineteenth-century Amherst material to examine? Things you haven't looked at before?"

"Well, good grief, when your family has been living in the same house for a couple of hundred years, you get bogged down in so much *stuff*. I try to sort through a little more of it every year."

"A *little* more?" Peter pretended to be scandalized. "But how can you wait? You should look at everything immediately. At once! There might be something of great significance among your family papers. Surely you owe it to the—what do you call your organization? The Amherst Women's Emily Dickinson Association? Really, there's no telling what treasures you might find."

"Well, of course, that's true. That's absolutely true. That's right, Elvis dear. Here we go, right around the corner." Through the trees at the bottom of the Dickinson garden they could catch glimpses of blowing white tablecloths and women running back and forth with trays. "Now that my last child is in college, I really should have time to explore the attic. Until now it's been impossible. Raising five children and teaching school—it's kept me terribly busy, as you can imagine. And then my husband was ill, and I nursed him for five years. It's only since he died last fall that I've had any time to myself."

They walked up the granite steps and strolled across the lawn in the direction of the picnic tables. "Oh, Tilly, guess what?" Carolyn Chin was rushing forward, her face anxious, her hair in a frazzle. "We forgot the sugar and cream. I thought there might at least be some sugar in the Homestead kitchen, but there isn't a *speck*."

"I'll run home and get some," said Tilly decisively. Reaching down, she swept up Elvis and turned to say good-bye to Peter. Then her face dropped. Putting Elvis down again, she apologized to Carolyn Chin. "Oh, I forgot, I don't have a car. Debbie took it. You know, Elvis's mother. She dropped me and Elvis at the cemetery and went off in my car to meet a friend."

"Well, then, *allow me*." Peter couldn't believe his good fortune. Once again heaven was smiling! "I have a rented car. Permit me to provide transportation. No, no, I insist. I positively insist."

"Well, in that case," said Tilly gratefully, "I positively accept."

A blue-and-white patrol car and a big police van were parked beside Peter's little Datsun on the other side of the house. "What do you suppose they're doing here?" said Tilly, getting into the front seat. "Oh, I suppose they expect a big crush at the picnic, and there'll be a lot of traffic and all."

"I expect that's it," said Peter smoothly, picking up Elvis, settling him in Tilly's lap. Getting in on the other side of the car, he smiled at the thought of the forged photograph in his pocket. It was warm over his throbbing heart. The opportunity was at hand. At Tilly's house he would delicately inquire if he might use the bathroom, and then surely he could make his way swiftly to the attic?

Grinning broadly, Peter swung the car around and headed out onto Main Street. His work of art, his handmade reproduction of the photograph of the woman with the dark eyes, was about to find a happy home.

My Hope put out a petal—

32

New feet within my garden go . . .

*T*he shadow of the white oak tree lay across the lawn. With its dangling infant leaves it seemed as much in flower as the pear tree, the apple tree, the umbrella magnolia, the lilacs, the Jacob's ladder, the bleeding heart. A pitcher was passing around again, another kind of wine, sweet malmsey this time, a heroic attempt by Barbara Teeter to follow a recipe of Mrs. Edward Dickinson's. Everyone made the same joke, *I taste a liquor never brewed—From Tankards scooped in Pearl.*

It was the last event of the symposium. The sun was warm. The participants were mellow. They seemed to have known one another all their lives. Their reverence for Emily Dickinson was turning sentimental. What a miracle it was that she had been born, right here in this house, and lived to become so great a poet; how staggering that her words had survived to become talismans for the condition of all their minds and hearts! When Dottie Poole appeared with an enormous memento on a tray, everyone cheered.

It was the pinnacle and masterwork of the picnic, an enormous black cake, made according to Emily's own recipe. Dottie had stayed up all night to finish it. In a giant plastic washtub

she had beaten together three dozen eggs, four pounds of flour, four pounds of butter, four pounds of sugar, ten packages of raisins, and a pint of molasses. Then she had tucked the cake in the oven and drowsed on the sofa for six hours, leaping up every now and then to test it with a broom straw. Recklessly at last she had poured over it every drop of her husband's precious Armagnac brandy at five o'clock in the morning.

Owen was doing his best. Hastening up and down the sloping lawn, he tried to speak to everyone, to Professor Nogobuchi, to the emeritus professor from Hokkaido, to Marybelle Spikes, to Helen Gaunt, to the Smith brothers, to the Swedish schoolteachers, and to Tilly Porch, who was holding a big baby in her arms.

"Your grandson?" said Owen, peering at the baby politely.

"No, just a little friend."

Owen's jaws ached from smiling. When Mary Kelly came

up behind him and took his elbow, he jerked convulsively and barked, "It's been so good to know you," before he recognized Mary and clasped her in his arms. "Mary dear, oh, Mary Kelly, thank heaven. I'm extremely pleased you're here at last. I've been enjoying Homer so much. Have you found him? Does he know you're here?"

Mary looked at him soberly. "Homer's in the house with Archie Gripp. Oh, Owen, that poor wretched girl, Winifred Gaw. You know, I think I met her once in your office, a long time ago. She had a missing finger, isn't that right? I thought I recognized her, just now, as they were taking her away. Pitiful. What on earth do you think happened to her?"

Owen flapped his hands in distress. "I have no idea. And now something else is worrying us. A young woman has disappeared. She simply vanished into thin air. She's engaged to my young friend, Tom Perry. Naturally, Tom is beside himself. He's gone to the police."

"Good heavens," said Mary, "do you think there could be any connection between her disappearance and the death of Winifred Gaw?"

"Oh, Mary dear, I can't imagine how there could be. Now forgive me, but I've got to say good-bye to everyone. They're all about to go home. I'll be so grateful when the whole thing is over." Owen squeezed Mary's hand and returned to his duties.

Owen was struggling with his feelings. He had promised Dombey Dell to say nothing to any of the participants in the symposium about the death of Winifred Gaw. And so far the lighthearted guests seemed unaware that anything was wrong. They had not heard of the gruesome calamity in Emily Dickinson's bedroom. They had not witnessed the removal of Winnie's body to the police van on the other side of the house. And, with Homer's help, Dombey had made a deal with Archie Gripp. Everybody who had not been staying in the Homestead could go home without interrogation, as long as Dombey supplied Archie with a list of names and addresses.

There was Dombey, sprawled under the magnolia tree. He was polishing off the last of the malmsey wine, waving the pitcher tipsily at one of the Smith brothers. Dombey obviously felt he had pulled off a great coup. But for Owen it seemed like treachery to grin and show his teeth while poor Winifred was on her way to a marble slab.

"Come, Professor Klaznik! Come, come!" It was the emeritus professor from Hokkaido. He wanted to take a group picture of the entire symposium. He had a camera with a 28-millimeter lens. Crowding everyone together, he pulled Owen Kraznik to the front with Dombey Dell, then ran around the outside, dabbing and patting, arranging and rearranging, shoving them all into a dense grinning mass. He took one picture, then another, and another.

"One more, please?" he said eagerly. But his orderly rows were falling apart. Someone was shrieking. It was Dottie Poole.

"Stop him!" hollered Dottie. "Oh, someone, please stop him!"

Startled, Tilly Porch turned around to look, and then she rushed up to the picnic table and reached for Elvis Buffington. Elvis was sitting beside the black cake, joyfully bashing his fist into the middle of Dottie's magnificent creation.

33

It was not Death, for I stood up,
And all the Dead, lie down—
It was not Night, for all the Bells
Put out their Tongues, for Noon.

*H*arvey Kloop had escaped at last. Yesterday, with his car barreling down Route 9, weaving a little with the weight of the boat-trailer behind it, he had felt an impulse to look back over his shoulder for possible pursuit, for some messenger calling him back to his duties, for Eunice Jane tearing after him in her little Honda, beeping and waving her arm out the window.

But no one had followed to summon him home. Now, out on the water, chugging northward past Mount Zion, Harvey could feel all the tension in his body give way. At the place where the east branch of Fever Brook entered the reservoir, he turned off the outboard and sat for a minute, gazing around and smiling in the bliss of being at last in the place he had dreamed about all winter long. Last night he had set up his little tent in the state forest at Petersham and stretched out in his sleeping bag, rejoicing in the distance he had put between himself and his wife, with all her punishing little eccentricities and her perpetual harping on Emily Dickinson. "The hell with Emily Dickinson," Harvey murmured happily to himself as he drifted off to sleep.

And this morning, waking up at dawn, he had muttered it

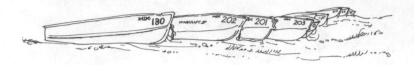

again—"The hell with Emily Dickinson!" And then he had turned over luxuriously, deciding not to get up early after all.

He had slept till noon.

Now, floating close to the shore in the brilliant sunlight, admiring the translucent tassels suspended from the oak trees and the separate puffs of needles on the white pines, Harvey lifted his head and shouted, "THE HELL WITH EMILY DICKINSON!"

The words drifted across the water and echoed from the shore and the surrounding hills. Another fisherman was putt-putting in the direction of the pass beyond Mount Zion. He looked up and waved his Day-Glo orange hat in greeting, and the gentle wash from his stern rocked Harvey's boat.

For a while Harvey just sat there, grinning, studying the shore, looking for some sign of animal life, a deer coming down to drink, a wildcat in a tree, an eagle lifting from a top-most branch. Someday, if he lived long enough, he might even chance to see that creature he was so curious about, a mountain lion—the beast the old settlers had called a catamount—and hear its legendary scream. But now there was nothing moving in the undergrowth, not even a bird hopping from branch to branch. The only sign of life was a jet going over, taking off from Westover Air Force Base, ripping the sky into halves like someone tearing a wide blue piece of cloth.

Harvey turned his attention to the water below the boat. Down there he could make out poising shapes—largemouth bass, decided Harvey. He had been hoping for lake trout, here in the cold water flowing out of Fever Brook.

The shallow water was wonderfully clear. Squinting, Harvey could see the bottom. There was a dark strip there—no, two dark strips with a lighter strip between. Immediately he knew what they meant, and he was charmed. The dark strips were the double track of a road, one of the old roads that had run through the Swift River Valley in the days before the dam was built, before the water had risen in the valley to drown the towns of Greenwich and Enfield and Prescott and Dana and make islands out of Mount Zion and Mount Pomeroy and Mount Lizzie. Harvey looked up curiously at the shore. Yes, there on the point he could detect a trace of the old road, coming abruptly to an end at the water's edge. Well, it was all a long time ago now. Forty years or more, wasn't it? No, fifty. More like fifty.

Harvey got to work preparing his tackle. Yesterday he had stopped at a bait shop along Greenwich Road for a jar of salmon eggs. Now, lifting his rod, he cast his line near the boat and watched the fluorescent eggs descend over the wheel tracks of the old road. He smiled. It seemed so queer that fish should be darting there now instead of birds, ten feet above the place where horses and wagons had once traveled with loads of hay, and tin lizzies had sputtered along on their way to Hardwick, and probably even Chryslers and Pontiacs in the streamlined nineteen-thirties.

Soon Harvey stopped reeling out his line. Hunched contentedly in the stern, he leaned a little to one side to gaze down into the shimmering amber depths. In his mind's eye he could imagine the old towns as they had once been, with their sunlit fields of white rye straw for the making of bonnets, their farmhouses and mills and box factories, their charcoal kilns and schools, and all the other buildings that had once housed a living population of three thousand souls.

Romantically, Harvey stared down over the side of the boat, letting his imagination rip, until he could almost see the lineaments of one of the old frame buildings wobbling under the water below him—a church, perhaps, with salmon passing in and out of the windows, and schools of silver smelt flashing into the door to nibble the hair of the ghostly sexton as he pulled down, down, down with his skeleton fingers on the slimy rope of the bell in the steeple to summon the long-dead flock. And then they would come floating along the road, those old parishioners, men and women with hollow eyes, their Sunday clothes spreading behind them in the watery depths. There now, hear the bell ring—muffled but penetrating—*bong, bong, bong*—farther down, out there in deep water, the drowned bell in the drowned steeple!

With a start, Harvey sat up. A bell? What bell? There was no church underwater anymore, there was no steeple, there was no bell. All the villages had been destroyed! There was nothing left but stone foundations and cellar holes. The people had moved away. Even the dead bodies in the cemeteries had been dug up and reburied somewhere else.

Why then was there a deep watery ringing that tingled into Harvey's finger ends, a reverberating hum that rattled the metal sides of his boat, a hollow jangling that tightened the very scalp under his duckbilled hat? Clutching his rod with one hand and the gunwale with the other, Harvey leaned over as far as he dared, and peered down at the old road on the bottom of the reservoir, twenty feet below. How could a bell be tolling mournfully, down there under the water?

Then something caught Harvey's eye, something bright, something white, a columnar white shape moving along the road. He caught his breath in horror. It was a woman! A woman was walking along the road under the water! A woman in an old-fashioned dress, a *white* old-fashioned dress, a woman with red hair flowing out behind her in a filmy torrent. *Jesus God, it was Emily Dickinson.*

A terrible shivering seized Harvey Kloop as the ringing grew louder, clashing sonorously, *bongety-bongety-bong*, as though the church were directly below him, as though the bottom of the boat were about to be punctured by the invisible steeple. And then Emily Dickinson lifted her great dark eyes to look up at Harvey, and now—dear God—she was lifting her arm, pallid and limp in its white sleeve, and now—HOLY MONKEY EYES—she was *waving* at Harvey! She was waving at him with the slow, languorous motion of the dead!

Harvey nearly lost consciousness. His hundred-and-fifty-dollar Fenwick rod slipped from his lifeless fingers and splashed overboard, carrying with it his forty-dollar Pflueger reel and his twelve-dollar lead-core line and his five-dollar Dave-Davis rig. But then, taking hold of himself, Harvey slammed the throttle to full speed and yanked on the starting rope. After a couple of false sputters and misfires, the engine caught and the boat zoomed away from Emily Dickinson, racing at full speed in the direction of the boat landing, skipping up and slamming down on the surface of the water, in Harvey's desperate eagerness to get away from the outlet of Fever Brook and the old underwater road and the apparition of the woman who had left the land of the living so long ago, a hundred years ago, *a hundred years ago today*, and the bell that was ringing her death knell.

The waters chased him as he fled,
Not daring look behind;
A billow whispered in his Ear,
"Come home with me, my friend . . ."

34

What triple Lenses burn upon
The Escapade from God—

*T*he flowers were still blooming in Emily Dickinson's garden, the grass was still soft and green underfoot, the trees cast down the same glowing shade. But the party was over. The Emily Dickinson Centennial Symposium had come to an end. Reluctantly, in knots and bunches, people began to leave.

Peter Wiggins was ready to go. He had accomplished his mission. He hovered at Tilly's elbow, saying good-bye, feeling a vested interest in Tilly, and in Tilly's old house on Market Hill Road, and especially in Tilly's attic, where his forged photograph was now tucked away in a dusty cardboard box, almost at the front of the wedged contents, sticking up invitingly from all the rest.

Tilly was polite, but her attention was elsewhere. She was keeping an eye on Elvis, who was toddling around on the grass. "Where do you suppose his mother is?" said Tilly, looking at her watch. "She was supposed to be here at one o'clock. Where can she be?"

"Why don't I drive you home again?" said Peter, smiling at Tilly like the old, old friend he felt himself to be. "After all, now that I know the way . . . ?"

So once again Peter Wiggins drove Tilly Porch and Elvis Buffington back to Market Hill Road.

"Now don't forget what I told you," he said roguishly as Tilly lifted a sleepy Elvis out of the car. "Just get right up there in that attic and go through all those old boxes of papers. Promise me?"

"Oh, yes," said Tilly. "I promise. I might as well start this very afternoon while Elvis takes a nap."

But even Peter could hardly believe his good fortune when Owen Kraznik came running out the back door of the Homestead at the sound of his returning car, with the announcement that another picture had turned up.

"Another picture like mine?" Peter was flabbergasted.

"Yes, more or less. But . . ."

Already? Peter grinned with satisfaction. Tilly must have galloped up the attic stairs two at a time and homed in on the right box and reached in to find his picture like Jack Horner pulling out a plum from his Christmas pie. Good for Tilly. "No kidding!" Peter beamed up at Owen. "Isn't that great!"

Owen didn't look happy. "Here, I wrote it all down. Telephone call just now."

What a magnificent woman, that Tilly Porch! Peter took the scrap of paper and glanced at it. The words blurred in front of his eyes. Owen's handwriting was almost illegible.

"You see, there was an inscription on the back," said Owen sadly. "Of course, it may not be genuine."

"Oh, I feel sure it's genuine," babbled Peter, leaning out of the car window, his glasses flashing with mad dancing lights. "I mean it just sounds so right, don't you think? *Emily don't like this much.* How *terribly* interesting. No signature, I gather? I can hardly wait to get my hands on it. I want to study the handwriting." Jumping out, Peter slammed the door of the car. He was dizzy with triumph. Once again everything in the world was shining with his good fortune, the needles of the hemlock tree, the sharp petals of the magnolia blossoms in the shrubbery, the sparkling windows of the garage. "'Emily don't like this much.' Well, good! That would explain why the picture disappeared, don't you see? Emily didn't like it. How perfectly *fascinating*."

Owen was puzzled. "But that's not what it says." He took his note back from Peter. "See here, it says, 'Mother before we moved to Topeka.'"

Peter gasped. "It says *what*?"

Pointing his finger at the words, Owen read them again. "'Mother before we moved to Topeka.' That's all. It was written on the back. That's what the woman said on the phone."

"But Tilly wouldn't—" Peter caught himself. "It can't be. It just can't be the same picture. It's some other picture."

"Well, this woman claims it's the same one. She says she saw your slide lecture. A woman named Helen Gaunt. Somebody put the picture in her mailbox with a note asking her to tell me. She didn't look in her mailbox until just now, she said, when she got home from the picnic."

"But it's—it's *impossible*." Peter flapped his hands. The sense of blessing in the sunlight had disappeared. The day had become hard and shrewd and glittering. "I'll bet it's a—a forgery. It must be." Peter gulped with dismay as the realization smote him that he had made the thing worse. He had turned an unfortunate situation into a disaster. He had given the whole thing away. He had spoken too soon. He had recited the inscription on the back of his own precious forgery. He had spoken the name of Tilly Porch. Too soon, too soon!

Owen turned away, distracted by the ring of the telephone. Peter followed him into the house slowly, dragging his feet, hardly able to walk. As Owen picked up the phone in the kitchen, Peter leaned weakly against the doorframe and looked on, dizzy with regret.

"Oh, Tilly, hello there," said Owen.

Tilly, Tilly Porch? Peter closed his eyes and prayed that Tilly had *not* rushed up to the attic, that she had *not* found his picture in the cardboard box. But his prayer was in vain.

"A picture?" said Owen. "You found a copy of Peter's picture?"

At the other end of the line Tilly was all excited. "Peter just dropped me off, you see, Owen, and then I went right up-attic the way he told me to, and the first thing I laid my hands on was this old photograph. I mean, it's the same one. It's another copy of Peter's photograph of Emily Dickinson. And listen to this, Owen. There's writing on the back. Wait till you hear."

Owen had a premonition. He could feel it coming. With his back to Peter Wiggins he stared at the refrigerator and mouthed the words to himself as Tilly pronounced them— *"Emily don't like this much."* Behind Owen's back Peter Wiggins was undergoing a transformation. From now on Professor Peter Wiggins of the University of Central Arizona was not simply a lame duck, he was a dead one, a dead, dead duck. Oh, the poor bastard.

"Isn't that wonderful?" said Tilly. "You know, Owen, I could swear I'd been through that box before. You'd think I would have noticed it. But I never did. What do you think of that?"

Owen knew precisely what to think of it, but he couldn't bring himself to say it aloud in front of Peter.

"He's not back yet?" said Tilly. "I'm dying to tell him."

Owen hesitated. "No," he said. "I'm sorry."

"Well, have him call me right away. I know he'll be so pleased."

"Of course." Owen hung up slowly, and stood for a moment longer with his back to Peter. The air in the Dickinson kitchen was thick and sickening with mutual understanding. Good God, what should Owen do now? Well, he would have to speak up. He would have to ask Peter for the truth. And the truth would be wretched and destructive. And then, somehow or other, Owen would have to find a way to be kind.

But the confrontation was forestalled. The phone rang again. Owen turned his head courageously to meet Peter's faltering gaze, then picked up the receiver, expecting still another photographic revelation.

But this time it was his cousin, Harvey Kloop.

Harvey's voice sounded strange and unnatural. It was high and thin and spasmodic, as though his teeth were chattering.

"Listen, Owen, I called Eunice Jane, only—she's in the—library, I guess. She always goes to the—library about—this time of day. Listen, Owen, I want you to—tell me something. Do you think—there are, like, holes in the—universe?"

"Holes in the universe? Harvey, what's the matter? You sound queer. Are you all right?"

"Well, no, as a matter of fact, I'm not. I ran my boat—into a rock. But that's not—what's the matter."

"Harvey, tell me, where are you?"

"And I busted my leg. But that's not it either."

"You broke your leg? Harvey, where are you?"

"And the boat sank, and I had to swim with my—broken leg, and I nearly drowned. But that's not what I'm—worried about—at all."

"Harvey, Harvey, I'm coming! Just tell me where to find you!"

Harvey's teeth were chattering uncontrollably. "It's the u-u-universe, you see, Owen, that's where the trouble is. Tell me, O-Owen, do you think sometimes the whole entire universe has sort of *cr-cr-cracks* in it, where the system as we know it breaks down? Dead people coming back to life, church bells under water, stu-stu-stuff like that? You know, maybe in retribution? For violating your Hippo-something oath? You know, times like that?"

"For God's sake, Harvey, I'll be glad to discuss the universe with you later on. Just tell me where you are right now so I can come for you, and then we'll discuss the whole thing."

"It's the boat dock. You know, at Qua-Quabbin, Gate Forty-three. You go out Route Nine, then turn left at Ware, and then you just keep going up Greenwich Road. There's this sign, Gate Forty-three."

"Oh, right you are. Just stay right there. I'll come right along."

Owen hung up and turned to Peter, putting out of his mind the nasty little problem of the multiple photographs and Peter's unfortunate new status as a dead duck. "It's my cousin," said Owen, running an anxious hand through his hair. "Harvey Kloop. I've got to go get him and bring him home."

"Harvey Kloop?" repeated Peter dully. His voice echoed meaninglessly in his own ears.

"He's a doctor. The medical examiner. My cousin. He's in some crazy kind of mental state. And he's broken his leg, so he can't drive. I've got to borrow a car."

"Borrow a car?"

"All I've got is a bicycle."

Then Peter spoke up in a dream. It was a nightmare, of course, not a dream, one of those nightmares where everything that happens is obviously insane, and yet at the same time intensely logical. "I'll drive you there," said Peter. In his personal crisis he had only one impulse left, to cling to the man who knew he had planted a forgery in Tilly Porch's attic. Owen's knowledge of Peter's dishonesty was like a bond of blood between them, a kind of open wound from which vital juices would flow, unless Peter pressed his hand over it, both his hands, unless he pressed up against it with all the strength in his body. Somehow he must keep the blood from leaking out and drenching everything. *Owen must not tell.*

"Thank you," said Owen, and then his face lit up with a happy thought. "We'll ask Dr. Oak to come along. Poor Harvey sounded as though he might be in a state of shock, with nobody there to take care of him."

But Harvey Kloop was not alone at the boat landing. The dock attendant had taken charge. He had heard the cry for help, he had seen Harvey struggling in the water, he had rescued him in one of the rental boats, he had helped him hop up the beach to the shack, he had sat him down and covered him with his own jacket, and then he had dialed the telephone for Harvey.

But Harvey had forgotten to tell Owen something. "Oh, damn," he said, reaching for the phone again with a trembling arm. "Gimme it again, Jimmy. I forgot—to tell him turn right. Somebody took the—bars down, across the road the other way.

He won't know—which way to go. If he doesn't know any better, he'll end up—at Shaft Twelve. What's that phone number again?"

This time there was no answer.

"He's already on his way, I guess," said Harvey, huddling down under Jimmy's jacket again, trying to control his shivering. "Say, Jimmy, listen here. You know the—way we get used to having everything happen according to physical principles? You know, atoms and—molecules obeying the laws of nature? Well, here's what I wonder. I mean, do you think those principles ever go wrong? I mean, do you think sometimes these really qu-queer things happen as if there were these really huge systems—of truth, only they kind of—collide with each other"—Harvey made a feeble whamming gesture in the air—"and cracks appear, and you get glimpses of, you know, another *universe*? Like black—holes or something? Come on, Jimmy, tell me what *you* think."

"Well, I don't know," said Jimmy, tipping his cap forward

and scratching his head. "My grandmother had this really weird experience in a haunted house once. Did I tell you about that? Like she heard music? And there wasn't anybody there? Spooky!"

35

It is a truth—of Blood . . .

*H*omer and Mary Kelly walked up the stairs from the subterranean police station in the Town Hall and stared at the Common on the other side of Boltwood Avenue.

A fair had appeared out of nowhere. Pieces of Ferris wheel were debouching from giant trucks. Somewhere a calliope wheezed and merry-go-round cymbals clashed. Down the street a fraternity house throbbed with recorded sound. The afternoon had grown still warmer. On Main Street and South Pleasant the students were thick on the sidewalk. They milled around the Common as the tents jerked up with a windy flapping of awnings. In the parking lot a guy on a motorcycle blatted out onto the street, leaning sideways.

Mary had to shout in Homer's ear. "That man you were talking to—was that Archie Gripp? What did he say?"

"That was Archie," rumbled Homer. "Come on, I'll tell you all about it in the car." Homer began loping along the sidewalk, moving into the shade of the giant katsura tree and out again, hurrying in the direction of Spring Street. "I want to go to Ware and talk to Mr. and Mrs. Gaw."

Mary was scandalized. She ran after Homer and grabbed

at his arm. "Mr. and Mrs. Gaw? Oh, Homer, don't you think that's ghoulish, probing into people's misery like that?"

"Well, I gather Winnie's father is more angry than grief-stricken. You know, he's really foaming with rage. Jesse Gaw, his name is. Works for the Quabbin Reservoir, runs some sort of garage on the side. His wife works in a knitting mill. He was just here, Archie says. Came over to identify the body before they took it away."

"Winnie's father owns a garage?"

"That's right. He's got some sort of car-repair business. Archie thought it was kind of interesting. 'Take a look around,' he said."

"What for? What does he expect you to find in Winnie's father's garage?"

"Well, Archie's just sort of interested in places like that, ever since the fire in Coolidge Hall. He's been working on it, interviewing people who might have had some nutty reason for trying to burn the place down. Fat women, for instance. Kids who work in gas stations where they do paint jobs on cars, spray jobs with cans of lacquer. Body shops. Well, it may not mean a thing, but this time we've got a fat woman and a car-repair outfit in one fist, so to speak."

On Spring Street a big chartered bus was parked beside the Lord Jeffery Inn. In a chattering, orderly mob, the Japanese Poetry Society was climbing on board, laden with luggage and thousands of miles of exposed film. Through one of the big tinted windows Professor Nogobuchi beamed and waved at Homer. Homer grinned and waved back.

Mary was still trying to understand the Gaws. "You say Winnie's father is mad instead of sad? Who is he mad at? Does he know who swung that axe at Winnie?"

"No, I gather he's just mad at the whole world. You know, a mean sort of cuss, Archie says. It was his own axe, did you know that?"

"It was? Winnie's father's own axe?"

"That's right. It was Jesse Gaw's own personal axe. He claimed somebody must have stolen it from his garage." Homer waved again and shouted good-bye to the wood-burning-stove man, who was striding along the sidewalk, going the

other way, heading for North Pleasant Street and a hitch to Lake Winnipesaukee.

"Bitter, he was," murmured Homer.

"What did you say?" said Mary. The hurdy-gurdy noise of the fair was still tweedling and thumping, making a racket all the way down Spring Street. "Bitter? Who was bitter?"

"Jesse Gaw. That's what Archie said. Bitter at the whole damned world. Rancid bitter. You know the kind of guy."

"Well, maybe he had good reason to be bitter."

"That's exactly what I mean. And you know what? Bitterness interests me. It goes back a long way in a person, that kind of ingrown, self-destructive, all-consuming grudge."

36

A Chill came up as from a shaft . . .

For Peter Wiggins the expedition to rescue Harvey Kloop at Gate 43 was a surrealistic journey. Plunging along Greenwich Road at the wheel of his rented Datsun, Peter was alert to every nuance in the conversation between Ellen Oak and Owen Kraznik. Without taking any interest in it at all, he was aware that something was seeping into the car, something large and warm and formless. It did not mix with the clammy air surrounding Peter. Coldly he sat beside Ellen in his envelope of isolation, adjusting his touch on the wheel with frozen fingers. The car obeyed his least command, but Peter felt out of control. Overhead the trees whizzed by in a blur of branches and sky. With them swept the dark eyes of the woman in his photograph, gazing tragically down at him. His year of work in her behalf had gone for nothing. In a moment of carelessness, in a single instant of failed caution, he had lost it all.

What was left for Peter now? Home and family? Trying to think of Angie, Peter could hear only the dull whine of her voice. His children's faces were blank blobs of pink.

The parking lot at Gate 43 was full of cars. The gate was open. Peter turned in and drove straight ahead, sparing only a glance for the road that branched off to the right. But his enhanced consciousness took note of every leaf on every tree and every uncurling fiddlehead fern. What the hell was going to happen now?

The road came to an end.

"That's funny," said Owen. "This doesn't look like a boat dock." There was no pier beside the water, no boats drawn up on shore. There was nothing but a solemn little building of gray stone. Owen stared at it. "Do you suppose Harvey's there inside?"

"The door's open," said Ellen. "Somebody must be in there."

Peter followed them up the steps, nearly treading on Owen's heels, clinging to Owen Kraznik like a wad of suffocating cloth, plugged into him like a bung in a barrel, a stopper, a cork. How long could he keep it up? The day would end at last, would turn into other days. Tomorrow Peter would have to remove himself, and then the oozing leakage would begin. Sooner or later Owen would let it be known that the word of Professor Peter Wiggins—as a scholar, as a teacher, as an instructor of young men and women—was not to be trusted. The news would go everywhere, to every college in the East, even to the University of Central Arizona in the West. The eager hope with which Peter had come to Massachusetts had been crushed. The Emily Dickinson Centennial Symposium had looked like the beginning of a new career, but instead it had become the end of everything.

"There's no one here," said Owen. His voice reverberated against the cement floor, the stone walls, the lofty ceiling. "We must have taken a wrong turn. This must be part of the waterworks. I'll bet the aqueduct is down there under those trapdoors. This must be the beginning of the tunnel that carries the water to Boston."

Ellen gripped his arm and pointed. A shoe lay on the floor, a woman's white sandal. "Alison Grove was wearing white sandals," she said gravely.

"Good God," said Owen. Together they turned to look at

the trapdoors. One of them had been pulled aside. It was only half-covering the opening underneath.

Fearful of what they might see, they walked across the floor and peered down into the shaft.

But they saw only the dark knobs of their own heads, reflected in the still water, ten or twelve feet down. Owen knelt on the trapdoor, trying to see below the surface into the depths. Ellen went to the window and stared out at the wind-driven ripples on the reservoir, half expecting to see Alison Grove in the water, drifting along with water lilies in her hair like the Lady of Shalott.

Peter Wiggins was not interested in the fate of Alison Grove. His only concern was with the man who was kneeling on the trapdoor. Coming up behind Owen, Peter stared at him with wide-open eyes, observing as with a hand lens every rib of corduroy in Owen's trousers, every pore in the sponge-rubber soles of Owen's shoes, every wiry strand of Owen's hair.

Then, shifting his glance to his own right shoe, Peter was astonished to discover that it had grown very large. And the foot inside it was quivering with eager strength. Cautiously, Peter lifted his foot until the toe of his shoe nudged the edge of the trapdoor. Then with a swift motion he kicked upward. The door dropped into the shaft, and Owen dropped with it, cracking his head on the edge of the floor as he fell. The room reverberated with the echo of Peter's shout, and the rumble of the trapdoor, and the splash of Owen's slight body in the dark water of the shaft.

"He hit his head," jabbered Peter as Ellen turned swiftly and threw herself down beside the hole in the floor.

Owen was nowhere to be seen. The water had closed over him. Ellen snatched off her shoes. "Go for help," she said quickly. "The boat dock must be right here somewhere." Putting her legs over the edge of the opening in the floor, she dropped into the shaft. Her narrow body made only a light splash, and then it too disappeared. The water slopped for a moment in widening rings, and flattened out again.

Peter was alone. For a moment he stared down at the still

water, and then he turned and stumbled out of the building. Panting in shallow gasps, he hurried to his car. Clever notions were boiling in his head.

With shaking fingers he lifted the hood of the Datsun and jerked out the distributor wire. Then he got into the driver's seat and went through the motions of trying to start the car. *Arahaha, arahaha, arahaha,* whined the engine, failing to turn over. Let them hear it, if they could, there in that watery hole! It was no use. It wasn't Peter's fault if his car wouldn't start, if he had to go for help on foot.

Abandoning the car, leaving the hood cocked up, he moved off slowly into the woods. Which way was the boat dock? Maybe it was this way. Maybe it was that way. Maybe it was some other way. Deliberately, Peter set out to lose himself in the wilderness.

Staggering in the ferny undergrowth, dodging between the trunks of trees, he headed away from the water. Help for Owen and Ellen would never come, not if Peter could help it. Not until too late, not until much too late. Lost he would be, for certain, wandering in a circle in the woods. Lost, and yet in some delirious way, once more in control of his life. Somehow or other, Peter Wiggins had once again taken a trembling hold.

37

Cool us to Shafts of Granite . . .

*T*he car was Homer's old red Volvo, but Mary was doing the driving while Homer consulted the map. He looked up as she turned off Route 9 into a side road. "Hey," he said. "What's this?"

"Quabbin Cemetery," said Mary. "I'm just curious. It's the place where they reburied the coffins from all the cemeteries in the Swift River Valley before they filled the valley with water. Thirty-four cemeteries had to be dug up! Did you know that?"

Homer looked around curiously at the headstones as the Volvo meandered slowly along the loops and byways of the winding drive. "It must have been hard on the living relatives, picking up their great-grandparents' bones, losing the places where their ancestors had lived, never being able to go back. Nothing but water rolling over the acres they planted and plowed." Homer read aloud the names on the tombstones— "Doubleday, Conkey, Wheeler, Goodale. Hey, look at that! What do you know? There's a Gaw."

Mary stopped the car, and together they stared at the names engraved on the polished marble.

JOHN GAW 1875–1937
EMMA GAW 1880–1930

"I'll bet they're Winnie's grandparents," said Mary. "Jesse
Gaw's mother and father. Maybe his bitterness begins right
here."

"Any more Gaws?" said Homer. "What's that one with the
lady on top? Gaws? No, Smiths. *'We shall meet on that beautiful
shore, Mother!'* Well, poor souls, I hope they're all up there right
now, somewhere in heaven, all those Smiths, frolicking on the
sand. But I suspect this shore right here is all they're going to
get, this high ground around the reservoir. Hey, look, what's
that wooden temple?"

Getting out of the car, Homer and Mary walked up the
steps of the little columned house and inspected the memorial
tablets on the porch. There were a great many names on the

tablets. They were honor rolls of the war dead from the lost towns of Greenwich, Prescott, Dana, and Enfield. One tablet bore only a single name—

To the memory of RICHARD GROVE, 1896–1936,
Civil Engineer for the Metropolitan District Commission,
who died in the line of duty,
this tablet is dedicated
by his fellow engineers.

"Hey," said Homer, "you don't suppose he was Alison Grove's father, do you? Her mother is a widow. That's what Tom Perry told Archie."

Mary shook her head. "Couldn't be. How old is she? Look, this man died fifty years ago."

"Oh, sure, right you are." Homer smote his forehead. "Common name anyway. Millions of Groves, probably. Billions."

They left the cemetery and drove to Ware, the melancholy little mill town Winnie Gaw had called home. Beside the Ware River the old mill buildings were still in use, still manufacturing shoes and knitted yard goods. But the ponderous brick Town Hall in the center of town looked half derelict, and so did the big brick church beside it. In the empty lot next to the defunct Casino Theater, a dead truck was engulfed in weeds.

The house belonging to Jesse Gaw was a sullen structure faced with asphalt shingle. The windows looked blind, their shades pulled down. The front yard was a litter of smashed cars.

Homer sucked in his breath with pleasure. "Hey, look at that sign. Jesse Jack Gaw, Collision, Front End Work. It's a body shop, by God. Not just a garage, a body shop." Getting out of the car, he looked longingly at the garage window, but he didn't have the nerve to go up close and take a look. He felt eyes on his back, looking out from the edges of the drawn shades.

"Come on, Homer," muttered Mary. "They're waiting for us."

Homer looked up to see Mr. and Mrs. Jesse Gaw framed in the open front door, staring down at them.

Mary walked up the porch steps and smiled ingratiatingly. "How do you do," she said. "I'm Mary Kelly. This is—"

"We already been interviewed," said Mrs. Gaw.

"I been up there already," growled Jesse Gaw, yanking his head over his shoulder. "I already talked to the police."

Homer fumbled in his pocket for an old card, dating back to his years of service in the office of the District Attorney of Middlesex County. He flashed it, then pocketed it quickly. "I just wondered if you would be so good as to answer a few more questions." Gently he moved forward an inch.

Jesse Gaw stood his ground, but Mrs. Gaw dropped back. Then, with a surly shrug of his shoulders, her husband gave in. Limping ahead of them into the living room, he sat down in a vinyl-covered lounge chair. Mrs. Gaw smoothed her thin hair and sat down too, on the edge of another overstuffed chair.

Her eyes were red. She was a sharp-featured rawboned woman. Mary guessed Winnie's clumsy frame came from her father. Jesse was a big man with thick muscular arms and a loose belly.

The Gaws' living room bulged with showy furniture. It was crowded with knickknacks. Mary hesitated, then sat down on the sofa, sinking in deep. Homer sank down beside her. Their knees were high. They didn't know what to do with their hands. The formality of the encounter struck both of them dumb—Strangers Confront Bereaved Parents In Darkened Parlor. Mary was desperate to say something, anything.

She turned to Mrs. Gaw. "Tell me about Winnie. I'll bet she was a good student. I mean, as a little girl."

Mrs. Gaw's eyes slid sideways to her husband, then returned to Mary. "Oh, sure, Winifred always liked school. Except she was sick all the time, you know?"

"Sick?" said Mary.

"Oh, you know." Mrs. Gaw had a flat, unblinking gaze. "Viruses, they used to settle in her chest. She was absent a lot. You know."

"Who you kidding?" Jesse Gaw spoke up roughly. "She run away. Kid was always running away."

"But she came back?" murmured Mary.

"Oh, sure. Police, they'd bring her back."

"And then he'd get out the strap," said Mrs. Gaw, looking peevishly at her husband.

"Well, what you going to do with a kid like that? Got to teach 'em. Listen"—Jesse Gaw sat forward in his chair and spoke with passionate resentment—"if the police was really going to do their duty, they'd find out who the hell is ripping me off. Shaft Twelve, my key to Shaft Twelve, somebody stole it off the wall of my garage."

"Shaft Twelve?" Homer's interest was suddenly engaged. Shaft Twelve! Somewhere there were a lot of shafts, twelve of them, twelve bottomless crevasses plunging into the bowels of the earth, twelve boiling pits with devils brandishing pitchforks. "What do you mean, Shaft Twelve?"

Jesse Gaw jerked his head backward. "Gate Forty-three, up Greenwich Road. Or you go out Route Thirty-two. It's where the water comes into the tunnel from the reservoir, goes to Boston. You know, sixty miles blasted through rock. No amount of money they wouldn't spend, build a reservoir, take the water to Boston. Do we get any water around here? Not on your life. All goes to Boston. All those millions of dollars they spent to build it, how much for the houses they tore down? Couple a thousand, that's all they give my father for the house his family lived in, you know, all their lives, going way back. Lousy couple a thousand. And look at this here, you see this here?" Jesse Gaw stuck out one leg. "That ain't my leg. That there's a prosthetic leg. One of *them* did that to me. You know. I was just a kid, playing around the old schoolhouse. I was picking up stuff, you know, the way kids do, and a wall fell on me. This big shot drove into me with his bulldozer. Didn't see me, he says. Well, my dad took care of him."

"You lost your leg?" Mary's self-possession had vanished. In the face of so much misery she felt like a callow ladylike fool.

But Jesse Gaw was off on another tack. "And how about the axe? And my bell? They took the axe and the key to Shaft Twelve and walked off with my bell."

Homer sat forward and looked mournfully at Jesse Gaw. "Your bell? Somebody stole your bell? What bell?"

Jesse fell back in his chair, his passion spent, and waved a surly hand.

Mrs. Gaw licked her upper lip and explained. "It's his old school bell. They knocked down the school. I mean, we both went there, the Greenwich Village School. When they knocked it down, he found the bell, only the thing that holds the clapper—you know—it broke, and yesterday, he—" She stopped and looked at Jesse.

Her husband spoke up again, with venom. "I fixed it. Welded a new piece on the inside. You know. And then somebody swiped it. Must of been still warm. Hardly even cooled off. I told the police just now, I told 'em, they don't find the shit stole my bell, I'll—" A nameless threat hung in the air. "They don't give a goddamn shit about my bell."

Mrs. Gaw picked nervously at a fold of her dress. "See, he really cared about that old bell." Suddenly she turned to her husband and whined at him. "More than about Winifred! He don't seem to care what happened to Winifred!"

"You shut your trap," said Jesse Gaw, without looking at her.

Mrs. Gaw's eyes were wet. She closed her lips and said nothing more.

Mary and Homer sat silent too, unable to inject any pious thoughts into the poisoned air.

But then the atmosphere changed. Jesse Gaw looked at his watch and stood up. He had become a man of affairs. "I got to go to Oakdale, throw the switch. It's my job, see, throw the switch. Chief engineer, he called me. Got to shut off the Ware River outlet, open the valve at Shaft Twelve. Oakdale, that's where it's at. Got to go throw the switch."

"Open the valve?" said Homer. "You mean it's been shut? Boston hasn't been getting any water?"

"Oh, Boston don't need no water. Not all winter long. See, all winter, Quabbin fills up at Shaft Eleven-A from the Ware River overflow. Only today you stop your flow that way, and you open up your valve at Shaft Twelve, so all summer the water goes to Boston. Four hundred billion gallons." For the first time the querulous note in Jesse Gaw's voice was gone, replaced by prideful know-how.

"Four hundred billion gallons?" Mary couldn't believe it. "You mean, all at once?"

"Oh, no, that's the head of water, see, in the whole reservoir. Eighteen miles long, the whole thing. Six hundred million gallons a day going through the pipe, after I throw the switch."

The man was a paradox, thought Homer. On the one hand there was his background of seething family resentment, on the other his pride in the massive statistics of the Metropolitan Water District, and in his own importance as the man with his hand on the switch. Homer had a vision of the entire population of Boston reaching out to Jesse Jack Gaw, millions of parched throats and open mouths, gasping for the water only he could supply.

And now he was departing, to throw that switch, to satisfy that thirst. Lifting and swinging his game leg, Jesse Gaw left the house. In a moment they heard his car start up and zoom backward out of the driveway.

Mrs. Gaw's hunched shoulders relaxed. Mary sensed her relief. Jesse Gaw's presence was the kind that filled a house, that bore down heavily on everyone else, no matter where one might hide, from attic to basement.

Mrs. Gaw was looking at Homer. For the first time there was a light in her sharp eye. "You want to see Winifred's darkroom?"

"Her darkroom?" Homer glanced at Mary. "Oh, that's right. Owen told me Winnie liked to take pictures."

"Down cellar," said Mrs. Gaw firmly. "Winnie did everything herself. Taught herself, you know, how to do it." Opening a door, she pulled a light string and led the way downstairs. "Come on, take a look."

The darkroom was a walled-off section of the basement. The space inside it was orderly and narrow. The three of them crowded in. Mary wondered how Winnie had managed to turn around. A camera was fixed to the stand of an enlarger. There were photographs pinned to a bulletin board, Winnie's work, obviously, mostly snapshots of a startled Owen Kraznik. Clothespins held negatives on a string over the set tubs. The overhead bulb shone through one of them, illuminating an image Homer recognized. "May I?" he said to Mrs. Gaw, reaching to take it down. Holding it carefully by the edges, he held it to the light for Mary to see. "It's Peter's photograph of Emily Dickinson, the one he talked about in his lecture." Homer turned to Mrs. Gaw. "I wonder why Winnie was copying this picture?"

Mrs. Gaw squinted at it and shook her head. She didn't know.

Homer hung the negative back on the line, then poked

furtively in a small cardboard box. The cover had a label, PROF. KRAZNIK, but inside there was only a miscellany of worthless objects, ends of pencils, rubber bands, bits of eraser, and a collection of little notes asking Winnie to do small errands or go to the library. Homer put the top back on the box. Winnie's crush on her boss was apparent. She had collected pieces of Owen Kraznik like fragments of the True Cross. Gloomily, Homer followed Mary and Mrs. Gaw upstairs.

Then he remembered the garage. "Oh, Mrs. Gaw," he said, "do you think we might look in the garage? You know, your husband seems to be having trouble with theft. I just wondered if—?"

"Oh, sure, help yourself. Wait a minute." Mrs. Gaw picked up her pocketbook and scrabbled inside. "Here's the key to the side door. Just stick it under the shingle when you're done, see? Loose shingle beside the trash can."

"Oh, thank you. Good-bye, then. Thank you again. Good-bye." Homer and Mary nodded and smiled, backing out the door.

But Mrs. Gaw seemed reluctant to let them go. "Winnie's finger," she said, whispering, glancing behind her as if her husband might suddenly reappear. "He done it."

"He—?" Mary blinked at Mrs. Gaw. "You mean her father? You mean there was an accident of some sort?"

"Wasn't no accident." The resentment in Mrs. Gaw's voice transcended the virulence of her husband's smoldering anger. "He got into this really bad mood, once when she run away and they found her and drug her home. He done it. He had this axe. You know. The one they found with Winnie."

Homer and Mary stared at Mrs. Gaw, too stunned to speak.

"And then he wouldn't let me take her to the doctor."

There was nothing more to be said. Mary wanted to put her arms around Mrs. Gaw, but the woman wasn't inviting comfort. Her eyes were dry. There was a fierce look of triumph on her face. She stood aside, and Homer and Mary left the house.

But on the front porch, Homer turned to ask a final question. "Mrs. Gaw, do you think your daughter killed herself?"

"Winnie?" The look of triumph disappeared. The corners of Mrs. Gaw's mouth turned down and quivered. "Honest to God, I just don't know."

They were glad to get away. Homer unlocked the side door of the garage and pushed it shut behind them. "My God," he said angrily. "I don't believe it. His own daughter."

Mary could hardly speak. "Maybe—maybe it was Jesse this time too. Maybe *he* killed Winnie. It was the same axe."

"But don't forget, the axe didn't kill her. And anyway Archie says no. They've looked into it. They know where Jesse was the whole time."

Glumly they examined the crowded interior of Jesse Jack Gaw's garage. A Chevy Impala took up most of the space. It was waiting for a paint job. Its windows were blanked out with cardboard. Against the wall a couple of narrow tanks stood beside a cluttered workbench. The floor was a tumble of chains and hoses and instruments for clutching metal.

"Tut, tut," said Homer in pious disapproval, picking up a greasy shirt, dropping it again. "The man doesn't know how to keep himself tidy. Where's the paint? That's what I want to know."

Mary pointed to the back wall. "There's a cupboard. Could that be it? Look, it's locked."

"Sign on it too," said Homer. "'No Smoking Private Keep Your Fucking Hands Off.' Well, isn't that nice." Stepping over the snaking tangle of hoses, Homer looked through the heavy wire grille. "It's paint, all right. Automotive lacquer. All kinds of colors, aqamarine bronze, apricot-pearl fleck, opal gold. Hey, that's the color of the can they found in the bushes, opal gold, I'll swear it is."

Mary sniffed. "That smell, it reminds me of high school. I used to paint my nails in the girls' room. This place smells like nail polish."

"Nail polish? Say, that's exactly right. Nail polish is lacquer." Homer picked his way back across the floor. "So maybe the fat girl in Coolidge Hall was Jesse Gaw's own daughter Winnie. Maybe she started here, right here in her father's garage. She unlocked the fucking cupboard with the fucking key, swiped the fucking can of lacquer, took it to Coolidge Hall, poured it into the buckets and set fire to it, and nearly burned down the fucking building. But, Christ, whatever for? Come on, let's get out of here before the fucking man gets back."

Dismally they got back in Homer's car. And then Mary had another idea. She fumbled in the glove compartment. "Homer, where's that map of the Metropolitan District Commission we used to have? Oh, here it is. I just wonder if we could find our way to Shaft Twelve."

Homer darted her a keen glance. "Shaft Twelve?"

Mary nodded. "I really think we should take a look at it. Look, Homer, somebody stole a can of paint from Jesse Gaw, and tried to burn down Coolidge Hall. Somebody also stole the key to Shaft Twelve, and—what's the name of that missing girl?"

"Alison Grove? My God, do you think she might be down the hole?"

"Well, why would you steal the key to a hole in the ground unless you wanted to get rid of something? Something big?" Mary jabbed her finger at the map. "Here it is, I found it. Gate Forty-three, that's what Jesse said. Where's Route Thirty-two? Oh, here it is. You'll have to turn around."

Route 32 was a paved country road, running in a straight line past forests and empty fields and signs advertising bait for sale, and small houses tucked into pockets in the woods. Homer gripped the steering wheel and stared at the road rushing toward him, struggling with a depression of spirits, thinking about Mr. and Mrs. Jesse Gaw.

Somehow they threw everything into question. Oh, it was all very well, reflected Homer, for Miss Emily Dickinson of Main Street in Amherst to sit in her garden, basking in eternity, but what about the Jesse Gaws of the town of Ware, and people like that? They had surely done very little basking. For the working people of Ware, life must have been an endless succession of long days in the mills, fastening heavy soles to leather uppers, or endless days at home, weaving palm-leaf hats by hand. Of course, sometimes the monotony was varied by national strife. Homer winced, remembering all the gold stars on the memorial tablets in the Quabbin Cemetery. In the grim company of Mr. and Mrs. Jesse Gaw, the ethereal respectability of Emily Dickinson seemed a cruel irrelevance. For an instant Homer saw a new Emily, cross-eyed with mystical rapture, clasping her hands at butterflies while her brother paid a substitute to fight in his place in the Civil War and her father drove hard bargains in his office in the Palmer Block. Homer snarled, and wrenched the car to the side of the road. "This doesn't feel right. I'll bet we've gone too far."

"Oh, Homer," groaned Mary, consulting the map, "we missed the fork."

Homer swore, and jerked the car into reverse. Swooping to the left in a clumsy curve, he careened back down the road the other way.

38

Death's tremendous nearness . . .

Blood was seeping from a great swollen bruise on Owen's forehead, but he was breathing. He was not drowned. At first Ellen wore herself out trying to tread water and keep him afloat at the same time. But then something nudged at her shoulder, and she grasped at it gladly. It was the trapdoor. It would do for a life preserver.

Heaving and hauling at Owen, Ellen managed to drag the upper part of him onto the trapdoor. Then she reached one arm over his chest, gripped the rope handle on the other side, and hung on.

It was a stable arrangement, decided Ellen gratefully. They could stay this way forever. And Owen was opening his eyes.

He seemed blissfully deranged. Rolling his head to one side on the trapdoor, he smiled at her and said, "My dear."

"We're all right," said Ellen, grinning back at him, tossing the wet hair out of her eyes. "No, don't move. Just lie back. Can you bring up your legs and let them float? Good for you. Peter's gone for help." She was speaking softly, almost whispering, to diminish the echo, the booming reverberation against the curving cast-iron wall. "Does your head hurt?"

"No," lied Owen. He leaned back again, feeling feeble and dizzy, and stared up at the square patch of light. The hole through which he had fallen looked small and far away. They were imprisoned in a dark circular room with water for a floor and a pitch-black ceiling. How deep was the water below them? Owen shuddered.

"Are you cold?" said Ellen quickly.

"No, no," he said, lying again. Then the trapdoor slipped out from under him, and water lapped over his mouth.

Swiftly, Ellen wrestled him up again. "Don't talk," she said gently. "Here, can you wrap your fingers around the other handle?" Skillfully she closed Owen's hand over the rope.

He was lifting his head, looking at her with concern. "You must be tired."

It was Ellen's turn to lie. "No, not at all. I can stay like this forever. And Peter will be back in a minute."

Dreamily it occurred to Owen that Peter was not the messenger he would have picked, if there had been a choice, but he merely gazed at Ellen and smiled. "Your face," he said. Then he closed his eyes and dropped his head back. "Beautiful. You shouldn't have—come down here—after me." Then his fingers opened on the rope handle. Letting go, he rolled off the trapdoor and his head went under.

Panic-stricken, Ellen seized the shoulder of his jacket and hauled him up again. And then she was aware of a change in the water around her. There was a noise, not just the hollow ricochet of their voices, but a deep shuddering echo, a tremendous booming that rattled against the metal walls. Below them, far, far down, there was a heavy rushing, a thundering, vibrating hum.

Around them the water had begun to move in a slow circle. Now it was swirling faster and faster. It dragged at Ellen, and she struggled to keep her place, paddling with one arm, splashing with her legs. The trapdoor was swept away. Like bathwater gurgling down a drain, the water was spinning in a descending vortex, guided by the helical vanes on the cylindrical walls of the shaft. Frantically, Ellen clung to Owen as they whirled in the sucking darkness, dropping lower and lower like chips of wood tossed into a whirlpool.

Far below them the valve at the bottom of the shaft was opening. In a mighty flood the water of the Quabbin Reservoir was bursting into the tunnel, gushing in a pouring tide fourteen feet high, surging toward the spinning blades of the hydroelectric station of Wachusett, and from there, plunging through deep rock, to the thirsty pipes and water mains of the city of Boston.

39

The River reaches to my Mouth—
Remember—when the Sea
Swept by my searching eyes—the last—
Themselves were quick—with Thee!

"*H*ere we are," said Mary. "This must be it."

In the clearing beside the reservoir stood a little building of gray stone. The door was open, banging against the granite wall in the chill wind that was lapping the blue water into whitecaps. A car was parked beside the building, its hood thrown high.

"I know that car," said Homer. "Did you meet Peter Wiggins? That's his car, I swear. I remember the fog lights, and the nick in the fender. What on earth is Peter Wiggins doing here?" Homer got out of the Volvo, then stopped to listen.

A huge sound was pouring out of the building, a thick liquid sucking, an appalling, terrible noise.

"My God, what's that?" said Homer, staring at the open door.

Together they ran up the steps and entered the building, then stopped short, their ears assaulted by a deafening roar, as though someone had pulled the plug in a stupendous sink.

The room was empty except for a scattering of shoes on the floor. Grasping Homer's arm, Mary shrieked at him, "Something's wrong."

Then both of them saw the hole in the floor, and they ran forward and knelt beside it to look down.

What they saw seemed not of this earth. *Black hole*, thought Mary. Below them was nothingness, and below the nothingness, water swirling, plunging down in a vortex like a whirlpool, and, spinning in the whirlpool, a square object and two small round ones, bobbing like corks.

Homer shouted, and the two round objects became infinitesimal pale spots, looking up.

Mary gasped and stretched her arm into the hole. "We're here," she cried, but her words were lost in the overwhelming noise that pounded on the iron shaft and dinned against the walls.

"Christ," bellowed Homer. "It's the shaft over the tunnel. The valve is open. Jesse Gaw opened the gate. He just opened the gate."

With one motion, Homer and Mary leaped to their feet and stared at each other. Wildly they looked around, their hands jerking involuntarily in grasping, saving motions. They were too far away. They couldn't reach. Then Mary saw the bucket, the great metal bucket, lying on its side on the floor.

Homer saw it too. "Overhead crane," he roared, pointing at the ceiling. "Runs along a rail, see? Kind of a trolley. How in the hell does it—?"

"Box on the wall," screamed Mary, and she ran for it, falling over the wood that was stacked beside it, barking her shins painfully, leaping up to throw open the metal door. "Overhead lights," she muttered under her breath, reading the labels beside the switches. "Outdoor lights—crane." There it was, the switch that controlled the crane. Swiftly, Mary yanked it up, then turned her head to see if anything had happened. The crane was shaking slightly. The power was on.

Homer found the ropes that worked the pulleys. It wasn't easy. Jerking too hard, he kept overshooting. The great hook raced past the bucket, while below them the vast sucking sound in the shaft grew lower in pitch and began to throb with deep harmonic overtones as the column of air above the descending water grew ominously longer and longer.

Homer Kelly had always been butterfingered, his muscular coordination was terrible, his mechanical know-how had been neglected, and he couldn't even repair a defective lamp cord. But in this crisis he caught on quickly, and soon he was jerking at the pulleys with clumsy effectiveness.

"More," cried Mary, her hands on the dangling hook. "A little more. Oh, ow, ow! What? Never mind!" Careless of her pinched fingers, she eased the hook under the heavy bail of the bucket. "Now, up, up! Up, first, then bring it over. No, no, Homer, not like that!"

Homer was dragging the bucket across the floor. The metal bottom shrieked on the concrete floor and struck out sparks. "Stop," screamed Mary, but it was too late. Bashing into Homer, the bucket knocked him down.

He hardly seemed to notice. He was up on his knees, yanking on the ropes, staring up at the crane, his face bleeding.

At last he had the bucket poised directly over the hole, hanging silently above the abyss, shaking gently up and down.

Gasping, Homer climbed in, and Mary ran to take over the guide-ropes.

Blood was running down Homer's cheek. He shouted at Mary, "The echo will be bad. You may not understand me when I yell at you. One yell for stop, okay? Two yells for go."

Mary nodded. With a jerk she started the bucket down, and then hurried back to the hole in the floor. Dropping to her knees, she peered past the bucket to catch a glimpse of the water.

Deeper! It was deeper down! Where were they, the two faces? Gone? Drowned and gone? No, no, now she could see one of them. It was much smaller than before, much farther away. Mary gasped as the head submerged, then reappeared. The second one appeared again too, dragged up by the hair. Then the bucket descended and the faces vanished.

Mary stood up again and watched with her heart in her mouth as Homer's frowsy head fell slowly out of the light into the hollow reverberating darkness of Shaft 12.

40

It sets the Fright at Liberty—
And Terror's free—
Gay, Ghastly, Holiday!

*P*eter Wiggins was lost in the wilderness.

Peter had meant to wander aimlessly for four or five hours, then find his way back to the road and flag down a car, and explain that two people had fallen into a hole, back there at the gate where people went fishing, only it didn't look like a fishing place, and he didn't know exactly where it was because he had been lost, but those two people certainly needed help and somebody should call the police or the fire department right away.

But at dusk Peter couldn't find the road.

When the stars came out, he was still stumbling in the middle of the square mile of roadless forest that lay south of Shaft 12. He was exhausted, but he didn't dare lie down on the ground and go to sleep. The thought of spending the night in the woods was too frightening. He had never slept in anything but a bed. He had never been a Boy Scout. He had never even gone to summer camp.

Peter was lost in the woods for forty-two hours. After the first blundering night of shivering cold and fear there was an endless day of mist and fog, and then a final terror-stricken twelve hours of utter horror.

If Peter had been a student of Calvinist doctrine, if he had agreed with the notion that God punishes the evildoer, or even if he had believed with Henry Thoreau in the moral lessons of nature—*Every zephyr speaks of some reproof!*—then he might have taken his misadventures in the woods as a personal reprimand, a kind of savage, enforced atonement for his misdeeds. But Peter was too close to those misdeeds to see them in a moral light. What he had done seemed perfectly natural to him, the necessary response to the circumstantial crises in which he had found himself. And of course during his two nights and a day in the forest, he was too galvanized with fear to think sensibly about anything at all.

The terrors of the first night were perfectly ordinary. In his ignorance, poor Peter failed to understand how trivial his misfortunes were. If he had known anything about the animal life of the New England backwoods, he would not have been so dismayed when he stumbled up to his knees in a beaver pond at midnight. Later on, struggling out of a swamp and shaking in every limb, he would not have screamed when a startled partridge flew up in his face out of the undergrowth. A few minutes later, he would have recognized the warbling gobble of a wild turkey, and then he might have been able to dodge the sharp beak that raked at his thigh. Of course the nest of bobcats that swarmed under his groping hand in the small hours of the night would have electrified anyone, but only an ignorant innocent like Peter would have run shrieking away from the wild howl that rent the silence of the deep woods just before daybreak. It wasn't a pack of wolves, it was only a coyote.

But Peter knew nothing about any of these creatures, and therefore at dawn he was a gibbering wreck. Dragging his bleeding leg from tree to tree, mopping his torn face with his bleeding arm, he was tearfully thankful to find himself alive.

A mist had formed during the night, and now there was a chill drizzle of rain. Peter was glad to sink down under the stone arch of an abandoned railway and try to sleep, before making another attempt to find the road that surely lay just within his reach over that way—or perhaps *that* way, or—of course, he was completely turned around—it must certainly be just a few hundred yards in *that* direction over there.

But when darkness came again, he was still lost. And his second night in the woods was a thousand times worse than the first. Or perhaps it was a thousand times better, since it was a succession of extraordinary adventures.

If Peter could have known the rarity of the things he was to behold that night, if he could have imagined the thousand failed attempts by sportsmen and nature-lovers to catch glimpses of the astonishing wonders he was about to witness, then perhaps he might have rejoiced when he was trampled by the largest deer in North America, a gigantic sixteen-point buck. He would have been thankful for his good fortune when at the top of a rocky ledge the only nesting eagle in Massachusetts rose above him, spreading her enormous wings, and dived at him, driving a beak like a dagger deep into the flesh of his shoulder.

And then there was a final miracle. As the mist at last dispersed, as Peter staggered, sobbing, into a moonlit clearing, bleeding from three places at once, he nearly tripped over a giant cat. He should have fallen to his knees in gratitude. Instead he stumbled backward in helpless dread as the catamount gazed at him with its luminous eyes, lifted its narrow head, opened its terrible jaws, and uttered a scream like a woman's.

The gracious greenwood of New England, the forest of leafy verdure for which Peter had hungered, had brought him to death's door.

41

No Wilderness—can be
Where this attendeth me . . .

On the second morning after Peter's disappearance, Owen and Ellen joined the search party that spread out to look for him, a network of volunteers and MDC police, fifty people strong.

Ellen's face was bruised from slamming against a corner of the trapdoor as she whirled, half drowned, at the bottom of the shaft. Owen's forehead was bandaged and one arm was set in plaster to support the shoulder joint, torn from its socket when Homer snatched him from the last guttering revolutions of the swirling water before it sank into the tunnel, to be swept away forever in the rushing underground river.

But now they were risen souls. It was a bright morning. Hand in hand, they crossed a meadow and entered a sunny patch of woodland. Red-winged blackbirds flew ahead of them, alighting to utter their piercing peep. Ferns unrolled in fronds of fresh pale green. Rabbits sat in trances.

At first Owen didn't recognize the pitiful apparition that tottered toward them, whimpering, his hair full of twigs, his face black and bleeding, one eye swollen shut, his clothing in shreds, his body poulticed with clusters of blood-soaked leaves.

But when the stranger said Owen's name in a feeble croak, Owen and Ellen ran to him and helped him to the road.

Owen had no suspicion Peter had ever meant him harm.

42

How much can come
And much can go,
And yet abide the World!

Next day the wind picked up, tossing the expanding leaves of the white oak tree in the Dickinson garden, blowing a shower of pointed magnolia petals onto the lawn. On the Common it snapped the flag on its tall pole and swung the traffic lights dangling over the crossing. In Ware the projecting sign of Astrella's Doughnut Snack Bar trembled on its supporting wires. All over the Connecticut Valley men and women students trudged to their final exams, their hair blowing this way and that. And at the Quabbin Reservoir the nesting eagle left her three white eggs to soar above the sunny wooded slopes on the rising thermals and gaze down with her golden eyes at a disturbance in the water.

A diver was dragging something out of the reservoir, depositing it on the stony riprap beside Shaft 12.

It was the body of Alison Grove. Taking off his face mask and flippers, the diver watched as the MDC patrolman picked up Alison and carried her to the police van. The bell on her ankle tonked dismally once or twice.

The chief engineer for the Quabbin branch of the Metropolitan District Commission was looking on, feeling a melancholy pride in the correctness of his prediction. As the

patrolman laid Alison in the back of the van and covered her with a blanket, the chief engineer explained with sweeping gestures how he had figured out where to find her.

"That guy in the boat—what was his name? Koop? No, Kloop. He sighted her right there east of the pass at Mount Zion. So she was sure to drift through and go south, because that's the way the current goes, and then I was positive she'd end up at Shaft Twelve sooner or later, especially since we opened up the valve. I mean, the pull in the direction of the opening was bound to create a swift underwater current and drag her right up against the screen, do you see?" Then the chief engineer was moved by the sight of Alison's childlike round arm protruding from the blanket, and his face fell. "Poor thing," he said.

The diver was unaffected. "That screen down there, it really needs cleaning, Jeez, you oughta see it. Choked with smelt!"

*　　*　　*

It was a good day for drying. Tilly Porch was hanging out the laundry, and she had to hold on to the sheets firmly to keep them from whipping out of her hands.

At the same time Tilly had her eye on Elvis, who was playing in the tall blowing weeds that had shot up overnight around the vegetable garden. Elvis was shrieking happily, chasing something. Suddenly there was a yowl and a wild tumble, and the neighbor's cat leaped as high as a house and bounded away. Elvis's head appeared again above the weeds. Grinning, he toddled after the cat.

"No, no, Elvis," called Tilly. "Time for your nap." Chasing him, she scooped him up and carried him, giggling, upstairs to bed.

Debbie Buffington had not come back. It was beginning to look as though Tilly was going to be stuck with Elvis. And stuck with her husband's old boat of an Oldsmobile Cutlass, because Debbie had disappeared in Tilly's little Toyota. Tilly wondered what her daughter Margie would say when she found out. Well, she would be furious with Tilly, tying herself down at her age with somebody else's child! "Mother, *really*, it's not *your problem*."

And of course Margie would be right. But somehow Tilly had become fond of Elvis. Of course he was a horrid child in many ways, but there was a curious new cheerfulness in him that looked promising to Tilly. When he choked the cat, he didn't do it out of malice, he was simply holding it firmly to get a good look at it. For the past few days Elvis had reveled in Tilly's house, and in the yard around it, inspecting everything with voracious curiosity, rolling over and over down the little grassy slope between the house and the driveway, entangling himself in the roll of chicken wire in the shed, climbing the grapevine to the shed roof, tugging at the plastic covering on the woodpile until the wood tumbled down on him, poking his finger in the nest of a house wasp and getting himself stung, pulling all the petals off the tulips, falling down the cellar stairs, eating all the crackers in the cupboard, breaking a Toby jug. Elvis reminded Tilly of that old explorer in the poem, the way he was looking at the world with a wild surmise.

Now he was safely asleep. Tilly smiled down at him in his crib and sighed with relief. For the next hour she would be free to indulge herself in the new pastime that was becoming so absorbing, her investigation of the old boxes in the attic. Tilly had begun it as a matter of duty. But now she was really enjoying her random study of life in the little village of Amherst in the old days.

And therefore, on the day the body of Alison Grove was removed from the Quabbin Reservoir, on the day Owen Kraznik and Ellen Oak drove Peter Wiggins to the emergency room of the Cooley-Dickinson Hospital, on the day Dr. Kloop was able to stump with his new crutches into the hospital morgue to do a postmortem on the body of Winifred Gaw, on the day all the lush grass in Amherst suddenly needed cutting for the first time—on that very same day, Tilly Porch came upon an interesting photographic negative, an old glass plate, in her attic.

Holding it up to the light, Tilly could see four small dark images, the same one repeated four times over. Darks and lights were reversed, of course, but it was obviously a photograph of a woman with a full face, her hair parted in the middle and pulled down and back in the fashion of the eighteen-sixties.

Climbing over a pile of her husband's ancient camping equipment, Tilly stepped boldly on a pillow of pink insulation batting and inspected the plate in the sunny attic window. Of course she couldn't really be sure, but the silhouette on the plate looked an awful lot like that of the *Emily don't like this much* picture that had been planted in Tilly's attic by Peter Wiggins. Owen Kraznik had said to forget about Peter's picture. It was just a mistake, he said. And then he had begged her not to say anything, just to keep quiet about it forever. Well, that was all right with Tilly. It was none of her business. But now she doubted the genuineness of what she had found. What if the glass plate, too, had been planted by Peter Wiggins? Was it just another example of his sly presence in her attic? Holding it firmly in both hands, Tilly went back to the chest and examined the big faded envelope in which she had found it.

The envelope was obviously an old one, yellowed and disintegrating at the edges. And surely that was Great-Great-Grandmother Louisa's handwriting on the outside? Tilly had already found sheaves and sheaves of Louisa's letters. There was no mistaking that tiny hand.

Tilly squinted at it, reading in the dark. Then she almost dropped the glass plate.

There was a date on the envelope, *February 18, 1860*. And the name of the woman whose image was recorded in quadruplicate was *Emily D*.

43

Life is deep and swift—

The wind was still whipping down Main Street when the party of five assembled in the Gaslite restaurant for lunch.

Harvey Kloop struggled out of his car and heaved himself up on the sidewalk with his crutches. The door of the restaurant gave him a hard time. At last he opened it a crack, but then the wind took it and slammed it against the wall, and one of Harvey's crutches went sailing away down the street.

"Good heavens, Harvey," cried Owen, jumping up from a table, rushing to the door. For a moment the two of them spun around each other, Harvey's plaster leg as helpless as Owen's plaster arm. Then Mary Kelly ran up with Harvey's crutch and Homer held the door open, and the two cripples at last achieved an entrance into the restaurant. At the table Ellen Oak slid over on the bench so that Harvey could sit on the outside and stretch his leg.

Dr. Kloop did not know Homer and Mary Kelly. There were introductions by Owen and Ellen, followed by joyful announcements and hearty congratulations. Then Harvey too had an announcement.

"I think," he said shyly, "my wife has gone away."

"Oh, Harvey," said Owen, "you mean Eunice Jane has"—it seemed too good to be true—"left you?"

"That's right. At least I think that's what she's done. She left this note. I guess it's a quotation from Emily Dickinson." Harvey drew a scrap of paper out of his pocket and passed it around. They all looked at it and shook their heads in mystification.

> *Good night, because we must,*
> *How intricate the dust!*

"I'm pretty sure it's some kind of farewell," said Harvey. "Anyway, all her clothes are gone. And her case of sauerkraut juice." Harvey smiled wickedly, then cleared his throat and got down to brass tacks. "I performed an autopsy on the body of Winifred Gaw this morning. Fortunately I had some familiarity with Winnie's medical history, since she had been a patient of mine. Not a very good one, I'm afraid. Terribly obese, as you know. Wouldn't take my warnings seriously. Of course I wanted to put her on a diet, but she claimed dieting gave her insomnia. She wanted diet pills. Well, I wouldn't give her the pills, of course, but I wrote a prescription for Secanol tablets to help with the wakefulness. And the other day when she requested a refill, I assumed she was taking them. But I gather she had been hoarding them instead."

"But, Dr. Kloop," said Ellen, "we suspect she didn't die from an overdose of Secanol. Is that right?"

"Yes, that's right." Harvey tucked into his plate of fried clams. "And of course, as you indicated in your report, it wasn't the axe. I'll tell you how the poor girl died. It was cardiac arrest."

"You mean a heart attack?" Owen was astonished. "Good heavens. Then she didn't commit suicide?"

"Well, I'm not sure what she meant to do with those pills. All I know is she succumbed from a coronary first. Sudden arrhythmia. This morning I was shocked at the condition of her arteries. I mean, she was such a young woman. And there was a lot of sugar in her urine, and an enormous amount of fibrous tissue in her pancreas. She must have been diabetic into the bargain. No wonder she keeled over." Harvey poured ketchup on his fried clams. "Did they ever figure out what happened in that bedroom? The axe and all? The overturned furniture?"

Homer picked up his beefburger club sandwich. "No, not so far. We can't think who could have been mad enough at Winnie to get into a real battle. Unless it was her father. I must say, he strikes me as a really sinister sort of bastard. But Archie Gripp claims Jesse Gaw was miles away all the time, working the night shift with a whole gang of men and a supervisor. And then he was doing a special job at somebody else's repair shop, working on a front end."

"There's one more thing." Harvey's face had lost its good humor. His melancholy eyes drifted vaguely from Ellen to Mary to Owen, then fixed upon Homer in a hollow stare. Reaching across the table, he gripped Homer's shoulders convulsively. "Listen, there was this amazing—I mean, you won't

2 2 4

believe it, but something happened at the reservoir, something strange, something really weird. Well, you know, it was a *miracle*."

Homer stifled an impulse to recoil and cry out, *I fear thee, Ancient Mariner, I fear thy skinny hand.* Instead he laughed. "Oh, sure, Owen told me. I gather the two of you were in the hospital together, having your miscellaneous broken parts patched up. I know what you're going to say—you saw Emily Dickinson, right? Walking along under the water? Wow, that was a big help. They found her. I just heard from Archie. Picked her up this morning from the water at Shaft Twelve."

Harvey's cadaverous face paled. He dropped his fork. Fried clams skittered across the table. "They found *Emily Dickinson?*"

"Oh, Homer, who was it?" said Owen, looking at him in pained anticipation. "Not—?"

"Yes," said Homer flatly. "It was Alison Grove."

Owen gasped, and his eyes filled with tears.

Then Homer explained it to Harvey. "Alison was a student at U Mass. She turned up missing a few days ago. Alison Grove, you see, not Emily Dickinson."

Harvey frowned, clinging stubbornly to his terrible vision of the woman in the white dress. "But she was walking, I tell you. She was walking along the road under the water. And the church bell was ringing. I heard it. I did, I really did. I figured it out. It's a big hole in the nature of things, you see. Like maybe sometimes there are these big cracks in the universe. I mean, it had to be something like that."

Mary Kelly exchanged an amused glance with Ellen Oak, and then Homer shed more light on Harvey's metaphysical dilemma. "Listen, don't worry. You're right. She *was* walking along the road. But it was because she had a weight attached to her ankle. It made her drift along upright. It was a bell, a heavy bronze bell. That's what was ringing. It was Jesse Gaw's own personal bell."

"No kidding?" Relief flooded Harvey as the universe

turned rightside up again and snapped into place in seamless perfection.

"The trouble is," said Homer, "we can't figure out how Alison's body got there. We think she was at Shaft Twelve sometime or other, dead or alive, because she left a shoe there. But her body couldn't have made its way into the reservoir from Shaft Twelve, because the valve was closed at the time. And, anyway, there's a screen over it to keep fish out of the water supply—deer carcasses, things like that. All we know is that somebody opened the door with a key stolen from Jesse Gaw. We can't help thinking of Winnie."

"But if Alison's body didn't get into the reservoir from Shaft Twelve," said Mary, "how did it get into the water?"

"Darned if I know." Homer scooped up a huge gelatinous bite of lemon meringue pie with his fork. "Musht have been toshed in shomeplashe elshe. Mmmm, izhn't thish delishioush."

Then Harvey Kloop gasped with understanding. "Oh, my God, I saw it. I saw the whole thing, and I drove away. Oh, Lord, my oath. I knew it, I violated my Hippo-something oath."

"Your oath?" said Owen. "Harvey, for heaven's sake, tell us what you saw."

"I saw Winifred Gaw pick up the body. I was too far away to see her clearly. But that's what must have been happening." Harvey groaned in tortured recollection. "I was going off on my little fishing holiday, you see, really anxious to get away, and I couldn't be bothered to stop and find out what was going on. Oh, Lord, there was this huge woman in the street, in front of a truck, a big van, right there at the traffic light. I sort of half recognized Winnie Gaw, but she had her back to me. She was bending down, picking up something. All I could see was something white. But that's what it must have been. It was the girl I saw in the water, later on. Winnie must have run her down. It all fits, do you see? And I just drove away, violating my Hippogriffic oath. Oh, Jesus, how could I do a thing like that?"

"Well, good for you, Dr. Kloop." Homer was ecstatic. "So that's it. Winifred Gaw set fire to Coolidge Hall. Winifred Gaw killed Alison Grove, and dumped her in the Quabbin Reservoir. Congratulations! That explains everything. Pippohoptic. Hippoticktock. I know the oath you mean."

Harvey reached for his crutches, and wrestled himself to his feet. "I'm sorry, but I've got to get back to the hospital. Work to do. My oath. From here on out, I swear I'm going to obey my Hippospastic oath, or whatever the damn thing's called. So long."

"Just a minute, Harvey." Ellen slipped off the bench and accompanied him to the cash register. Then she held the door open for him and followed him onto the sidewalk. "Hippocratic," she said firmly, helping him into his car. "I swore one of those things myself."

She came back to find Owen staring at Homer in shocked disbelief. "But surely it wasn't Winifred. It couldn't have been Winifred. Winnie couldn't have killed Alison Grove. Why would she do such a thing? And why on earth would poor Winnie set fire to Coolidge Hall?"

"Damned if I know." Homer grinned at Owen. "I suppose there are things we aren't meant to understand in this world. Holes in the nature of things. Yawning cracks and voids in the rational universe. Like the axe. We'll probably never know what that crazy girl was doing in Emily Dickinson's bedroom with her father's axe. All we know is that she stole it from his garage, along with the can of paint and the bell and the key to Shaft Twelve. But whatever for?"

"The axe?" said Ellen quickly. "I think I understand the axe. It was a metaphor."

"A metaphor?" said Mary, astonished. "The *axe* was a metaphor?"

"That's right. Even poor old Winnie was clever enough to know a good image when she saw one. Remember, Homer, the book on the floor in Emily's bedroom? *The Letters of Emily Dickinson*? I shouldn't have touched it, I suppose, but I did. I picked it up and noticed that one passage had been heavily underlined. It was in one of those three mysterious love letters Emily wrote to someone she called 'Master.'" Ellen closed her eyes and tried to say the passage by heart: "*Tell me my fault, Master. You send the water over the dam in my brown eyes. I've got a Tomahawk in my side, but that don't hurt me much. My master stabs me more.* Something like that. Winnie underlined the words and put the book on the bedside table as a kind of suicide note. I think she meant to take a lot of pills and go to sleep with the axe on the bed beside her."

"I see," said Mary, nodding wisely. "The axe was supposed to represent the tomahawk. You mean it stood for the pain some perfidious person had inflicted on her? Someone she loved?"

"Ah, but how do you know Winnie did the underlining?" objected Homer. "And how do you know it was that particular page she meant someone to read?"

"Simple," said Ellen. "It was covered with blood."

"Oh," said Homer. There was a mournful silence, and then Homer slapped the table and snickered in callous sarcasm. "A metaphor, by God. Listen, you know what? Maybe Lizzie Borden's axe was just a metaphor too. I mean, maybe Lizzie was just thinking about poetry when she gave her mother forty whacks, did you ever think of that? And then when she saw what she had done, maybe it was just another pretty little figure of speech she had in mind when she gave her father forty-one. How about it?"

Owen clutched his throat and gagged, struggling to breathe. Mary kicked Homer under the table. "Shut up, dear, it's lunchtime."

"Oh, sorry," said Homer. He looked at Ellen inquiringly. "But who was Winnie's message for? I mean, who was this loved one, this 'Master?'" And then, as Owen moaned and got up from the table, his face ashen, Homer murmured, "Oh, of course," and reached for his wife's hand in remorse, remembering the keepsakes in Winnie's darkroom, the bits of eraser, the ends of pencils, the scraps of notes, *Dear Winnie, would you please call the library—Dear Winnie, this book is overdue.* Homer was ashamed of himself.

But it was too late. Owen was breaking down. Ellen had to take him outdoors and sit him down on a park bench on the Common.

44

Given in Marriage unto Thee
Oh thou Celestial Host—
Bride of the Father and the Son
Bride of the Holy Ghost.

And Owen was destined to shed more tears at the funeral of Alison Grove. As he entered the sanctified gloom of the memorial chapel, he could feel them welling up.

"That must be Mrs. Grove, Alison's mother," murmured Ellen. "Doesn't she look like the mother of the bride?"

It was true. Alison's mother seemed to have planned her daughter's funeral as if it were the splendid wedding reception she had been denied. In her powder-blue dress she stood behind the casket in queenly grandeur. Beside her, the groom, Tom Perry, looked uncomfortable in morning coat and striped trousers. Between them Alison lay like a lovely doll, her white wedding dress foaming around her in clouds of net and lace.

The viewing line was long. One by one the guests shuffled forward to exclaim at Alison's loveliness and touch the glove of Mrs. Grove. Owen joined the line timidly, gripping Ellen's arm. Warily he studied Alison's mother as she listened hungrily to exclamations of sorrow and took greedy note of weeping eyes. No tears were falling down the ivory cheeks of Mrs. Grove, but her hands were never at rest. Again and again they darted forward to rearrange Alison's hair, or smooth her lacy gown, or fluff her tissued veil.

It was Ellen's turn. "I'm so sorry," she said to Mrs. Grove.

Alison's mother closed her eyes and nodded majestically. But Tom Perry was waiting for Ellen. Hurrying around the casket, he took her arm. "Listen, Ellen, I want to talk to you."

Ellen hardly saw him. Beside her, Owen was dissolving. He was leaning over the casket, sobbing, "Poor child, poor child."

"Oh, Owen dear, sit down," said Ellen. Once again she helped him to a chair.

Homer and Mary Kelly were late. Homer refused to join the line filing past the open casket, but Mary decided to do what was expected of her. When it was her turn to take the hand of Alison's mother and encounter Mrs. Grove's large tragic eyes, she was at once reminded of Mrs. Jesse Gaw. And that was strange, because Mrs. Grove was a strikingly handsome woman, utterly unlike Winnie's scrawny mother. It was in the rapacity of their grief that the two women resembled each other, decided Mary. Nodding at Tom Perry, she moved away, as Mrs. Grove reached out her hand again to the casket and fiddled with Alison's ring, turning the flashing diamond up to the light.

At the other end of the chapel two women were pouring tea. Mary made her way past the sobbing organ, accepted a cup gratefully and introduced herself. Soon she was chatting comfortably with Barbara Teeter and Dottie Poole.

"It should have been Alison's wedding, don't you agree, Mrs. Kelly?" said Dottie Poole. "Lemon and sugar?"

"Sponge cake?" said Barbara Teeter. "Oh, Mrs. Kelly, isn't it terrible? When you think of all the sorrow she's been through. Poor Shirley Grove."

"Sorrow?" said Mary. "You mean, there have been other—?"

Dottie Poole leaned forward confidingly. "First it was Alison's grandfather, and then it was Alison's father, and now it's Alison herself. It's like a curse on the family." Dottie lowered her voice to a whisper and leaned still farther in Mary's direction. "And they couldn't even *bury* Alison's grandfather."

"Why not?" whispered Mary, bending over Dottie. "Did he die at sea?"

"*Would* that he *had,*" said Dottie with melancholy emphasis, rolling her eyes at Barbara Teeter.

Barbara crooked her finger at Mary. Obediently, Mary came closer and bowed her head until her ear was next to Barbara's lips. "He was a civil engineer, you see," hissed Barbara. "Alison's grandfather, I mean, during the construction of the Quabbin Reservoir. You know, clearing the land, building the dam. And there was this tragic accident. He fell into the concrete core while they were pouring the cement for the dam."

Mary gasped and withdrew a few inches. "How terrible."

It was Dottie's turn. With solemn pride she touched Mary's sleeve. "They never found him."

"They never found him? You mean he's still there in the dam, buried in the cement?"

Dottie and Barbara nodded regally.

"But how did it happen?"

"Nobody really knows," said Barbara. "Some of the people say there was this man, one of the people who were forced out of the villages in the valley, and they say he was driven mad with the injustice of it all, and they say he was standing next to Alison's grandfather on the dam when it was under construction, and he gave Alison's grandfather a little push. But of course nobody actually saw it. I mean when it was happening. Nobody was ever prosecuted. There's a nice memorial plaque to Alison's grandfather's memory in the Quabbin Cemetery, only it doesn't say what happened."

"Well! So much for Alison's grandfather," said Dottie Poole, picking up the story eagerly. "Wait till you hear about her *father.*"

"Her father?" whispered Mary. "What happened to him? Did he drown in the reservoir or something?"

"Oh, no." Dottie's solemn expression gave way to cruel giggles. Barbara Teeter laughed. "All *he* did," said Dottie, "was run away with another woman."

"Nobody could understand it," offered Barbara. "She was plain as a mud fence. She had, you know, these big buckteeth and bulgy eyes. And Shirley Grove is so beautiful."

"Inscrutable," murmured Mary, "the ways of the male sex. May I have some tea for my husband?"

She found Homer standing dolefully in the corner beside a gigantic basket of white pompom chrysanthemums. Homer gulped down his tea thirstily, and inclined his head to hear the sorrowful history of the death of Alison's grandfather, while the organ played the wedding march from *Lohengrin* at a funereal *largo vibratissimo.*

"Do you suppose it was Jesse Gaw's father who pushed him?" said Mary. "You know, in retribution for crippling little Jesse with his bulldozer?"

"Are you suggesting that Winnie Gaw killed Alison Grove, and Winnie's grandfather, by some zany trick of fate, killed Alison's grandfather?"

"It does sound ridiculous, when you put it that way."

"God knows what really happened," said Homer. "You know, we're surrounded by cracks in the universe on all sides, holes in the rational undergirding firmament, fundamental anomalies in the—*whoops!*"

"Oh, Homer, watch out!"

It was too late. Homer's teacup was falling from its saucer, exploding on the floor with a hideous crash, fracturing the reverent mood of the soprano as she sang "O Promise Me." Reaching for a high note, she squawked instead, and muffed it.

45

So give me back to Death . . .

"Sorry, you people," said Dombey Dell. "You've all got to leave today. The people at the College, they want to start the regular tours again."

The front door was open. Another mild spring day glistened outside. Sunshine streamed through the parlor windows, glowing through the translucent porcelain of the Dickinson china, filling the hollow cups with light. Invisible pollen drifted into the front hall, mingling the fragrance of lilacs with the hot smell of tar from the truck that was cruising down Main Street, repairing winter potholes. The lilacs themselves were turning rusty. The flowering trees had dropped all their petals and put on a thick new growth of leaves. Grass rushed up out of the ground. An employee of the buildings and grounds department at the College was taking care of it, running a noisy lawn mower around the garden, guiding it deftly with one hand under the bushes, leaving a few tall whiskers between the elephantine toes of the white oak tree. In the narrow front yard a sprinkler whirled, sparkling in pulses in the sunlight, making a light pattering on the ground.

Tom Perry was ready to go. He came down the stairs

heavily, lugging his suitcase. Sourly he looked at Dombey Dell. "Did you hear about the job at Harvard?"

"No," said Dombey sharply. "What about the job at Harvard?"

"There isn't any job at Harvard. You know that guy they were going to fire, Rexpole? He just won the Nobel prize."

"Oh, my God."

"So relax."

"Well, what the hell," said Dombey Dell. "*C'est la vie.*"

Owen, too, had packed up his slender possessions. Sitting on the top step of the back porch, he waited for Ellen. It was broad noon. A fly buzzed around his head. Leaning against one of the porch pillars, he closed his eyes.

When the door opened behind him, he was too sleepy to turn around. But he looked up as the long white skirt rustled past him, flowing easily through the floor of the porch. Yes, that made sense, because the porch wasn't old. There had been nothing here a hundred years ago but a pair of granite steps. The white skirt rippled with the briskness of the woman's forward motion as she walked away from Owen and hurried past the barn. Now she was climbing into the field beyond the stone wall. Soon she was only a determined bobbing note of white, farther and farther away, walking firmly in the direction of the cemetery.

Owen's head jerked up. Getting awkwardly to his feet, he stared at the place where the barn had been so clearly visible a moment ago. It had vanished. There was only the garage on the other side of the driveway. Beyond the stone wall lay the backyard of somebody's house, with its green lawn and swimming pool. The spell dissolved.

Owen smiled. His dreams were improving. This one was particularly satisfactory. Emily Dickinson was burying herself again. From now on she would lie in her own alabaster chamber, *Untouched by Morning And untouched by Noon.* Untouched at least by anybody at the Emily Dickinson Centennial Symposium, because the symposium was over. Even Dombey Dell was abandoning Emily Dickinson, getting ready to rip and claw at somebody else. This time it was Julia Moore, the Sweet Singer of Michigan.

But, decided Owen, it was not just Dombey's greedy territorial ambition that was to blame for the indignities Emily had suffered, and for the tragedies that had engulfed them all. Blame, too, the passions of mind and heart, those very same terrors and fervors that reeled in her poetry. Those ardors were still raging in Amherst, tormenting the strong and maddening the weak. Blame disappointed yearning, *the drop of Anguish That scalds me now—that scalds me now!* Blame the frustration of reaching without achieving, of longing for the impossible. *I'll clutch—and clutch—Next—One—Might be the golden touch.* And as for the nightmares and fatalities of the last few days, who had known better than Emily Dickinson the terrors of death, *the supple Suitor That wins at last?*

"Open the screen door, would you, Owen?"

Owen turned hastily to open the door for Ellen. She was carrying a bag and a slide projector for Peter Wiggins. Peter stumbled after her clumsily, moaning a little under his breath.

"Now, see here, Peter," said Owen, taking the slide projector, following him to his car. "Are you sure you can drive all the way back to Boston?"

Peter smiled wanly, and climbed into the front seat, favoring all his bandaged places. "Oh, yes, no problem."

Owen felt sorry for Peter Wiggins, his newest lame duck. He stood beside the car with Ellen and rested his plaster arm on the open window. "Oh, Peter, I forgot to tell you the good news about that picture that turned up. You know, the one that said, *Mother before we moved to Topeka.* You can forget about it."

"I can?" Peter's drawn face brightened.

"You certainly can. Helen Gaunt brought it over and showed it to me, and there's no question about it. It's brand new, not nearly as sharp as the original. And the cardboard backing was just cut out of a shoe box or something. It's a very crude job. Helen said somebody left it in her mailbox. Homer Kelly assures me it must have been Winifred Gaw."

"Oh, so that's what Winnie meant by documentary evidence?" Peter smiled faintly, and then hunched his shoulders, waiting for Owen to say something about another embarrassing forgery. But Owen was silent. Impulsively Peter burst out, "I hate to leave." And then all his frustrated hopes came gushing forth. He looked up at Owen with his sad rabbit eyes. "You see, the truth is, I was hoping to get a teaching job somewhere in the East. You know, around here." Peter gestured at the woodsy confusion of light and shade beyond the garage. "Someplace with trees and flowers. Things like that."

Owen didn't know what to reply. But Ellen looked at Peter in surprise. "You mean you don't like it in Arizona?"

"No," said Peter, closing his eyes and shaking his head from side to side. "I don't like it in Arizona."

"But that's such great country out there," exclaimed Ellen. "Why don't you enjoy it? Why don't you just wallow in it?"

"Wallow in it?" Peter stared at Ellen, and blinked. Once again he shook his head in clumsy protest, and then he recited the names of his gods, Henry Thoreau, Herman Melville, Emily Dickinson. "They all belong here, you see. Here in New England."

"No, they don't," said Ellen quickly.

"They don't?" Peter gaped at her.

"They don't?" said Owen, amused.

"Of course not. Emily Dickinson isn't here. She's not in this house anymore. She's not distilled somehow in the fragrance of the flowers in the garden. She's not folded into the pleats of that white dress in the bedroom. Emily Dickinson is dead."

"Dead," agreed Owen sagely.

"Dead," agreed Peter, nodding his head up and down.

"Stone dead. She only comes alive when some kid in Anchorage, Alaska, or Nashville, Tennessee, or Brooklyn, New York, or—where do you come from?—Pancake Flat, Arizona!—opens an anthology of American poetry and reads one of her poems for the first time. It's all the life she's ever going to have. Listen, you idiot, Emily Dickinson is alive and well in Pancake Flat as long as you're there to pass the book around."

"Pancake Flat," said Peter dreamily. "Alive and well in Pancake Flat."

"That's where she is," concluded Ellen, beaming at him kindly. "Not here."

"Pancake Flat," said Peter again, nodding sleepily. Owen and Ellen watched him as his car floated backward, then drowsed forward out of the driveway like a piece of mesmerized machinery.

"My dear, you were superb," said Owen Kraznik.

46

I had a guinea golden—
I lost it in the sand . . .

*T*he black glass negative on the mantelpiece was gathering dust. Tilly couldn't seem to get time to examine it carefully. At first she was kept busy by her duties in the Amherst Women's Emily Dickinson Association. Marilyn Wineman, the chairperson, had asked her to write up an account, for the minutes, of the historic march on the Homestead. And then it was Tilly's daughter Margie. Margie sent Tilly three yards of fabric and a dress pattern, urging her to make it up in a hurry. And then it was the clothing exchange at Grace Church. Tilly was in charge of collecting all the stuff.

All of these things had taken one hundred percent of the time left over from the care of Elvis Buffington, who was such a little go-getter Tilly had to keep an eye on him every minute.

But today for sure, decided Tilly, she would get a look at that glass plate during his afternoon nap. The trouble was, when Tilly at last dumped Elvis into his crib, she felt so tired herself that she couldn't resist lying down just for a couple of winks.

And then her nap turned into a really good snooze.

Elvis woke up first. Taking hold of the bars of the crib, he tried hoisting himself over the top. It was easy. Elvis was proud

of himself. Clambering quickly down to the floor, he turned around and looked across the room at Tilly. Her eyes were shut. She was still asleep. Toddling to the stairs, Elvis negotiated them rapidly, scrambling down backward on hands and knees.

Downstairs he explored the house, looking for something to play with. In the living room he climbed a chair. Behind the chair a bookcase offered easy handholds. On the top of the bookcase he stood up carefully. A jar of flowers wobbled. A statue thing tipped back and forth, then righted itself. Elvis stood silently on the bookcase watching it, a drop of water suspended from his lower lip. Then he turned his head. Beyond the bookcase, on the shelf over the fireplace, he saw something interesting. A black thing, shiny and flat. It was made of glass. It would break. It looked like "No, no, Elvis!" Edging sideways along the top of the bookcase, Elvis leaned his stomach against the edge of the mantel and grasped the piece of black glass. Miraculously he carried it to the floor without mishap.

Where to now? Outdoors! Holding the piece of glass carefully in both fists, Elvis made his way purposefully to the kitchen door. With extreme care he set the glass on the floor and undid the hook of the screen. Then he picked it up again, clutched it to his stomach, and pushed the door open.

The sun was high over the treetops, yellow and bright. A dog was barking up the road. Elvis slid down the grassy slope to the driveway and got to his feet. What next?

And then he saw something worthy of his epic journey. Once again the neighbor's cat was stalking beside the field. Catching sight of Elvis, the cat froze, then streaked across the street.

Dropping the piece of glass on the driveway, Elvis took off after the cat. Soon he was toddling along a path on the other side of Market Hill Road.

And therefore it wasn't until much later that afternoon, it wasn't until the neighbors had been summoned to look for Elvis, it wasn't until the police had organized a search party along Cushman Brook and were wondering whether or not to drag Factory Hollow Pond, it wasn't until Elvis turned up at Whittemores' Store at the bottom of Market Hill Road and the people at Whittemore's called the police and the police called Tilly and Tilly rushed down to get him and hug him and scold him and take him home for supper and a bath, it wasn't until she put him to bed and locked the bedroom door—it wasn't until then that Tilly discovered the disappearance of the glass plate from the mantelpiece in the living room. Only then did she begin to look for it all over the house. Only then did she find it at last in the driveway, crushed into a million splintered shards by the wheels of the police chief's car.

"Oh, well," said Tilly regretfully, stirring the pieces with her foot, "who cares what Emily Dickinson looked like? It's the poems that count, after all."

> *I reckon—when I count at all—*
> *First—Poets—Then the Sun—*
> *Then Summer—Then the Heaven of God—*
> *And then—the List is done—*

2 4 1

But, looking back—the First so seems
To Comprehend the Whole—
The Others look a needless Show—
So I write—Poets—All . . .

Afterword

꧁꧂

The photograph that appears at the front of this book and on page 247 became famous when it appeared as the frontispiece for the second volume of Richard Sewall's 1974 biography of Emily Dickinson. Below the picture, on the same page, Professor Sewall displayed the scribbled, misspelled identification from the back of the photograph, *Emily Dickenson 1860*, but he took no position as to the genuineness of the attribution:

> This frontispiece is an enlargement of a 3″ x 1¾″ photograph reproduced here by the kind permission of Mr. Herman Abromson, who bought it "some years ago" from a bookseller in Greenwich Village, New York City, since deceased. The name and date (in handwriting unknown) appear on the back of the photograph. Opinions vary as to whether it is an authentic picture of Emily Dickinson, the poet. . . .

The Greenwich Village bookseller was one Samuel Loveman, who actually did not die until 1976, at the age of eighty-nine. According to his former partner, David Mann, Loveman had owned and cherished the picture for a long time before he offered it for sale in 1961. The catalogue for his Bodley Book Shop listed it incorrectly as a daguerreotype, *an unknown daguerreotype portrait of Emily Dickinson*, and described it like this:

> 95 DICKINSON, EMILY. Original Portraits of Emily Dickinson, are, alas, all too Few—a Daguerreotype or Two, a Drawing or a Verbal Description, and the Sum of Portraiture of this Unique American Poet is Complete. We offer a Completely Unknown Photographic Portrait of Emily Dickinson on a Crad [sic] de Visite (4 x 2¼ Inches)—an Exquisite Likeness of One of the Loveliest Faces recorded in Early Photography. This is a Bust-Portrait, and a Pencilled Inscription on the Verso reads: *"mily* [sic] *Dickinson, 1   ."* $25.00

Mr. Loveman failed to explain that the inscription on the back of the picture had been written, and misspelled, by himself. His handwriting has been identified by David Mann.

How did Samuel Loveman acquire the photograph and why did he think it a likeness of Emily Dickinson? Among Loveman's surviving friends, no one seems to know. As a self-taught scholar, he made attributions that are sometimes dismissed as naïve or overly optimistic. Lorraine Wilbur of the Gramercy Book Shop in New York remembers an example. When she asked Loveman why he claimed that his unsigned landscape had been painted by Albert Bierstadt, he said, "I feel it."

At the same time, Loveman had a considerable reputation in New York as a cataloguer of rare books. An occasional poet himself, he was a close friend of the poet Hart Crane. After Crane's suicide and after the death of Crane's mother, Loveman became his literary executor. Many people attest to his interest in the poetry of Emily Dickinson. Perhaps he "felt" that the woman in this photograph resembled the seventeen-year-old Emily as she appears in the famous daguerreotype of 1848.

And then, perhaps he made a guess at the date of the *carte de visite*. Or perhaps, on the other hand, he had a solid reason for his attribution.

Unfortunately there is no photographer's insignia on the back of the little card to help with a more positive identification. It is unlikely that the photograph was taken by Amherst photographer J. L. Lovell, whose studio was patronized by other members of the Dickinson household. Amherst scholar Ruth Owen Jones has studied the friendship of Lovell with David Todd and his wife, Mabel Loomis Todd, Emily Dickinson's first editor. The three were such close friends that the Todds wrote a brief biography of Lovell after his death. Surely if he had taken such a picture of Emily Dickinson, Mabel would have sought it out.

The photograph remains mysterious.

A daguerreotype of Emily Dickinson taken shortly after her seventeenth birthday in 1848.

A photographic carte de visite. *On the back, someone has scribbled in a careless hand,* Emily Dickenson 1860.